BLOOD
TIES
AND
DEADLY
LIES

BLOOD TIES
AND
DEADLY LIES

A BLUE PALMETTO DETECTIVE AGENCY NOVEL

ANG POMPANO

LEVEL
BEST BOOKS

First published by Level Best Books 2025

Author Photo Credit: Sara M. Photography

First edition

ISBN: 978-1-68512-988-0

Cover art by Level Best Designs

This book was professionally typeset on Reedsy.
Find out more at reedsy.com

To my family—thanks for not killing me while I wrote this. Any resemblance to actual people is purely coincidental... probably.

Chapter One

Thursday, June 23

"DeLucia, we picked up a guy claiming to be your brother."

Lenny Rodriguez's call caught me mid-coffee.

"I don't have a brother," I said.

"Yeah? Didn't think you had a father either."

My old coworker from the New Haven PD wasn't wrong. Big Al had walked out when I was eight, and I'd spent most of my life thinking he was dead. Then last year, I got a call from Savannah—Big Al was alive, had dementia, and wanted me to take over the Blue Palmetto Detective Agency. I'd planned to sell it and retire in L.A. Instead, I stuck around to see what might develop with my girlfriend, Maxine Brophy. Thanks to Big Al's odd arrangements, I owned the agency, but Max was the senior detective and effectively my boss. I took that as another jab from my father, but after he risked his life for me, I started a fragile truce with the old man.

"Look, dude, everyone tries to say they have some connection to a cop when they're arrested."

"I'm just passing on what he told us."

"Who's this guy, then?"

The guy's name is Abe Cromwell. Ring a bell?"

More like Big Ben. Abe and I had grown up in Sachem Creek, a seaside village east of New Haven. He'd always lived on the edge of trouble, and in high school, I made the mistake of standing up to him. He never forgot it.

1

For him to claim me as his "brother," he must've been desperate.

"What's he in for?"

"Threatening an attorney. Said he'd kill anyone responsible for him losing his land."

"That sounds like Abe, all right."

"Prosecutor's still deciding if he meant the lawyer or someone else, but either way, Abe's in deep. And it's not just him. The whole village is hurting. Amanda Kittle's buying up land like she's hoarding gold."

That wasn't news. Even before I left for Savannah, Amanda Kittle and I had locked horns over her development projects. When I lived in Sachem Creek, I had been on the Town Board and we'd often clashed over the gentrification of the village. She was transforming the town, driving out the locals and bringing in wealthy out-of-towners. But I had to laugh at Lenny's Captain Kidd reference. Sachem Creek's treasure stories go back three hundred years, from when the Yale crowd started going there.

"You still buying into that pirate tall tale?" I asked.

"Poor choice of words," Lenny laughed.

"That's okay. I grew up with the stories, and sometimes even I wonder if they're true."

"Anyway, you are coming back for the race?"

"The Pirate's Day Race is on this year?"

"Yep. They decided to bring it back and get this; there's a twenty-five grand first prize, thanks to some electric car startup. Figured you'd want another shot at Donahue.".

Tom Donahue. My ex-wife's boyfriend and the guy who cheated me out of a win the last time we raced pre-COVID.

"I'll think about it," I said.

"I figured you'd say that."

Before I could answer, Lenny cut me off. "Gotta go. We'll talk when you get back."

I never planned to return to Connecticut—too much baggage. Savannah felt like home now, and I didn't want to dig up old ghosts. But something about Abe's claim, and Amanda's land grab, had me reconsidering.

I decided to tell the crew what the plan was. When I pushed open the door to the outer office. Big Al was playing solitaire the old-school way—real cards, not a screen. He didn't say anything when he saw me.

"Where's Max?" I asked.

"Atlanta," Greenleaf replied, without looking up from her computer.

"What's she doing there?"

"Do I look like her mother?"

I didn't press. Greenleaf always knew everything, but she wasn't giving me any more details today.

"I'm heading to Connecticut," I said.

"Good for you," Greenleaf muttered, still typing.

Big Al glanced up. "What for?"

"Pirate's Day Race. And a guy from high school, Abe Cromwell, got himself in a jam.

Told the cops he's my brother."

That got their attention. Greenleaf froze. Big Al knocked over his coffee.

"Brother?" Big Al echoed, grabbing a napkin. "What kind of jam?"

"He threatened someone."

"I'm going with you," Big Al said.

I should've seen that coming. Even though he handed me the agency, Big Al still thought he was my partner.

"Oh no, you're not. I can handle this."

Big Al crossed his arms. "I'm going."

"Where?"

"Where you're going."

I sighed. "Connecticut?"

Big Al gave me a blank look. "You said it."

"I've got it covered. You don't have to go all the way up there for some nut job."

"That's no way to talk about your brother," Greenleaf said."

I glanced between her and Big Al. "You mean Abe is your son?"

Greenleaf kept busy on the computer, and Al kept his head down as he cleaned up the spill.

"Well, is he?" I pressed.

Big Al furrowed his brow. "He's my brother."

"No way. Abe's my age."

Big Al often mixed up the past and present, but this "brother" business threw me.

"Then he's my brother's son. Big Al said, tossing the wet towels into the sink before returning to his cards. Conversation over.

I wasn't giving up. "You said Cromwell was my brother. You've known this all along?" I asked Greenleaf.

"Your daddy might've mentioned it. A game of Truth or Dare or something."

I slumped into Max's chair, lost. "I don't know what to think anymore."

"What are you afraid of?" Greenleaf asked, softer now.

I rubbed my temples, trying to clear the fog in my brain.

Greenleaf motioned toward the porch. "C'mon. Let's talk."

Outside, her tone was gentler. "I know this is a lot to drop on you, but Big Al needs to go with you. His doctor said he's carrying too much baggage. This trip might help him unpack it."

"I'm not his therapist."

"You're his son," Greenleaf said, stamping her foot.

I scoffed. "I don't need an entourage for some crap case. It'll probably end up pro bono."

"You're doing it for family," she said, firmly. "And peace of mind. His and yours. I'll hold down the fort with Max."

"Looks like we're going on vacation," Big Al said, stepping out from behind the screen door.

I called my Aunt Phoebe, my late mother's twin sister, back in Sachem Creek. After Mom passed, Phoebe and I grew close. When Kim and I divorced, I even lived above her garage for a while. She was more than happy to offer the space again.

With that settled, that afternoon, we hit the road in the '92 Mercedes sports car that came with the Blue Palmetto. Never one to make things easy for me, Big Al had refused to fly, so instead of a two-hour flight, we were looking at a fifteen-hour drive. Big Al slept most of the way, leaving me with too much time to stew about what to say to Abe—the guy who used to make my life hell as a kid and now claimed to be my brother.

Hey, how about that? We're brothers! No way. *Welcome to the family?* Doubtful. Sorry we missed out on a lifetime? A lifetime of what? We had zilch in common.

Somewhere in Maryland, Big Al woke up, stretching. I decided to broach the subject.

"So, Abe might be your brother's son?" I asked casually.

"I said that?"

"Yeah. I didn't even know you had a brother."

Big Al furrowed his brow. "I forgot more than you'll ever know. Got blamed for plenty of his crap, too."

I was treading carefully. "So, you had a brother?"

"Twins. Couldn't tell us apart."

I sighed inwardly. He was mixing things up again. My mother had the twin, not him.

"Okay. What happened to him?"

"He died."

"But is Abe Cromwell your son?"

"No."

"No, he's not your son? Or no, you don't remember?"

"I don't have a son."

"But I'm your son."

He blushed. "So you keep telling me."

"And Abe's not my brother. Right?"

Big Al gave me a tired look. "Like they say, it's complicated."

Chapter Two

I was already ten minutes late for my 9:00 meeting with Abe at an eatery called Tide and Griddle Tavern when we pulled into Sachem Creek the next morning.

Although I was late, I stopped at Phoebe's place, a Painted Lady with violet shingles and lime green shutters on Buena Vista Road, a few blocks up the hill from the harbor. She was waiting for us on the porch.

"Where the hell have you been?" Phoebe yelled as she came down the steps to the car.

When I had made the arrangements, I didn't mention my father was coming along because I had suspected bad blood between them. It appeared that my worst fear of bad blood between her and Big Al was real. I positioned myself between her and Big Al worried things might get mean.

Instead, she gave him a big hug and kissed him on the cheek. "Al. It's good to see you. How are you?"

"Hangin' in there. That's all we can do." His voice was cheerful, but he didn't call her by name, and I wondered if he remembered her.

That's when I realized her anger was directed at me.

"You could have called to let me know you'd be late. Aren't you supposed to be down at Tide and Griddle Tavern?"

Looking at Phoebe, who didn't like being called aunt, I couldn't see my mother as I remember her, despite their identical twin status. Unlike my mother, she never felt she needed to be married. Until her retirement, she owned the Sachem Creek Garage, which she inherited from my grandfather. Throughout the years, she kept most of the vehicles in town running. These days, she keeps busy running people's lives. Phoebe insisted that Big Al stay in her guest room, and I should stay in the apartment over the garage where I had lived after the divorce. I dropped off our bags and left my father with her to catch up.

* * *

Main Street, unlike other parts of the village, hadn't changed much since I was a kid. The road ran only three-quarters of a mile, starting at the Amtrak underpass. One side boasted little shops in what had been old homes, a granite church, a post office, and a summer stock theatre facing the water and the Nutmeg islands on the other side.

A little past the beach at the boat ramp, Main branches off to tiny Wharf Street, forming a triangle. In the center of the triangle was a trefoil fountain made of the pink granite that once made the village famous, a gift of Anderson Kittle, the late owner of the Sachem Creek Quarry.

Tide and Griddle Tavern was the first building on the wharf. At Island Marine Services next door, Paul Hartt was testing an outboard in a barrel of water.

"You better hurry," he called to me. "Abe's pissed and fixing to leave."

There it was. I hadn't been in town for fifteen minutes, and probably the whole village knew what was going on. Gossip is an Olympic sport in Sachem Creek.

I waved him off. Then, after mustering enough nerve, I opened Tide and Griddle Tavern's wooden screen door to the smell of frying bacon. I can do this, I told myself.

To the left, below the front windows, was a makeshift narrow wooden shelf with painted stools where customers ate, looking across the wharf to the boat slips.

In the middle of the linoleum floor, so crooked that you walked uphill to get to the serving counter, were three small tables. Under the windows on the right wall were two booths that looked across the green and the public beach to the gingerbread cottages and a mini mansion on the north shore of the harbor.

Abe sat by a shelf that held I'm-A-Creeker T-shirts and souvenirs. It was hard to believe anyone looked up to this guy when we were in school. Hardly forty years old, he had that hardened look that usually comes with old age and tough work. He wore cutoff jeans and a blue t-shirt that showed off the navy tattoos on his bulging biceps.

"It's about time you got here," he said in a husky smoker's voice.

What was I supposed to do? A man hug was out of the question. Years ago, the storefront had been a bait shop. I looked around, remembering the sandworms with two large pincer teeth I bought there as a kid. If I could handle the bite of a sandworm, I could handle shaking hands with my *brother*. I put out my hand. He looked at it. For a while, I thought he wasn't going to take it. He finally offered a calloused paw. The shake was so brief it was more like a palm slap.

I sat and the table rocked. I looked down and noticed the cardboard that leveled it had slipped from under the leg. I bent over and shoved it back in place. I sat up. Time to get this over with.

"Well," I said.

"Well," he repeated.

"Seems you think we're related."

He scoffed. "Seems? We are. We're brothers."

"Look, you don't have to keep up this game. I'm going to help you out if I can."

"Good. I appreciate that. But that don't change the facts. You going to listen?"

I listen to get it over with. "Let's hear where this is coming from."

Abe lifted his shoulders and took a deep breath. "My mother died a couple of years ago. That's when I found my adoption papers. She never thought to tell me."

"Yeah. Must be tough. I found out my father was alive after thinking he was dead for twenty-eight years."

"You know, that's why I never liked you. It's always all about you. Who cares about you?

Me for one, I thought. "Look, you contacted me. If you don't want to talk about it, I'll get out of here."

"Do I have to spell it out? They raised me a Cromwell, but I'm a Benchley. Your mother was my mother."

Benchley was my mother's family name. But that didn't prove anything. "So, you're a Benchley. That doesn't make you my brother. It doesn't even make you my cousin."

"I got proof. Doreen, one of the bartenders at the Lobster Pot, gave me a DNA kit. I told her I didn't believe in that crap. She asked what it could hurt if I spit in a bottle. What could it hurt? The test comes back and claims I have a brother. You! Damn it! Of all people, you."

"Are you trying to say, my mother—"

"Our mother."

I wasn't about to accept that yet. "Are you trying to say *my* mother had a baby who lived in the same town she lived in and never acknowledged him?"

"She never acknowledged me."

"No way does that sound like her."

"Listen, man, I'm not lookin' for nothing if that's what you think. I'm stating a fact. And I'm not blaming nobody. The bartender told me back then Family Services never gave the mothers information about where their babies went. She even told me about two guys who were best friends for sixty years before they found out they were brothers. It happened."

We were hardly best friends. "You're saying we're half-brothers and nobody realized it the whole time we were growing up. That's hard to swallow."

"You're not listening. I said we're brothers. Not half-brothers. Your mother and father are my mother and father."

"Come on now. It must be a mistake. A false result. Something. I have to go." I was almost whispering because it seemed the whole place was listening. It was so quiet that you could hear a mouse fart.

"Go then. I didn't expect you to help."

Something about his look got to me. I imagined I saw a resemblance between us. Big Al had called the situation complicated. Talk about an understatement. I sat down again.

"Look, I can't deal with this same mother/father stuff right now. I may never be able to. Talk about something else. Tell me what's going on with your pinch."

"Does that mean you're going to help?"

"It means I'm going to listen."

Abe gave a nod that told me he understood what I meant. This was a courtesy call. No strings and no promise of warm fuzzies.

"I don't want no favors. I'll pay you."

He didn't even have coffee in front of him, so I figured he didn't have money for breakfast, let alone to pay me. "We'll work it out."

"Okay, but I'm going to keep an eye on you. Brother or no brother. I'm gonna keep an eye on everybody from now on!"

"You do that, Abe. You keep an eye on me. Have some breakfast, and you can tell me about it."

Abe glanced at the handwritten menu on a big piece of white tagboard that hung on the wall next to the counter.

"You're buying, right?"

"Sure. Whatever you'd like."

"Good. Then I'll have a Western omelet. And a side of ham and bacon."

I went up to the counter at the far side of the store and put in Abe's order. For myself, I ordered two eggs, over easy, with hash browns and toast. The hash browns at Tide and Griddle smelled great. I suspect that's because they're fried in bacon grease. In deference to my arteries, I asked for the whole wheat toast dry. I poured two large coffees into paper cups at the self-serve coffee counter where the bait box used to be. Then I returned to Abe's table to wait for the order.

"I understand you assaulted someone," I said, eyeing Abe as he leaned back, hands clasped over a slight beer gut bulging over his belt. He looked like a man who'd seen his fair share of troubles.

For a moment, I thought he'd drifted off, head drooping down. But then his eyes snapped open, and he gave a grim shake of his head.

"Verbally. Just verbal. She had it coming," he said, his voice low and tight.

"She who?"

"A lawyer type. I was down at the town hall, trying to sort out my tax bill, and she starts asking Chelsea about land records. It didn't take me long to figure out it was about my place."

I leaned in, intrigued. "And then what?"

"Then Chelsea tells me I don't own the land anymore."

Chelsea, I knew her well. She was the lynchpin that held this little village together. She practically ran town hall by herself. If she said it, it was gospel.

"So you confronted the lawyer in town hall?"

Abe gave a bitter laugh. "Nah. Saw her in the parking lot later, told her to mind her own damn business."

I arched an eyebrow. "That's it?"

"I was mad," Abe said, shrugging. "Don't remember everything I said."

"And then you tried to get out of a jam by using my name."

"Hey, isn't that what brothers are for?"

I frowned.

How was I supposed to know? My best friend, Charlie, and I were like brothers, but I'd never had a real brother. I wished I did when I was eight and my father took off. Now? Now, I wasn't sure I needed a brother. Especially this one.

Again, I wanted to get up and leave, but something kept me there. On the one hand, I didn't want to think about my mother having a baby at a young age. But on the other, I realized the irony that this former nemesis of mine might be one of the few only living connections to her left.

"I'm here to listen. Start at the beginning."

"Okay. When Mom Cromwell died, I had to pay off some uncles who had claims to the farm."

I knew the farm on the edge of the marsh had been in the Cromwell family since before the Revolution.

"I'll give you families can be tough," I said.

11

Abe scoffed as if to say tell me about it. "I worked hard to keep it going. So did my wife. It damn near killed me and did kill Becky. I was in a mess after she passed, but I held on to it for her. The uncles got paid off, but I got behind in my taxes. They've been sky-high since the New Yorkers moved in. I had seventy thousand dollars in back taxes. I got a mortgage to catch up."

"Then what?"

"Everything was fine until I get this paper in the mail two weeks Saturday. It says that my house ain't mine. It belongs to some bank. Where's my omelet?"

"It's coming."

"Did you ask for the side of ham and bacon? I wanted a side."

I downed half a cup of coffee while the server placed the omelet with a side in front of Abe. He smiled for the first time since I walked in. He didn't wait until she handed me my order to tackle his food.

"So, you were saying now a bank owns your home."

"Yeah. Aren't you listening? They tell me the house belongs to the bank. How can it be? I took a loan from a mortgage company. Not the bank. The taxes are all paid up, and I worked night and day to pay up the mortgage. But they say I'm evicted. If Becky was alive, she'd kill me."

"Who gave you the loan?"

"Something Apple. They're out of New York."

"Could it be Big Apple? Think, Abe."

"Yeah, that's it. Big Apple Mortgage. I got the catch-up loan and paid the taxes. I got a receipt from the town hall. You can check."

"Why'd you go out of town to get a loan?"

"I didn't want the whole Creek to know I didn't have the money for the taxes."

"Listen, a lot of people must be in the same boat."

"Don't know about other people's business. And don't care. All I know is I'm up the creek without even a paddle."

"You must have signed something. If I'm going to help, I'll have to see those papers."

"They're in my tackle box on the boat. I brought them to the town hall first thing when it opened. They said the house ain't mine and I got to get out."

Abe pushed away his empty plate. "Thanks. Ya didn't have to do that."

He was wrong there. I did have to. I was glad I did.

I finished my breakfast, and we headed out to his boat on the docks across the wharf so I could look at the papers.

* * *

I stood on the dock as Abe hopped into his boat, a Boston Whaler. The open runabout with a center steering console was the boat of choice in Sachem Creek. He went into his tackle box and retrieved the papers he had brought to town hall earlier. "Here, take a look."

He handed me the crumpled envelope, his hands shaking with anger and confusion. I took out the documents, an eviction notice, and mortgage papers, and read them over carefully. Big Apple Mortgage and Loan, the name alone made me skeptical. They had given Abe what they called a Catch-Up Loan, but it looked more like a setup to me. In return, he had signed his property over to the mortgage company, which rented it back to him. The whole thing reeked of a scam.

I looked up at Abe, his eyes pleading with me for some kind of explanation. I took a deep breath and began to break it down for him in terms even a layman could understand.

"Well, Abe, nobody is going to give you a loan without some kind of security. You should know that. But what you didn't realize is that when you were paying rent every month, it wasn't like a mortgage payment. You were paying rent to live in your own house. You sold them the house and the land for the price of the taxes due."

"Ain't so," he said, his voice rising with indignation. "I own the house free and clear. And the taxes are all paid up. I went down to the town hall, and they said I sold the house. I didn't sell it. If I wouldn't sell it to Amanda, why would I sell it to this mortgage company?"

I could see the confusion in his eyes, the anger building up like a thunderhead on Long Island Sound. It was clear that someone had pulled a fast one on him, and I needed to get to the bottom of this, fast.

"Wait a minute," I said in a low voice, trying not to rile him further. "Amanda wanted to buy your farm?"

"She offered me good money, too. And I needed it, but I wanted to hold on to the place." His voice softened a little. "Becky. Ya know?"

"Why would Amanda want your property?"

"I don't know," he replied, his voice softening a little. "I figured it was to build more fancy houses for her friends. I told her no thanks. That land had been in the family for four hundred years. Funny thing is, it turns out it's not my family after all. But Becky and me worked hard for that land."

I knew Amanda Kittle all too well. She was a bulldozer, plowing through anything in her way, with no regard for the people or the history of the village. Before I moved to Savannah, I had clashed with her many times over the gentrification of the village, and the destruction of many of the historic homes that had made this place so special. And now it seemed like she had set her sights on Abe's property.

"Do you think Amanda is behind this?" I asked, trying to keep the suspicion out of my voice.

"What do you think? That's why I brung these papers to town hall. And they tell me I sold the house. Sold and I have to get out!"

"Because Big Apple sold the house to the bank, and now they're selling it to someone else. That's why you got the eviction notice. How did you get mixed up with this Big Apple in the first place?"

"The antique guy told me about him."

"What antique guy?"

"A guy comes around. I sold him some old tools from the barn. They were all rusty, and he was willing to give good money. I needed to pay the taxes, so I sold them. He told me he knew a guy who gave loans to pay taxes."

"Hold on a minute, Abe. Let me see if I can talk to someone at the mortgage company."

I looked for a telephone number on the papers and punched it into my cell phone. I wasn't surprised to find that the number didn't work. I checked the

Internet. There was no listing for a Big Apple Mortgage and Loan Company in New York or anyplace else. I put the phone back in my pocket and turned to Abe.

"That was a waste of time. Listen again, Abe. A Catch-Up loan gives you money to catch up on your taxes. But you sold them your house and land to boot!"

"You mean I don't get it back when I pay up the mortgage?"

"There is no mortgage to pay up. You sold them the house and were paying rent. Now they sold to the bank, and the bank wants you out."

It finally sank in. I'd never seen a man look more defeated.

"Don't give up, man. There may be something you can do. I'm not promising, but at least you can try. Tell me about this antique dealer."

"Not much to tell. I know he buys antiques."

"Well, that's a start. Do you know anything else about him?"

"That's it. He had a nice car. A white electric car. I know it was electric because it didn't have a grill."

From what I could see in the brief time I'd been back, the electric vehicle now seemed to be the car to own in Sachem Creek, and many of them were white, following the "Apple Effect"—where drivers matched their high-tech cars with their devices.

"Did you notice the make?"

I don't know. Every car looks alike nowadays. I used to know every one of them at a glance. Year, make, model. No more. That's when cars were cars, not computers."

"Abe, focus on his car. Was there anything else?"

"It had his initials on the door under the window. Fancy writing. DW."

"Did you see the plate number?"

"I don't remember, but..."

"What, Abe?"

"The frame on the license plate said Litchfield Autos. I remember because I always heard about the harvest fair up that way. Been meaning to get up there some year."

He gave me a wistful look. He didn't have to say it, but I knew he wouldn't go up there without Becky.

"I hate to say it, but you have to tell this to a lawyer."

Abe reeled back. "Oh, no! No, no, no, no!

"I'm sorry, Abe. Sometimes you need a lawyer."

"Not that. Her."

I followed Abe's gaze down the dock, where Doris Page was walking toward us. Doris made history a few years back when she became the village's first female resident state trooper. Under Connecticut's State Trooper system, a municipality can contract with the State Police to supervise its police officers or constables. She'd followed in her father, Isaac's footsteps. He had made history as the village's first African American trooper.

I'd known Doris all my life.

"Good morning, gentlemen." Doris has a tone that keeps you guessing about what she's thinking. "Nice day for fishing."

"I'm not fishing," Abe said. "I'm talking to my brother."

Doris ignored the remark and turned toward me. "Glad to see you back, Al. I heard you two are newfound relations. May the Lord help you."

"I can use all the help I can get," I said.

Doris dropped our conversation and addressed Abe again. "It seems the prosecutor is going to let you off with a simple verbal assault."

Abe nodded and seemed relieved.

"Hell, I was just blowing off steam, and everyone made a big deal out of it."

But Doris was giving him no chance to celebrate.

"You've still got that other little matter to straighten out, Abe. I can't give you much longer to get out of the house."

"I'm working on it."

He started the engine. I helped cast off his lines and threw his fenders, an odd flat rectangular style of blue vinyl, into the boat. I'd seen that type in a catalog. They cost a lot less than the more common inflatable cylinder-shaped fenders. It's ironic how someone so good at pinching pennies could end up in the situation he was in.

As Abe's boat moved away from the dock, I called out to him.

"Tell me, if you had known I was your brother, and I'm not saying you are,

16

would you still have beaten me up when we were kids?"

Abe threw on a crooked smile that reminded me of Elvis.

"Every day," he said. As the boat made its way up the harbor channel, Doris looked at me and shook her head.

"I don't know…"

She left it at that and headed toward the Sachem Creek rescue boat at the end of the dock. I walked up the dock to the wharf, thinking I might have to stay in town for longer than I had expected.

Chapter Three

While I was on the wharf, I decided to stop by Neal's barbershop—not just for a much-needed trim but because the old barber was the unofficial town crier. Neal was a scissors-and-clippers kind of guy: no washing, no blow-drying. You got a solid haircut, a dusting of talcum powder down your collar, a splash of rosewater, and you were on your way. He prided himself on keeping the same hours as the town dump—eight to four, Tuesday through Saturday. Walk-ins only.

The shop hadn't changed a bit since I'd gotten my first haircut there as a kid. Two gleaming white porcelain chairs with ornate cast-iron footrests stood beneath hanging lamps with milk glass shades. A grand mirror stretched across the wall, its frame cluttered with faded photos and yellowing newspaper clippings. Beneath it, a slim shelf held Neal's neatly arranged tools, while an intricately carved cornice above the mirror added an air of bygone elegance.

Neal was reading the paper in one of the chairs when the bell over the door jingled. He blinked, then sprang to his feet with a wide grin.

"Hey-hey! It's Dick Tracy. Heard you were back."

"Just got in," I said. I'd only been here an hour, but news traveled fast in this village.

"How's business?" I asked, keeping it casual.

"So-so," he admitted, his eyes flicking to the mirror. "Guess scissor-and-clipper joints are too old-school for the New Yorkers."

"Amanda's crowd. I hear ya." I glanced around the shop, wondering how much longer this piece of history could hold out against the tide Amanda had unleashed.

"But you look like you could use a quick trim."

"That's right," I said. Neal motioned for me to take a seat. He chuckled, a glint in his eye. "Promise you won't jump out of the chair when I'm halfway through?" he teased.

I smiled, thinking of my first haircut when I was just a year old. Although I had no recollection of the incident, Neal never failed to remind me of it. But I didn't mind—sometimes it's good to hold onto legends.

"I'll do my best to behave," I joked. "But I expect to leave here with both ears."

Neal threw a seersucker apron over me. "So, how do you want it today?" he asked.

"Number 5 clippers on the sides and trim the top," I instructed.

As he worked, I closed my eyes a few times and let my thoughts wander. Nobody's ever called me nostalgic, but this connection to my past stirred up memories as well as a few questions.

"You're pretty quiet," Neal observed.

"Just thinking," I replied. "Hey, do you remember who brought me in for my first haircut?"

"What do you mean?" Neal asked.

"I mean, was it my father or my grandfather?"

Neal's face turned red as a baboon's ass. "Uh, I guess it was your old man," he stammered. "Yes, definitely. Hey, I heard you found him. That's great. How's he doing?"

"He found me," I corrected. "But he's got some memory problems. He's hanging in there, though." I decided to keep the details to myself—it would be interesting to see how the story evolved as it spread around town.

The conversation stopped when Buster and Walter walked into the shop. They were a couple of older guys who ran a handyman business, specializing in restoring historic homes the old-fashioned way. I glanced from one to the other, sizing them up. From their expressions, it looked like there might be trouble in paradise.

Neal picked up on it, too. "Everything all right?"

"Car shopping. Need I say more?" Buster's response was tense.

"I could see Walter wasn't happy. 'Mr.-Keep-Up-With-the-Joneses is insisting on a BEV just because everyone else is getting them. Ridiculous!"

Neal had no clue what they were talking about, so I decided to enlighten him. "Battery Electric Vehicle," I said. "It does seem there are a lot of them in town.

"He's a tree hugger," Walter said, his voice dripping with the disdain of someone set in their ways.

Buster came back with, "And he's stuck in the fifties. Our generation caused the hole in the ozone layer, and we should fix it."

"Okie Dokie, so did you see who's here?" Neal pointed to me in the chair. Smart move not to get involved in a domestic, I thought.

"I hear you quit your job and moved to Florida," Buster said.

"Savannah. Savannah, Georgia."

"There's a community down that way called The Burbs. All the retirees there drive electric vehicles, Buster said."

"The Burbs is in Florida, and they use golf carts, not electric cars," Walter said.

"Same difference!" Buster seemed as if he had had enough. "So, how'd the meeting go?" He asked.

"It went fine," I replied, not surprised that he knew about it.

Walter slumped into one of four chrome chairs, their red oilcloth seats worn with use, placed against a wainscot wall layered with so many coats of green paint that it resembled alligator skin.

"It looked like Abe took off in a huff after Doris chewed him out," Walter added.

"She was only talking to him," I said.

"If you say so. I could have seen it wrong," Walter replied.

I don't know if Neal changed the subject because he lost interest or if he had an agenda. He turned the chair so that I was facing the window.

"Bill's got the right idea. He's headed for Vermont. He wants to avoid the wedding madness this weekend."

I watched through the plate glass with reversed gold lettering that spelled out Neal's Barbershop. Bill Lester, of Pot Island, one of the handful of locals who hadn't sold his island to Amanda, was on the wharf with his wife and three kids. They were loading luggage into the back of a car.

"What wedding? I asked

"You don't know?" Neal had a skeptical expression on his face.

I didn't know what Neal was trying to tell me, but I knew I'd soon find out. I hoped this conversation wasn't going to become one of the all-too-familiar rides on a merry-go-round that I experienced with Big Al. I tried to keep my voice calm. "No. I'm not following you."

"The wedding. Out there."

"A beach wedding?"

"No. Out there on Kittle Island. At Amanda's place." He pointed his comb out to the nearby island.

Long Island Sound was tranquil as a kitten on Paxil. Many small craft lay idle at cedar mooring poles driven into the harbor bottom. Kittle Island looked as if it, too, was only temporarily moored, ready to float away on the next tide.

"Amanda is getting married again?"

"Not Amanda. But she's throwing the shindig for the bride." In the mirror, I could see that Neal had a weird look on his face.

"So, who's getting married?"

"I don't know. A friend of hers," Neal said.

Walter came up to the chair and put a hand on my shoulder. "Someone has to tell you this. Kim's marrying Tom Donahue."

Before Kim and I split, Amanda had formed a friendship with Kim. She used to egg her on about how bad I was, and she encouraged her to take up with Donahue. I'm sure it was to get even with me because I always stood up against her development of the village. I processed it for a minute, then burst out laughing.

"No shit. I wish them luck. They'll need it.

"It's not your fault, so no sense getting upset over what might have been," Buster said.

"I'm not upset." I really wasn't. I had gotten over it long before I moved to

21

Savannah.

"It probably is your fault. You and Kim should have gone to marriage counseling like we did," Walter said.

Buster waved him off. "That's exactly why we went to counseling. You always contradict me."

"You got yourself an invite to the wedding?" Neal asked. In the mirror, I could see that he winked at Buster and Walter. They were sitting on the edge of their chairs, taking in every word. It was obvious they had nothing to do at home that morning.

"No. I didn't know anything about it."

"And here I am thinking it's nice there are no hard feelings and you're here to wish the happy couple luck." He put the comb in a jar of blue water on the counter and then turned on the clippers.

"No hard feelings at all. I've moved on. But I'm not going to the wedding." I glanced over to Kittle Island. The mansion's red slate roof barely showed above the trees.

"Didn't think you'd get invited," Walter said.

I tried to make my voice sound as if I didn't give a damn about what they thought.

"I'm here for the race and to find out what's going on with Abe. That's it." Under the seersucker cape, I gripped the arms of the chair so hard my fingers went numb.

"That's some coincidence about Abe's problems, Kim getting hitched, and the race all falling at once," Neal said.

"Yeah, kind of the perfect storm if you ask me," Walter put in. "Not that I'm saying they're all connected."

"And what business is it of ours if Al wants to go to the wedding?" Buster asked.

Why would they think I cared if Kim was getting married? "Not too close on the top," I said to Neal.

"I hear it's going to cost a bundle to put on that shindig." Neal clipped away, not indicating that he heard my instructions.

"It sure is! It's going to be a whopper of a classy deal. It'll be written up in Connecticut Magazine and The New York Times." I could see a bit of pride on Buster's face as he walked to the window and looked toward Kittle Island. I'm sure he was trying to imagine the grand event.

Buster was probably right about the write-ups, though, since it would bring together the Creekers, my ex-wife's Yankee family, and the New York Society part-time residents, the groom's side. This had never happened around here before.

"Not too close," I repeated.

"They say it's going to cost upwards of two hundred and fifty-thousand dollars. The biggest thing in the Creek since old man Kittle's funeral," Neal said.

Two hundred and fifty thousand dollars! I could think of a lot of better things to do with that kind of money than blowing it on a wedding.

"He's going to be at the wedding, I suppose," Buster said.

"Who?" I couldn't imagine who he was talking about.

"Old-man Kittle."

Neal had a serious look on his face. "He has to be. It's part of the will. He has to be at every family occasion, or all the money goes to charity."

"That's right. I understand they even got him a formal urn for the occasion," said Walter. "Heard the wife cracked the old one. Amanda kept it under the bed while she was banging the gardener. She figured if he wanted to be there for every occasion, so be it."

Neal began to cackle. "Yep, can't you hear him shouting from his urn under the bed? 'Hey, cut out the bouncing up there.'"

Buster took up the conversation on old man Kittle's behalf. "Hell-low-ah, I'm not a dust bunny down here. Let's stop the bouncy bounce!"

The three of them burst out in laughter again.

"I guess when you have money, it makes you do stupid things, even after you're dead," Walter said. For a second, envy flashed in his eyes.

"The summer people are no better than us. They just have better boats." Buster turned back from the window. "She didn't like all the talk when she married Old Man Kittle. Some people called her a gold digger."

Neal snipped away. "People around here talk too much. That's why I mind my own beeswax."

"Absolutely," Buster said. "I do the same. Still, the whole Kittle marriage thing has flared up again since she's been using the old man's money to snatch up every piece of property she can get her hands on."

"When I drove in this morning, I noticed the Peterson and Wald places were gone. So is the Robinson homestead. That's a lot of change in the west end of town since I went down south."

"You're telling me," Buster said. "Every time she grabs one of those fine old Victorians, it's one less home we can restore—and one more mansion for her New York friends to flaunt their money in."

Walter shook his head. "She's tearing down history just to build show-pieces. This village is losing its charm brick by brick."

I was eager for their take on Abe's situation. "Do you think she's behind Abe losing his farm?"

"It wouldn't surprise me," Buster said.

"Ha!" Neal gestured with his clippers. "You haven't seen the half of it. She's been tearing down every cottage she can get her hands on.

"Ouch!" I threw my hand to my ear.

Neal had nicked my ear, but he went right on talking. "Some people say she's doing it to get back for the gossip when she married Kittle. Rumor has it, there's talk of an upscale housing development to lure even more of her rich New York friends away from the Hamptons. Imagine that!"

Buster nodded. "Property values and taxes to shoot up like crazy. Families who've been here for generations will be forced out. I say it's a real shame. I just hope Walter and I can manage to hold on to our place."

Walter leaned in close to my ear as if he were going to tell me a secret but his voice was anything but a whisper. I think he was assessing the damage. "You wish it was *only* a housing development. I heard Amanda's got some real big plans for that land."

Yeah, well," Neal muttered, as he trimmed the back of my hair. "Word around the wharf is that she's got an eye for land that might hold 'historical treasures,' if you catch my drift. Some even say she's been reading up on the old Captain Kidd rumors."

I raised an eyebrow. "Kidd's treasure, huh? Thought that was just talk to keep the summer people entertained."

"Yeah, I've heard a few things too," Buster said, a glint in his eye. "On the wharf, the word is that she also wants to reopen the Old Man Kiddle's granite quarry. They say there's been some action up there. Folks like Amanda don't spend big money on old stone pits without a reason."

"Nonsense, The quarries are history, Neal said. "Nobody wants this to be a quarry town again. Don't forget, at one time, we had four of them here. We're through with that chaos. People nowadays are for protecting the land. It's all about the Killer View. That quarry rumor is a smoke screen. Get the tree huggers riled up about a quarry, and then they're fine with a housing project, even if it means more taxes."

I looked at a smear of blood on my finger from where Neal had nicked my ear and wiped it on the seersucker apron.

Neal turned off the clippers.

I kept looking in the big mirror in disbelief.

"What? Not what you wanted?"

"I wanted the top done by hand."

"What do you mean? Oliver Welles never complained. Look at this." He pointed to a faded brown and white photograph hanging on the wall. "Do you know who that is?"

I reached to the counter and grabbed a hand mirror to check the back. I didn't want to see that stupid picture again.

"That's me and Oliver Welles. Back in the day. Every time he came to the Playhouse, I gave him that same haircut I gave you. And he never complained."

I'd heard about Welles all my life. Every summer, he brought his troupe to the village theater before moving on to New York. He even made a movie in town. He was a local folk hero, but I didn't want to look like him.

"If the good old days ever come back, I'm all set."

I saw the hurt look on Neal's face and gave him a bigger tip than he deserved, or I could afford. He took it, noted how large it was, and figured he owed me some advice.

"Look, you're a Creeker. You don't belong there."

"Where?" I said.

"At the wedding."

"He's right, you know," said Buster. "The Creekers have no business getting mixed up with the summer people."

"I'm not getting mixed up with them. My ex is."

"Well, then enjoy the wedding!" the three of them chimed as I walked out of the barbershop in a huff.

When I got to my car, I took a close look in the mirror; my hair had more divots than the fairways of the new Sachem Creek Country Club, another innovation of the part-time residents.

I looked at my hair in the mirror again. God help anybody who broke them on me today.

Chapter Four

When I went back to Phoebe's place, the note on the door told me she and Big Al had taken off for the day. I climbed the steps to my old apartment. It looked smaller than I remembered. But the old stuffed chair was still there, along with the faded rug and the coffee table covered with rings from my wet beer bottles.

I needed to decompress. The trip had been rough, and the meeting with Abe had been even rougher. And now, on top of everything else, I had to deal with the news that my ex was marrying my rival. I took a deep breath, trying to push those thoughts aside. I needed to clear my head and figure out my next move.

I still had a few things stored in the garage under the apartment, including my kayak from before I left for Savannah. I had to get ready for the race anyway. Maybe being out on the water was just what I needed to calm me down and give me the clarity I needed.

I drove back down to the wharf, where I could only find a parking space in front of a dumpster. No one was going to be dumping it before morning, so I parked.

I bought a ham and cheese sub along with a bottle of water from the Tide and Griddle walk-up window and stowed them in my dry bag for later. After that, I hauled my kayak and other equipment to the postage-stamp-sized beach that served as the only authorized launch point for kayaks. This beach lay nestled between the village green adjoining the seawall and the wharf, a domain overseen by Bart Frisbee, the village's self-proclaimed dock master. God forbid you should set your kayak down on the grass. Bart would never let you hear the end of it.

I was putting on my safety device when I noticed Bart standing on top of the seawall. Bart can be a pain in the ass, but he has this uncanny talent for accurately predicting the weather. So much so that people call him Bart the Barometer. It's a name that he seems to like. His arms folded over the I'm A Creeker t-shirt that strained to contain his belly, he called down to me.

"What do you think you're doing?"

"I'm going out."

"For how long?"

"Until I get back. Why?"

Bart motioned to my vehicle. "Your car is parked on the wharf in front of a dumpster."

"Now listen, Bart, the wharf is full, mostly with cars from out of town, I might add."

Bart was no dummy. "Your car is from out of town. It has Georgia plates."

"Well, there you go. It fits right in."

"It's still in front of a dumpster." Bart seemed hell-bent on giving me a hard time.

"That dumpster shouldn't even be there. That used to be two public parking spaces before it was dropped there." Dropped there for the convenience of the people on the islands, I should have said, but he knew what I meant. "Nobody is going to empty that dumpster until morning. My car will be long gone before then. I mean, the wharf is a public parking place."

"Not after dark, it isn't. Make sure you're back by then."

"Come on. What's the difference if I get back after dark, as long as the car is gone before morning?"

"You know what the difference is. The wharf is closed after dark unless you're an island resident."

After sundown, the parking spaces on the wharf are by permit only for the people who live out on the Nutmegs. Living on the islands is nice, but the drawback is that everything has to be schlepped out there by private boat or on the water taxi. So most islanders do their shopping in the evening when

28

they're guaranteed a parking spot near the docks.

"I'll be back on time."

"Kayaks don't belong on the water after dark," he said.

I held up my dry bag so he could see my flashlight in it. "I'll put my light under my deck line so I can be seen. What can go wrong?"

I set off from the shore, propelling myself with steady paddles until I reached the far end of the docks, sailing past the Lavinia Warren. This cruise boat was christened after General Tom Thumb's wife, a famous couple who once worked for P. T. Barnum. They had tied the knot on one of the Nutmeg Islands.

Captain Bruce, a rugged man in his late fifties, with a sun-leathered complexion and piercing blue eyes, spotted me as he boarded passengers for a sunset tour. His faded navy captain's cap, complete with an embroidered anchor, and salt-and-pepper beard set the tone for the bullshit stories of the islands his passengers were about to hear.

"I heard you were back!" He called out.

Of course, he had. I gave a wave and headed up the channel. I made a circuit of the inner islands as I had done so many times as a teenager. Victorian gingerbread is the norm in the Nutmegs. Neal had complained about mainland Sachem Creek losing one fine old house after another. From what I understood, the same fate was in store for the islands.

As I glided past Governor Island, I spotted a kayaker who had bottomed out. It was a safe bet they were from out of town. Most locals knew how easy it was to misjudge the depth. The danger of boating in the Nutmegs was that one minute the depth was sixty feet, and the next six inches.

I had a towing harness in my dry bag. I put myself through college giving paddling lessons, so I knew the value of keeping one in the kayak to use as an emergency tow rope.

I attached the Y end of the rope to the chocks behind my cockpit. Then I tossed the single end of the rope to the guy in the other kayak. I told him to clip it on a sturdy handle. I paddled slowly until the rope was taut. Then I put more strength into it and pulled him off the sandbar. My "rescue" mission accomplished, I went on my way.

I maneuvered through the calm waters between the remains of sturdy granite piers that had once supported a footbridge that connected the divided halves of Cut-In-Two Island. The Great Hurricane of '38 had reduced the bridge to memories, leaving behind only remnants of its existence.

As I continued paddling through the narrow channel, one of my favorite spots, Davis Island, President Taft's summer White House, came into view. The history of the islands, spanning from the summer encampments of Native Americans to clandestine hideouts of pirates, and further to the seasonal retreats of presidents and celebrities, always fascinated me.

With determination, I set my sights on Outer Island, the furthest one in the chain. I liked setting challenges for myself and reaching Outer Island and returning to the wharf before dark, so I wouldn't get a ticket, had become my personal "Bart Frisbee Challenge."

After gliding past Horse Island, Outer Island was in sight. One of the few uninhabited large islands in the Nutmegs, there had been a house on it at one time, but all that remained was a fireplace chimney standing like a periscope in the center of the island. Several years before, it had become a wildlife sanctuary, and a large sign marked it as off-limits to the public.

The sun was beginning to dip below the horizon, and I couldn't ignore the fact that there was only about an hour of daylight left. I knew I was pushing my luck, so I picked up my pace and focused on each stroke. The water around me glistened with the hues of the setting sun. The thrill of the adventure, mixed with a hint of anxiousness, urged me onward.

Although now based in Savannah, I still keep tabs on the goings-on at home through the "Simply Sachem Creek" Facebook group. Recently, my friend Jamila Cambridge shared a post stating that endangered Piping Plovers had nested on the island. Jamila is in charge of the refuge and writes a newspaper column for the Sachem Creek Gazette. As I rounded the island, I noticed someone on the rocks. When he saw me, he hopped into a small yellow and red kayak and headed toward open water.

People trespassed on the islands all the time. It was hard to control. But his genie's slipper-shaped kayak caught my attention more than anything. It was a strange-looking kayak for these parts. I'd read enough kayaking magazines to know it was a rodeo kayak used for doing tricks on white water rivers. He handled his kayak like an expert and had already put a good distance between us. It wasn't my place to pursue him out into Long Island Sound. But I would mention it to Jamila when I saw her.

I headed down the narrow channel. On its eastern flank lies Pot Island, marked by smooth, rounded outcroppings of rock with deep potholes carved into the surface by glaciers during the Ice Age. Across the channel to the west, High Island stands with its sheer rock palisades jutting out of the water to heights of twenty-five feet or more. Along the reddish rock face, crooked pine trees cling, their roots finding a foothold in the cracks. The towering walls of High Island remain unbroken, save for the entrance to Hidden Cove, aka Kidd's Harbor, a secret haven nestled within.

Come the weekend, boats from Long Island would crowd the sheltered area. But for now, I was alone and glad of it. I stopped in the channel to eat, even knowing I was sure to get back after dark if I did. I'd have a ticket on my car, but I'd handle Bart when the time came. I pulled the sub and my phone from my dry bag. As I wolfed down a few bites, I pressed video call and keyed in Max's number. Big Al and I left Savannah while she was in Atlanta, and I didn't get to say goodbye. Max answered, and even though the sun was low in the sky, the day got a little brighter. Although it was well after 8:00 pm, I could see she was still at the Blue Palmetto.

"Hard day?" I asked.

The right side of her mouth twitched in a brief, halfhearted smile painted with a touch of sadness.

"No more than any day."

"Hey, I miss you," I said.

"It's quiet around here without you, too. How's Big Al making out?"

It wasn't quite the response I had hoped for, but I learned a long time ago not to read into what people say. For all I knew, she had other things on her mind.

"He's fine. Listen, we may be staying up here a little longer than we had expected."

"So, okay. You're bonding with the newfound brother. I'm happy for you."

"Not exactly. Abe is getting evicted from his farm, and he's disappeared. I want to find him before he hurts himself or someone else."

"Take all the time you need. Family first."

I lost my train of thought when someone stood behind Max. His face was out of the picture. She turned around and took his hand.

"Who's that?" I tried to make my voice sound casual, but my insides were reeling because I had a pretty good idea of who it was—Phil Malkovich. Phil was a TV journalist from Atlanta. He was also Max's ex-husband, who stole an Emmy from her by taking credit for a story she broke. In a pecan shell, she left Atlanta and TV, and my father gave her a job as head detective at the Blue Palmetto. All this was before my time in Savannah.

Phil leaned down and stuck his chiseled face in the camera.

"How's it going, old sport?" Phil's grin was nowhere near as melancholy as Max's attempted smile had been.

"Would you mind pulling back a bit? I just had my dinner."

"Did Max tell you the good news? We're giving it another go."

Max pushed him away. "I was going to get to that, Al. Phil is like a new man, and he asked me to give him another chance. I owe it to him. So…" She inhaled deeply. I wish I knew if her hesitance was because she was trying to find the words to tell me or because she wasn't sure if she was doing the right thing. "So, we're going to give it a try."

"Right. I think you should. Hey, listen, I have to get going. I'll keep you in the loop." I hung up thinking, that's more than she'd done for me. The day dimmed as quickly as it had brightened.

As I disconnected and threw my phone back into my drybag, the thunderous roar of an outboard engine shattered the air. My eyes shot up, catching sight of a sleek Boston Whaler hurtling up the channel. In a split second, I realized it was too late for evasive maneuvers. Bracing myself for impact, my heart raced as the boat cut across my bow, the proximity sending shockwaves through my body. With a heart-pounding swerve, the vessel accelerated, slicing through the narrow channel towards Long Island Sound. In its wake, a monstrous swell consumed my kayak, flipping it over without warning. So much for the no-wake zone.

Submerged upside down in the murky depths, disoriented and disheart-ened, I desperately clutched the edge of the cockpit, pushed off with my legs, and fell free. As I gazed at my overturned kayak, looming ominously above me, Bart's haunting words echoed—a cruel reminder of my predicament. *"I told you kayaks shouldn't be on the water at night."* Screw Bart.

"Bubbles up," I thought, pushing myself upward, limbs straining against the water's resistance. Bursting through the surface, gasping for air, I searched for my paddle. Luck was on my side, and I snatched it before it slipped away. I swam towards the overturned kayak and, reaching my vessel, I placed the paddle atop it, a small victory amidst the turmoil.

High Island, shrouded in darkness on the other side of the channel, offered no solace. Through the trees that clung to the cliff, a dim glow of gaslight flickered in a cottage window, teasing my hopes. Yet, there was no sign of a helping hand, no indication that anyone had witnessed my plunge into the murky waters. Abandoned to my resourcefulness, I steeled myself for the back-breaking task of salvaging my flooded kayak.

My heart pounded with a mix of anger, frustration, and determination. I had to get the water out of my vessel. My drybag with my hand pump was gone. Pumping was a slow process anyway. It was possible to paddle a flooded kayak, but the water inside sloshes back and forth, creating a momentum of its own. It's slow, strenuous work, and the fight to keep it from tipping is constant. That would be the last resort.

Summoning every ounce of resilience, I swam with the waterlogged vessel, pushing it against the current towards Bill Lester's small dock on Pot Island. It was a slow and challenging process, but I refused to give up. Finally, climbing onto the dock, I tugged until I got the bow of the upside-down kayak onto the boards. I struggled to pull the kayak higher until the water seal between the flooded kayak and the surface of the water broke, allowing the water to flow out. With most of the water out, I pulled the kayak fully onto the dock to drain the rest of the water.

As I worked, my senses on high alert, something caught my eye—a form on the small beach obscured by the shadows. I dashed off the dock toward the still figure in a white two-piece bathing suit. With instincts ingrained in

33

me from my days on the force, I approached with caution, my mind buzzing with uncertainty. Even in the dim light, I could determine that the woman resting against a large boulder had reddish hair and appeared to be in her mid-thirties.

"Can you believe that guy?" I said, attempting to establish a connection. She remained eerily silent, unresponsive to my presence.

My senses heightened; I took in every detail of the scene. Moving closer, I studied her form, body slumped over, completely motionless. My eyes scanned for any signs of life. With a mix of urgency and dread, I reached out, my fingers searching for a pulse, for any sign of vitality. None. Still, I started chest compressions hard and fast, all the while my eyes observing the scene. "Someone help!" I shouted, hoping someone on High Island across the way would hear. No response.

After several rounds, I had no doubt. She was dead.

Chapter Five

For my money, she had been deliberately positioned there, carefully arranged. My phone was in my drybag and gone. I had no way of calling 9-1-1. I knew Bill had taken his family to Vermont, but hoped he had a house sitter who would let me use his phone. I ran to the house and banged on the door. The house was deserted. The natives had been a trusting lot until the interlopers came to town. Once upon a time, the place would have been wide open, but even so, they weren't cynical enough not to leave a spare key hidden in plain sight. I trailed my hand along the top edge of the doorframe, and sure enough, the key was there waiting for me. With relief, I let myself into the kitchen, confident that Bill wouldn't object—no question about it. I used his phone to call 9-1-1.

I knew help from shore would take at least half an hour, so I called Max to fill her in. Sitting alone with a dead woman wasn't exactly my idea of a good time—or so I told myself to justify the call. She picked up on the second ring.

"Really, Al? Calling me to check on Phil? He's gone."

"This isn't about Phil," I cut her off.

"Then what?"

"I just found a body on the beach."

There was a pause, long enough for her to process. When she spoke again, her tone was sharp. "Wait—what? Are you serious? Where's Big Al?"

"Dead serious. My father's with Phoebe. I already called 9-1-1. Thought you should know. It's a woman, propped against a boulder. Doesn't look like an accident."

She exhaled. "Are you okay?"

"I'm fine. Didn't touch anything. The cops are on their way."

"Good. Let them handle it."

"I will. I just want to get through this mess for Abe, finish the race, and come home."

"I wish I could believe that, but I know you."

"Yeah, but you don't know Doris. She wouldn't let me get involved even if I wanted to."

A brief silence, then her tone softened. "Listen, about Phil—if you're worried, don't be. We're just clearing the air, saying things we should've said years ago."

"Phil who?" I shot back. "I've gotta go."

"If you need backup, say the word. I can be on a plane tonight."

"I'm fine. The cops will be here soon."

"You've got this. Just…don't do anything stupid."

"Wouldn't dream of it."

"Good. And for the love of God, keep me in the loop."

"Will do."

I hung up and jogged back to the beach to wait. Doris fooled me by arriving with a team of volunteer firefighters and EMTs in just fifteen minutes. As usual, she was all business.

"I understand you discovered a body. You've been back what, a day?"

If she was trying to bait me, I wasn't going to give her the satisfaction. "More or less."

"What were you doing out here?"

"I was kayaking."

"I understand Bart gave you a warning about going out so close to dark."

"Bart says a lot of things. That body didn't end up there because it was dark."

I glanced toward the EMTs, standing by while waiting for instructions. "I already know she's dead."

"They're not here to determine cause of death. Let them wait for the medical examiner."

"Were you alone together?"

"What are you getting at, Doris?" My irritation flared, but I tamped it down. In my previous life as a cop, I'd been just as blunt in similar situations.

"You know I had to ask," she said without apology. "I assume you preserved the integrity of the scene?"

"You have to ask that? I left the force, but some instincts stay with you."

"So, you didn't touch anything?"

"Not other than laying her down to give CPR. Preservation of life overrides crime scene integrity, or has that changed? When I determined it was hopeless, I immediately called it in."

"Did you notice anything about the body or the surroundings?"

"Female, mid-thirties maybe, propped against a boulder at the end of the beach. It looked staged. No sign of a struggle, no personal belongings nearby, and the only footprints were mine. Someone cleaned up. The body's above the high tide line, so the water didn't erase the footprints."

"And the victim certainly didn't," Doris muttered. It wasn't much, but it felt like a concession.

"So, you're thinking what I'm thinking."

Doris pursed her lips, studying the beach. "Homicide."

"That wasn't so bad, was it?"

"What?"

"Sharing your thoughts."

She ignored me, her expression unreadable. The subtle wave of her hand signaled the EMTs to stand down and wait. Minutes later, the medical examiner arrived, a wiry man with a focused demeanor. He crouched by the body, taking notes and photos before nodding to the EMTs.

When they finally loaded her onto the rescue boat, Doris turned back to me. "Don't get any ideas, Al. This is my investigation."

"Wouldn't dream of it," I lied.

Doris and I rode back on the ferry, which plied between the dock and the Nutmegs every two hours between 6:00 a.m. and midnight. The ancient flat-roofed boat usually toted everything from passengers to groceries to lumber. That night, with my kayak tied to the side like Santiago's marlin,

Doris and I were the only passengers. I told her everything. I shared about the Boston Whaler, my plunge into the channel, struggling to get the water out of the kayak, spotting the body, and going into Bill's place.

I couldn't help feeling that if I had gotten there sooner, I would have saved the girl's life. Would I have been there in time if I had taken a different route? What if I hadn't towed the kayaker, or if I hadn't wasted time arguing with Bart? I couldn't know, but I felt guilty, and even though I had never felt seasick before, right then, only pride stopped me from puking.

When we arrived at the dock shortly after 11 p.m., a rescue truck was waiting. No flashing emergency lights, but the motor was running. As they transferred the girl's body from the rescue boat to the truck, I looked the other way, watching the ferry head back out for its last run of the evening.

"Be at the dock by 9:00 a.m.," Doris said. "We'll go back out there in the daylight. I want you to show me step by step what happened."

"I told you I don't know what happened. I found her on the beach propped against that rock. I couldn't revive her. That's it."

Bart Frisbee's annoying voice interrupted the conversation. "Storm tomorrow!"

I turned to see Bart, standing behind me, all too close to my personal space. Doris looked toward the star-filled sky.

"Not a cloud up there, Bart, and Channel 8 said it would be clear."

"Storm tomorrow!" Bart repeated. "Barometer 29.8, falling quick. Wind from the East. Storm tomorrow!" Bart was becoming agitated because Doris didn't seem to believe him.

Captain Bruce was on the dock checking the Lavinia Warren's lines. It was late for him to be there since the sunset cruise had ended hours ago. "If Bart says a storm is coming, it's coming."

Doris gave the captain a nod, conceding that Bart usually was right. Then she turned toward me. "Storm or no storm, we shove off at 9:00 a.m. And Al…?"

"Yeah?"

"I don't have to tell you not to be late, do I?"

"You've known me long enough, Doris. I'll be here at 9:00 a.m. tomorrow.

Rain or shine."

Chapter Six

Saturday, June 25

At 2:00 a.m., I was still awake. To no avail, I had put away a half bottle of Grey Goose in the hopes of falling asleep. My stomach was killing me. Every time I moved my head, I felt like I was in the whirlpool out at the Race where the Atlantic pushes into Long Island Sound. When I could stand it no longer, I crawled to the bathroom, and with my head suspended over the toilet bowl, I stuck my fingers down my throat.

After throwing up, the room didn't spin anymore and I went to bed. My sleep was fitful. Awake or not, I saw the girl, propped against the rock like a discarded mannequin, the sand stuck to her skin.

At 6:30 a.m., I awoke to thunder and lightning. Bart was right, and Channel 8, despite its Doppler radar, was wrong. I don't know why they don't hire Bart to do their forecasts. By 7:15, the rain had stopped, but the winds were still pretty heavy, and I knew that the water was going to be rough. I also knew that Doris would still want to go out there even though there wasn't going to be much to see. I figured I would humor her and show her where I was when the Boston Whaler almost crashed into me. I didn't know if the reckless boat driver was involved in the victim's death. But I owed it to the girl to help Doris find out.

I was hoping to make a quick exit from my apartment above the garage without encountering Big Al or Phoebe, but as I descended the outside stairs, they were waiting for me on the porch.

"Are you all right?" Phoebe asked.

"Fine."

Phoebe looked doubtful. "The way I see it, the individual who discovers the victim is also a victim in their own right."

I felt a weight of sadness pass over me. At that moment, I wasn't sure if I should be mad at Phoebe for pointing that out or thanking her.

"It's not the first body I've seen. You'd think I'd be used to it by now."

Big Al seemed to be staring off into the clouds as the whole conversation seemed to go right over his head. I was thinking that it was just as well that he was oblivious when he spoke up.

"This work," he said. "We don't do it because we like bad shit. We do it because we don't. If you get used to death, you're in the wrong business."

Phoebe and I exchanged glances. Sometimes, when you think he's lost in his own world, he comes out with something that makes sense.

"Why didn't you tell us what happened when you got in last night?" Phoebe asked.

"It was late when I got in."

"I know it was late. I left the light on for you," she said.

It was bad enough that I'd have to go over the story again when I saw Doris. I didn't feel like giving an account to my father and aunt right then.

"I'll tell you when I get back. I have an appointment. "

"You don't have to meet Doris until 9:00."

It seemed that the Sachem Creek rumor mill had been churning all night long.

"I'm going with you," Big Al said.

Just what I was afraid of. Big Al may have given me the Blue Palmetto on paper, but in his mind, we were partners.

"Sorry. No can do. Doris won't allow you to go with us. You weren't a witness."

Big Al made a face. I was sure there would be fireworks until Phoebe put her hand on Big Al's. "We'll meet him for breakfast on the deck at Tide and Griddle when he's done. How about that?"

He nodded. Phoebe seemed to have the magic touch when it came to calming him down.

"Sounds like a plan," I said and got out of there while the getting was good.

* * *

I was at the wharf by 8:00. It was too early for Doris, although I had no doubt she'd be there before our 9:00 appointment. I parked next to a beautiful pearl-colored electric SUV. It must kill the rich people who own houses on the islands to have to leave their gorgeous vehicles unattended on the wharf.

The water in the harbor was choppy, and I knew it would be worse out there. I didn't see Doris, so I decided I had time to duck into Tide & Griddle for a coffee.

Inside, Captain Bruce, Buster, Walter, and a few other regulars were yakking up a storm. It got quiet when they noticed me.

"What?"

Chaos broke out as they all threw questions at me.

"I know as much as you do. Or less," I told them. "Let's drop it."

Walter hopped up from his table and shouted like a trial lawyer.

"Drop it! It's not like a dead body shows up around here every day!"

"Well, I have nothing to say about it." I walked to the counter and bought my coffee, then sat down.

It was quiet again. All eyes were on me, and I needed to break the silence.

"Has anyone seen Abe this morning?"

"Not yet," Captain Bruce said.

"He was in quite a state yesterday. I'm a little concerned," I said.

Bruce waved it off. "He probably headed up to the casino. That place has been his second home since Becky died."

I thought that might explain some of his problems, but I didn't want to go there.

"Doris's been waiting for you since eight," Captain Bruce said.

"She told me nine. You were there."

Bruce scoffed. "You know Doris."

I didn't see her black and white on the wharf, so I knew the guys were pulling my leg. I brought my coffee with me and went out to meet her anyway. Feeling smug about being early, I walked down the weathered dock toward where the Sachem Creek Rescue boat lay tied up at the end. I was surprised to see that Doris was already on board.

She cast a glance at her timepiece, then back at me, a subtle reproach lingering in her expression.

"I was in Tide and Griddle." I'd tried to lace a tinge of nonchalance in my voice. But she came back with an undisguised tone of annoyance and frustration.

"I saw you."

"Why didn't you come in and get me?"

"I reckoned it was your responsibility to arrive punctually,"

"Well, I made it with time to spare."

While Doris busied herself with fueling the boat, I took the opportunity to ask about the unidentified girl, her presence in my thoughts growing by the second.

"Has she been IDed?"

"She has," Doris mumbled.

"Are you going to enlighten me?" I pressed.

"Not until the family is duly informed." Her voice was solemn.

"Do you know how she died?"

"They're doing the autopsy up in Farmington."

"When will it be back?"

"Couple of days."

I knew further prodding would yield no more information than the storm clouds looming overhead.

We pushed off on the dot of nine o'clock.

* * *

Doris was careful to keep the speed down as we headed up the channel. Police business or not, she'd observe the no-wake policy in the harbor. I thought of how the guy in the Boston Whaler had swamped me. Either the jerk didn't give a damn about damaging the shoreline, or he was in a big hurry to get out of there.

As we passed the green buoy marking the end of the channel, Doris opened up the twin outboards. The aluminum bow lifted out of the water, and she put on the wipers to clear the spray from the windshield.

The exhilaration of the hull slapping on the choppy water and the cool, fresh air lifted my spirits a bit. I took a deep breath, trying to further drive the evil events of last night from my brain. I consoled myself by thinking that with water this rough, I wouldn't have been able to train for the race anyway. Hopefully, tomorrow's weather would be better, this mess would be settled, and I could take a trial run across Long Island Sound.

I glanced over at Doris. Was she thinking, as I was, that the Boston Whaler had something to do with the girl's death? She looked straight ahead, giving away nothing, as we sped out to Outer Island so that we'd enter the Channel from the same direction as I had. As we got near Outer Island, I asked Doris if I could borrow her binoculars. She reluctantly gave them over with a grunt.

"Those babies cost me five hundred dollars. Be careful with them."

Normally, I wouldn't have let the remark go unchallenged, but under the circumstances, I thought it best to do so. Instead, I searched the island where I had seen the trespasser the day before. I was curious to see if he had returned. Sure enough, I spotted someone.

"Hold up, Doris. Someone is on the island again!"

Doris had already cut the engines a little, being in a channel once more.

"I didn't need glasses to see him. And what do you mean again?"

"There was a guy out on the island yesterday, just before I found the girl. He took off in a weird little kayak."

Doris glared at me. "You didn't think you should mention that?"

"Well, no." The Kayaker was on Outer Island, and I found the girl on Pot Island a good ways down the channel where the Boston Whaler had swamped me. My money was on the guy in the Whaler as the killer, but now Doris was seeding doubt in my mind. Was I slipping or just too overtired to overlook that possibility?

44

Doris grunted again.

The interloper must have spotted us because he ran over a low rise of glacier-smoothed rock toward the other side of the island. I couldn't be sure if it was the same joker as the day before or not.

Doris sighed. "Never one problem at a time."

We pulled up to the small dock and got out, not far from a chicken wire enclosure that protected the piping plover nesting area. As we stepped on the sandy shore, Doris grabbed my arm. "Watch out where you step."

A faint, high-pitched peep caught my attention. My eyes scanned the area until they locked onto a tiny bird, its gray and white feathers blending in with the sandy terrain. Its wing was cocked at an awkward angle, as if it were broken. I watched, wondering if the trespasser had stepped on the little thing. There was a reason why this island was off-limits during this time of year.

"She ain't hurt, she's drawing you away from her eggs," Doris said.

Sure enough, there in a little nest hollowed out in the sand were four speckled eggs. It looked like the chicken wire enclosure would have to be expanded. As we made our way around the nesting area and climbed to the top of the rise, we heard the roar of a boat motor.

"Doris, look!" I pointed to a Boston Whaler as it sped off into the Sound. Doris didn't seem excited. "He won't get far."

I was about to protest that she was allowing the guy to get away, as the boat hit a rock outcropping at full speed. The boat became airborne, turning direction forty-five degrees while still in the air. It slammed into the water with a loud thud that resonated across the water. The occupant flew over the bow and into the drink.

Doris looked at me as if to say, I told you so. "I guess we should get back to the boat and go fetch him out of there," she said. We hadn't walked thirty feet back toward the rescue boat on the other side of the island when we heard the boat start. We turned to see the Boston Whaler as it fled off toward Long Island.

"I'll be damned. He was able to get back in." Doris said.

He was lucky. I'd give him that. "You saw it, Doris, A Boston Whaler. Now do you believe me?"

"Never said I didn't believe you."

"Well, anyway, it's a Boston Whaler like I saw yesterday."

"There are a lot of Boston Whalers around these parts."

"But that one was flying the Jolly Roger."

"It's not illegal to fly the Jolly Roger. Was the Whaler you had a run-in with last night flying the Jolly Roger?"

I should have seen that one coming.

"I was too busy trying to save myself from drowning to notice."

"There ya go."

"Let's get him."

Doris glared at me as if to say she didn't need me to tell her what to do.

"You know, there's no law against being stupid. Besides, we'd never catch him. He'll be halfway across the Sound by the time we get back to the boat."

"Unbelievable," I grumbled.

"I told you we couldn't catch him. What is it you'd like me to do?"

"Call the Coast Guard for starters."

"I can handle what goes on in these islands. If I find out that there's more to this, I'll get the Coast Guard involved, if it's their business." She thought for a while, gave a huff, and then took out her cell phone."

"Chelsea, I don't want this over the air. Notify the Coast Guard that a damaged Boston Whaler may be calling in for assistance somewhere between Sachem Creek and Long Island. If they get such a call, I have some questions for the operator of the boat." She hung up and turned to me. "Happy?"

If Doris was thinking that there was any connection between what we had just witnessed and the death of the young lady, she wasn't about to share it with me. I was fuming. I was sure that was the same boat that swamped me.

"Now let's you show me just what happened over there in that channel."

We headed down the channel toward where I had been swamped. Unlike the night before, the water was pretty rough, even in the sheltered channel. To make things worse, it began to drizzle.

I showed Doris exactly where I was when the Boston Whaler swamped me.

"I was just about here, off the inlet to Hidden Cove," I pointed to the entrance of the cove.

"The Whaler ripped out of there like Captain Kidd on a mission."

"Not here for a history lesson." Doris seemed intent on giving me a hard time. I could see the worried expression on my face reflected in her sunglasses. I quickly changed it to a smile. I wasn't going to let her think she was getting to me. Why should I be worried?

"I'm just sayin'," she said.

She knew I only meant that I couldn't see the Whaler coming out of the cove until it was right on top of me. What was her problem?

"Look, Doris, I don't know why you had to drag me out there. I told you all this last night."

Doris grew up in the village, the same as her father and grandfather, and she probably was boating out here before she could walk. Oh yeah, Doris could picture exactly where I was talking about as I explained it to her the night before.

"You said you got swamped." She reached for her binoculars.

"His wake flipped me, is what happened."

"And you swam over to Bill Lester's dock?"

"Right. To empty the water from my kayak. Do you think I killed the girl?"

"I didn't say that, but right now I have to check out everything I've got."

"Which isn't much, Doris!"

"There ya go! So, what I got, I gotta check out, so cool your jets there boy. I'm not trying to give you a hard time. I'm doing my job."

"You're giving me the impression that you don't believe me one hundred percent."

"I'm just gathering facts. It's my job whether you like it or not."

I knew she was right. It was her job. I also knew that it didn't make any sense to alienate her. She put the boat in idle and peered toward the shore through the binoculars. She adjusted her binoculars and studied the small jetty that protected the beach where I had given CPR to the girl. Suddenly, Doris put the boat into drive, and we slowly rumbled in closer.

Doris anchored as close to the jetty as she could get. Then she took an inflatable dinghy off the roof of the boat and put it in the water. She grabbed a couple of paddles and got into the smaller boat. I started to climb in with her.

"Don't even think about it."

"I'm coming."

I guess she saw the resolve on my face as I hopped into the rubber craft.

She rowed us to shore and landed on the beach. Once again, I pictured the sand that stuck to the dead girl's skin as I tried to revive her. It was that image that had kept me awake most of the night. Doris headed straight for the jetty. Slimy black rocks had been placed on the south side of the beach long ago to prevent what little sand there was from washing away. I had no idea what she was after.

"You stay here," she said, making it clear that I wasn't to follow her as she climbed up the rocks. Doris slipped several times as her feet popped the air bladders of the seaweed left behind when the tide receded. With each slip she swore, and with each cussword I became more and more uneasy.

She climbed to the top of the boulders, looked around, and then, bracing herself with her hands on the rocks, scrambled for a small piece of driftwood. She used the stick to reach for a clear plastic dry bag with a blue bottom that was caught in the rocks at about the mark of the last high tide. Doris carefully made her way back down the rocks to the beach. She got back on the sand with the dry bag hanging from a piece of driftwood. As soon as she laid it on the ground, my heart sank. I wished I could read the expression on her face.

"Yours?"

"I lost it when I capsized." I tried to sound like it was no big deal, but my guts were churning.

Inside the dry bag, I could see my white canvas Gilligan hat, my phone, the pump, and the half-eaten sandwich from Tide and Griddle.

Doris pointed to the dry bag. "What's that rope?"

"A towing harness. I used it to pull a guy off a sandbar not long before I found her."

Doris looked from the dry bag to my eyes.

"Mind telling me again how you think this accident may have happened, my friend?"

My friend. I wished that she meant it. I was in no mood to tell her the story again until she had me make a formal statement. I wanted to get back and train for the race.

"No."

Doris gave me a sarcastic frown.

"No? No, you don't mind or no, you're not going to tell me."

I spotted a bit of blue in the seaweed that marked the point of the last high tide on the beach.

"What's that?" I asked in a loud voice as I pointed to a spot on the other end of the beach from the jetty.

Doris dropped her train of thought and looked toward where I was pointing.

"That wasn't there last night. The tide must have brought it in," she said. She marched toward the high-water line, where the color of the sand changed from oil-slick grey to tan, with me right behind her.

As we got closer, I could make out a blue, rectangular-shaped vinyl object about eighteen inches long and six inches wide in the seaweed. The object, about two and half inches thick had a grommet on the top of the narrow side so that it could be tied to the cleats of a boat to protect the hull and gunwale.

I bent near it to get a better look.

"Don't touch it!" she growled.

She didn't have to tell me that. She knew damn well I had been a police detective before I became a P.I. Even though it was most likely just a piece of flotsam washed ashore, the same as my dry bag was, I knew it could be evidence. She pulled a pair of rubber gloves from her pocket and put them on.

"You ever see a fender like this one?"

Yeah, I had seen four just like that yesterday when I helped Abe cast off his lines, and it would surprise me if Doris hadn't noticed as well that Abe used fenders just like this one.

Chapter Seven

The boat ride back was rough, both physically and emotionally. Even though I'd promised myself not to go over it all again, I ended up telling Doris everything anyway, beginning with the haircut that had landed me out near the scene where I'd found the girl. I relayed every detail I could recall about the guy I'd seen on Outer Island, every flicker of memory, every sight, sound, and smell, taking her through the events until the moment she'd arrived herself.

"There was nothing I could do, Doris. Really," I said, staring out at Long Island Sound, unable to meet her eyes. I didn't want her to see how much I felt I'd failed.

Doris sighed, her voice soft. "I believe you did what you could, kid."

From her, even a sliver of sympathy meant a lot. Still, the term "kid" stung a bit, only adding to the disappointment I already felt in myself.

As we neared the dock, it became clear we had an audience. Half of the village had turned out, including Bart, Buster, and Walter. Walter was the first to walk over as we stepped off the boat.

I shook my head. "Surprised Neal isn't here. He wouldn't want to miss any part of this."

Walter chuckled, pointing towards the shore. "Oh, he's here in spirit. He's watching from his shop window."

Sure enough, across the wharf, Neal stood by his shop's front window, peering out from behind his gold-lettered sign. Ignoring the crowd, I made my way toward my car, but Doris wasn't about to let me off so easily.

"Hold on there," she said. "I'm taking you back to the station for a formal statement."

She gestured toward her vehicle—a new, pearl-colored SUV. Though I'd seen it before on the wharf, I'd never seen her behind the wheel. Surprised, I climbed in without protest, letting my hand rest on the plush leather seats as I buckled in.

"Upgraded your ride, huh?" I remarked, eyeing her with curiosity.

"Don't overtax your brain thinking about it," she said with a faint smirk.

The Sachem Creek Police Station, located in the Town Hall just north of the Amtrak bridge on School Street, was technically outside the central village. The building had originally been the town's elementary school when I was a kid, until about twenty years ago when they'd repurposed it. As we stepped inside, we were greeted by Chelsea, who, despite being wheelchair-bound since a teenage accident, managed the place with precision, juggling the responsibilities of town clerk and police dispatcher.

Her usual warm smile brightened her face. "Nice haircut. That the style down in Savannah?"

"Not sure it's a style anywhere," I replied, running a hand through my hair with a grimace.

Chelsea grinned. "I mean it—looks good. Makes you look young."

I raised an eyebrow, not buying it for a minute. "Yeah, right."

Seeing my lack of enthusiasm, Chelsea dropped the teasing.

"There's coffee over there. Help yourself."

Doris shot her a look, and Chelsea turned her wheelchair back to her desk, saying, "And there's a bagel toaster over there if you're starving."

Apparently, Doris didn't think I was stressed enough to deserve a cup of coffee from her budget. "He's fine, Chelsea. He needs to give a statement first. Did you notify the Coast Guard?"

"Done." Was Chelsea's curt reply.

Doris nodded and led me into her office. "Did you want that coffee?" she asked, motioning for me to sit.

"I'm fine. Let's get this over with."

I went through the entire story again while she typed up my statement one finger at a time. It felt like it took forever. I leaned forward at one point.

"Look, Doris, I've written plenty of these reports before. Just let me finish it myself so I can get out of here and grab some breakfast."

She glared at me over the top of her reading glasses. "I don't think you're in any position to be telling me what to do here, Al. I need this statement done properly."

My stomach growled, and I reluctantly continued with the story, my mind drifting to the breakfast I'd promised to have with my father and Phoebe. Finally, Doris looked up, a note of finality in her voice. "You know you're in the clear, right?"

"Good to hear," I said with some relief. "But do you think Abe's involved?"

Doris shrugged. "I don't know. Do you?"

We were interrupted by the ring of the phone, which Doris answered immediately. After a brief exchange, she put down the receiver and gave me a slight nod. "I have to give a safety talk at the library. You're free to go but make yourself available if I have any other questions."

As we walked into the outer office, Chelsea waved me over, waiting until Doris had left before speaking. "Got a minute to catch up?" she asked, her tone serious now.

"Sure, what's on your mind?"

Chelsea leaned closer, her voice low. "There's something you should know. Last week, a lawyer came in to do a title search—specifically, for Abe's property. She was working for Amanda Kittle."

My eyes narrowed. "Amanda? That sounds strange, but not impossible."

Chelsea nodded, glancing towards the door as if to make sure Doris wasn't coming back. "It was more than a standard title search, Al. This attorney, Ginny Lawson, didn't just go back fifty or sixty years like most abstractors would. She was eyeing maps and documents dating back over three hundred years."

I felt a chill go down my spine. "Did she say what she was looking for?"

Chelsea shook her head. "No, but here's where it gets messy. Abe came in while she was here. He was really upset when he left. Later, I saw him outside in the parking lot with Ginny—he looked like he was about ready to explode. The room was getting stuffy, so I opened a window to get some air." She cracked a wry smile. "That's when I overheard part of what he was saying. He was waving his arms around, saying he'd kill anyone involved in taking his property. I figured it was just frustration talking, but still..."

I crossed my arms, recalling Abe's recent moodiness. "So, what's the connection?"

Chelsea hesitated, then nodded. "Doris hasn't told you the dead girl's name, has she?" She leaned in, her voice barely a whisper. "The girl you found on the island was Ginny Lawson, Al."

It was all pretty interesting. If Ginny had been looking into historic properties for Amanda—maybe ones connected to the rumored treasure near Sachem Creek—it added up. Amanda had been buying up land like crazy for her new development. I didn't think she actually believed in the old tourist legend, but what if Ginny had found something historic that could mess up Amanda's plans?

"Chelsea," I said, "are you saying you think Ginny's work on these records could be why she was killed?"

Chelsea didn't hesitate. "It's possible, Al. If Ginny was getting close to something that threatened Amanda's plans, then Amanda could've had a motive—especially if Abe made any threats in front of her."

I let that sink in. Amanda was known for her single-minded ambition, and if she thought Ginny was a liability... well, it would explain the lengths she might go to keep things quiet. "Did Ginny leave anything? Any notes or files she was working on that might help?"

Chelsea frowned. "I don't know, but it wouldn't hurt to take a look in the records room."

The records room was tucked in what had been my third-grade classroom. In spite of the light from the large windows, the room had a gloomy look, and the musty smell of old paper and dust greeted us as we entered. Rows of metal filing cabinets lined the walls, covering the slate blackboards at which I had spent many after-school sessions writing the words, *I will behave in class*" over and over when I was a kid.

The file drawers were packed with faded folders and thick binders. A single desk sat in the corner, cluttered with more paperwork, its surface barely visible. Chelsea shook her head as she rifled through the last stack of papers in one of the cabinets. "I'm telling you, there's nothing here. If Ginny left anything behind, it's long gone."

I leaned against the file cabinet, frustration building. "There's got to be something. She wouldn't just disappear without leaving a trail."

Chelsea paused, thinking. "What about her home office? Ginny always said she did her best work there. If she had anything important, that's where it would be."

I straightened. "You know where she lived?"

"She mentioned Whitfield Green a couple times, but I have no idea where."

My mind raced. If Ginny had uncovered something in those old maps or records, it could explain why Amanda might've had her silenced. I had to find out what Ginny had been working on if I wanted to help Abe. I just hoped I wouldn't find anything that pointed back to him. But if it did, it was a risk I'd have to take.

Chapter Eight

I left town hall more concerned about Abe's plight than ever. The sun was out, and the wharf was less than a ten-minute walk from the police station, so I hiked to Tide and Griddle, looking forward to a peaceful breakfast. On the way, I called the Blue Palmetto to see how things were going back in Savannah.

Greenleaf picked up without saying hello. "Is Big Al okay?" she barked.

"He's fine. Is everything okay there?"

"Don't you think we can survive without you?"

"I'm just checking in," I said.

"Oh, so you're checking up on Max. Why didn't you say so?"

"I'm not checking up!" I protested, my voice louder than I intended. Greenleaf had an infuriating knack for reading my thoughts. The truth was, while Max had asked me to keep her in the loop, I couldn't deny my own curiosity—especially about her rekindled relationship with Phil.

"Good. I'll tell Max you called when I see her. By the way, the place seems weird without you and Big Al."

I knew that was the closest thing to a compliment Greenleaf would give. Before I could respond, I heard a click on the other end of the line. I sighed, grateful that she hung up. I'm no better at stuff like that than she is.

* * *

When I arrived at Tide and Griddle, Big Al and Phoebe were having breakfast at a picnic table on the deck.

"Hey, look who's here," my father said to Phoebe.

When I first reunited with my father in Savannah, it didn't take me long to figure out that he sometimes found it difficult to recognize people when he saw them in an unfamiliar setting. *Look who's here* was Big Al's way of saying he'd forgotten my name.

Big Al picked a piece of bacon off his plate and casually popped it into his mouth. He chewed slowly, pretending to savor the flavor as he searched the recesses of his diminishing memory. He pushed the plate toward me and pointed to a piece of bacon.

I shook my head. "Nah. Not for me."

"Why not?"

"I don't eat things that are as smart as I am," I said.

He scoffed. "What the hell are you talking about? It's a piece of bacon."

"Which comes from pigs. Pigs are intelligent animals."

"Big deal, they also have twenty-minute orgasms. Hurray for them. Bacon tastes great. Hurray for me." He stuffed two pieces into his mouth.

Meanwhile, a voice came from behind me. "I appreciate the gentleman's way of thinking," I recognized it as Charlie's voice.

I stood, and my lanky friend wrapped me in a quick man hug.

"Hear that, Dad? He called you a gentleman."

Big Al shook hands with Charlie. "He calls me Dad because we have the same name."

My friend squinted and studied Big Al for a bit, then his eyes widened with understanding.

"Of course, Mr. DeLucia."

Big Al gestured toward Aunt Phoebe. "My wife," he said.

Phoebe gave a weak smile but didn't correct Big Al. "I know Charles. I used to fix his cars."

Charlie nodded. He hadn't seen my father in years, but of course, he knew the story of him reappearing out of the blue.

I shrugged. "He forgets his son, but he remembers pig trivia. I thought you were in Frisco."

"I was. I got into New York last night and stayed at the Yale Club, then I

56

took Metro North from the city this morning. Come, I want you to meet someone."

Charlie brought me to his table to meet his breakfast companion. Her long blond hair, deep tan, and teeth so white I thought I'd go snow-blind gave her the girl-next-door look, but the twinkle in her blue eyes made me envious of good old Charlie Brown.

"Summer Townsend, this is Al DeLucia. Summer is from New York."

"Sit," Summer said. "Is that your dad over there? He's cute."

"I'm glad you noticed the resemblance," I said.

Any chance that I might have to engage Summer in any further banter was cut off by a shout from inside.

"Charles!" Charlie got up to get his order, but Summer interrupted. "No, you two catch up. I'll get it."

I watched her walk across the deck until she opened the screen door and went into the restaurant. Charlie picked up on it.

"How's Maxine?" Charlie had never met her in person, but of course, he knew all about her from me.

"You know how it goes."

Charlie gave me a knowing look.

I glanced toward Big Al's table. He was playing with a golden retriever. A couple at a nearby table spotted their dog. The woman called, "Here, Chopper." The golden ambled over and sat at their feet. I almost wished that Aunt Phoebe didn't have everything under control so I'd have an excuse to get out of the conversation.

"I'm semi-out of circulation. Tell me about Summer." It was my turn to pry.

"There's not much to tell." He glanced toward Kittle Island. "You do know Kim's getting married?"

"I heard. I suppose you're going," I said.

"I was invited. Yes."

I saw Charlie's expression change for an instant. Then I heard a familiar affected uptown New York accent behind me. "It's Amanda, right?"

"It is."

Given my history with Amanda, talking to her wasn't my idea of a fun time. I had two choices. I could either meet her face to face, in which case I might say something I'd regret, or I could turn and leave from the other end of the crowded deck. I decided I wasn't going to let her think she'd made me run. Especially since she was hosting my ex's wedding.

Amanda stopped at Charlie's table. As always, she appeared refined with her chestnut brown hair in an updo that highlighted her high cheekbones and angular jawline. When Charlie stood to greet her, she made a great show of air-kissing him. Then she turned her piercing eyes on me and snickered.

"Charles, dear, you should watch who you associate with."

"I don't understand," Charlie said.

"Didn't he tell you about the dead woman?"

Charlie's mouth dropped. "What dead woman?"

"I was about to tell you," I said.

Amanda took over before I could say another word. "An attorney I employed, and he insists he 'discovered' her body on Pot Island. I'm not saying anything, but his missing brother seems to be the major suspect."

"Abe's not my brother, and nobody said he's a suspect," I replied.

"Whatever you say. All I know is something strange is going on, and I'm going to make sure you both pay."

Charlie looked at us with his mouth agape. "Wait—how is Abe involved?"

"Abe's missing, but that doesn't mean he killed her. And Doris still doesn't know how she died," I said.

Amanda smirked. "Maybe not yet. But she—and the rest of us—know you've always been obsessed with the village's history. Maybe there's an old map or some treasure here you're dying to get your hands on." Her eyes locked on mine, challenging me to say something.

"A map?" Charlie repeated, looking between us.

I kept my tone even. "She's reading too many mystery novels."

Amanda arched an eyebrow. "Just making sure you understand, Al. Some of us know more about the past here than you might think."

The deck was quiet, and all eyes were on us. I knew that Amanda's implication that I had something to do with what was going on would soon be on everyone's lips.

"Well, no wonder you looked stressed." There was genuine concern on my old friend's face.

Amanda had to get in one more jab. "You'd be stressed too if you were mixed up in murder."

"First, nobody knows yet if it was murder. And second, I found the body. Nothing more," I said.

Charlie set his jaw. "Well, I for one will go on record as saying I don't believe Al had anything to do with it."

The couple with the golden retriever was all ears. The woman leaned toward her companion. "Did you hear what she said?" She reached under the table for her dog and pulled him closer to her. "Good boy, Chopper."

I didn't realize that Big Al was standing next to me until he put a hand on my shoulder.

"Who's this?" He spat out.

"Well, you must be The Father of The Year," Amanda said.

"I don't like her," Big Al said to me. I'd seen several examples of his lack of filter often over the last year or so. Sometimes I've wondered if it's his natural personality or a symptom of his dementia. I suspected it's a little of both.

By this time, Phoebe had her hand on Big Al's arm and was trying to lead him away. My father insisted on one parting shot to Amanda.

"I don't like you. And my son doesn't have to answer to you."

My son. How about that?

Chapter Nine

Ernie Fitzgerald burst from the door to see what all of the ruckus was about. The veins in his neck were bulging as he shot me a look that said I'd better stop disrupting his business. I shrugged, pretending I didn't give a shit what he or any of the others thought. I turned to Charlie. "I've got to go."

I motioned for Big Al and Phoebe to follow. As we walked down the steps to the street. I caught Big Al stopping to give Ernie a one-finger salute. Under other circumstances, I might have thought it was funny, but I never did get my breakfast, and I was hangry.

"Come on." I grabbed my father by the arm.

I was still trying to process that after a year, he realized I was his son. Had he been faking when he thought I was just his "friend" who was also named Al, or was it one of the oddities of his illness?

Charlie's voice called out, urging us to slow down.

"Don't mind Amanda's dramatics. You know her tendencies. You two have crossed swords for years. Now that you're back, she's taking it up a notch."

I had no intention of allowing Amanda's accusations to dictate the course of my life. I steered the conversation in another direction.

"New wheels?" I gestured toward an elegant European sports car parked on the curb.

His response held a hint of surprise. "How did you know?"

I didn't need to be Sherlock Holmes to come to that deduction. The license plate marked B 322 was a dead giveaway. The number 322 seemed to be Charlie's number and held some kind of meaning for him. He incorporated it into everything.

"A shot in the dark. Electric?" I probed.

He nodded with conviction. "The only sensible choice." His fingers formed a Namaste gesture. "Remember, don't worry about Amanda. This, too, shall pass. We'll catch up later." With that, he returned to the deck.

"Damned stupid Yalie," Big Al muttered under his breath.

"He has a few quirks, but he's a good guy," I said.

Phoebe broke in.

"Hey, it's best if you take some time to cool off. Big Al and I are heading back home." Phoebe's gentle voice reminded me of why she had always been my favorite aunt.

Phoebe was right. I realized that I needed some time to myself to cool down, so I headed for the Trolley Trail. There I could clear my head of all the shit that was going on by soaking in the trail's history. Plus, I could get in a little running to train for the race. Paddling is as much about the legs as it is about the arms. Win. Win.

The trail was built on a hundred-fifty-year-old trolley bed that used to run between the village and New Haven, twelve miles to the west. Although the tracks had long been removed, a small portion of the gravel bed remained and had been repurposed into a jogging path. It stretched from Main Street, passing by the ballpark, and leading up to an iron trolley bridge and beyond.

The sun was blazing, and it promised to be a scorcher of a day. I soon reached the iron truss bridge that crossed over the river, which drained the salt marsh to the north. The thick mat of sedges and rushes was now flooded by the high tide. The trolley rails on the old truss bridge had been replaced by a wooden walkway laid over the bridge deck so that the trail could continue over the creek some twenty feet below.

Hanging from the top of the bridge's framework was a heavy rope used by kids to swing out and plunge into the water during high tide.

I decided to pass on the temptation to relive those old memories. Instead, I looked south and saw the islands and a cargo ship out on Long Island Sound. I couldn't help but notice the similarities between my tiny hometown and the much larger Savannah. Sachem Creek was on a tidal estuary with marshlands and views across the water to New York. My office at the Blue Palmetto, at the mouth of the Savannah River, offered a similar view of South Carolina. Even the container ships heading to the port of Savannah felt familiar, like those on the Sound.

It made me wonder if that was why Big Al had exiled himself there all those years ago.

I continued my jog and eventually arrived at a shady cut that had been blasted through a hill for the old tracks. Here and there, ferns had taken hold in weeping cracks in the rock walls. The water collected in skunk cabbage-filled ditches that line each side of the path. Emerging from the cool, shady dampness, the trail crossed the marsh on the west side of the village. This was the marsh that abutted Abe's property.

I jogged on until I reached Abe's farm. I didn't expect to see him, but I walked around agonizing over how I could help him when I didn't know where he was.

Abe's place was a relic of the past, as indicated by the placard on the front facade, declaring it to be the handiwork of Samuel Cromwell in 1693. The front of the house was painted red, but the other three sides were covered in unpainted clapboard siding that had aged into a mellow brown-black hue. The front sported a door flanked on either side by a lone window, with three windows on the second floor. Along the left side, positioned close to the front corner, was a coffin door. The roof had weathered wooden shingles and a bowed ridge line from which emerged a massive central chimney.

The weight of history seemed to have taken its toll on the structure, giving it a gloomy feeling that was inescapable. Yet, amidst the melancholy, one inviting aspect could not be denied—a brick sidewalk leading to the front door. The pathway was adorned with colorful marigolds, planted between pretty purple-pink stones with glittering speckles of mica. I couldn't help but wonder if they were a legacy of Becky, whose spirit still lingered amidst the shadows of the old home.

I saw someone walking from the barn and realized it was Tyler House, a high school kid who did odd jobs around the village. He was carrying a bucket. It looked heavy.

I was surprised to see him and was going to ask what he was doing there but caught myself realizing cop mode was no longer my thing.

"Seems like you've got a pretty good yard business going, Tyler."

"I do. But this isn't part of it. Are you looking for Mr. Cromwell?"

"That's right."

"He's not here. When Mom told me Mr. Cromwell was missing, I got worried about his stock. She said it was all right to come by and feed the animals and do a few things around the place. That's okay, isn't it?"

"Yeah, of course, it is. Pretty nice of you if you ask me."

"I like doing it."

He bent and picked up a pile of pulled weeds and put them in the bucket.

"I was looking at those rocks. They're interesting. Do you know what they are?"

"Some kind of mica. They're all over the farm. I never thought much about them. A lot of things around the village are made of pink granite."

"Right." I reached into my wallet and pulled out seventy-five. This is for you. For helping out."

"Thanks, but I can't take that. I want to help Mr. Cromwell."

"Good for you. But this is for helping me. You keep your eyes and ears open, okay? If you see anything unusual around here, let me know. Okay?"

"Unusual like what?"

"You'll know when you see it."

Chapter Ten

A bit of the gloominess of Abe's farm stuck with me as I headed back on the trail. I started to think about Max and tried to put the situation with her in perspective. She had every right to explore what would make her happy. While I defended that right, I didn't have to be happy about it.

As I approached the Little League field, I noticed a huge black pick-up truck with a crew cab and dual rear wheels. Taking note of vehicles is a habit I picked up while on the force. I know a guy back in Savannah who has a similar fat ass truck. He owns a construction company and has his fitted out with heavy diamond plate toolboxes. This one, though, had a massive high-rise cap, making it look like a hearse on steroids. Someone was sitting in the truck, but its darkened windows made it impossible to make out their appearance.

Navigating around a good-sized mound of dog crap, I found myself confronted by a drenched American Bulldog emerging from the salt grass. The dog, predominantly white with brown patches, appeared taken aback as it fixed me with its pink-rimmed gaze.

A tall, skinny guy with a shaved head and what appeared to be a week's worth of growth on his ginger beard jumped from the truck. As he approached, my attention was drawn to a tattooed snake on his neck, its design seemingly slithering from beneath his collar toward his ear.

"Get over here, Abby."

The dog slinked to its master.

"It's cool, I said. "She was curious. That's all."

The guy was staring at me with glassy eyes. Then a look that I couldn't read flashed across his face.

"You!"

Me? Did he know me? I certainly didn't know him.

He took in a deep breath and then bellowed. "Leave my dog alone!"

I studied his face to see if I knew him. He wasn't someone I knew from the Creek. But that didn't mean anything anymore. Those days of knowing everyone in the village were long gone.

"Hey, what's your problem, man?"

"You heard me. Leave my dog alone!"

I had recently found a body, I'd lost a girlfriend, a newfound "brother" was losing his house, and might be a murder suspect, plus I was tired. Add hungry to that, and you pretty much can guess my demeanor. My attempt at being friendly evaporated like piss on a griddle. I was in no mood to deal with someone who seemed a little too irrational to handle. "Later, man! I'm out of here!" I was headed up the trail when the guy pulled the unimaginable.

"Go, Abby! Sic 'em!"

Was he freaking kidding? It took all my willpower to stop and face the dog as it charged. I used my deepest, most authoritative mean-cop voice. "You stay!"

The dog stopped but had its front legs planted like it intended to spring at my throat. They say you shouldn't run when a dog goes after you, but that's easy to say when a tooth-baring canine isn't eyeing your Adam's Apple.

I glanced up the trail, narrowed by the encroaching marsh grass that all but blocks it at this time of year. The old trolley bridge lay about two hundred feet ahead. I knew that there was no way I was going to outrun the dog, so I slowly backed toward the bridge, not making eye contact, yet never taking my sight off that mass of muscle and teeth.

When something in the high grass distracted him, I saw my chance to take off for the bridge. It wasn't long before the dog was nipping at my heels. It ripped the leg of my shorts as I reached the ancient span. My first thought was to snatch the rope hanging from the framework and swing out into the water, but that dog didn't look like it was afraid of getting wet. It didn't look like it was afraid of anything.

Instead, I leaped onto the two-by-four crosswalk railing and attempted to climb the iron framework, all the while the dog snapping at me. Its jaws managed to grasp the back of my t-shirt and held on. As I climbed, the dog was lifted nearly a foot before it eventually dropped back to the boardwalk. I continued my climb while the dog remained at the base, emitting low growls in my direction.

Trying to keep my voice soft and soothing, I tried to convince Abby that I was her friend.

"Good dog, Abby," I repeated over and over again. I knew diversion was my only chance. Perched atop the intricate ironwork, I sent my water bottle sailing down the trail. Abby dashed after it with enthusiasm. My pride in concocting such a successful diversion was short-lived, however, as she bounded back to the bridge with the bottle in her mouth. I was resigning myself to spending the night clinging to the rusty girders when I noticed Abby crouching, front legs lowered and rear end raised, tail wagging in anticipation.

"So you want a game of fetch. You could have said so," I told her, making my way down through the lattice of girders.

Abby let me grab the bottle, and I threw it again. This time, it landed right at Snake Guy's feet, who had followed us up the trail. He called his dog, and it quickly ran over to him.

"I told you to stay away from my dog!" He sounded annoyed, but I couldn't figure out what it had to do with me. Then it clicked. Maybe he was connected to Amanda. Could he be hired muscle, making sure no one got too close to whatever she was hiding with her land deal?

I was bracing myself for another round with the dog when Max appeared on the trail. Last I knew, she was back at the Blue Palmetto in Savannah.

"Stay back," I said to her for her safety, my voice had lapsed into police mode and was a little harsher than I had intended. She ignored my warning.

"What a splendid creature," she exclaimed as she came closer. "Did someone mention her name is Abby?"

With a slap on her leg, the dog came to her. She lavished praise upon the animal as her hand caressed its fur. Extending her other hand to the man, she commanded, "Leash."

"Same goes for you. Keep your distance from my dog," the guy said.

"Leash, please," she said again, her tone unyielding.

Though he scoffed, he handed her the leash. She fastened it to the dog's collar and handed the opposite end to him.

"It's time for you to leave," Max told him, her voice full of the authority of an irate parent.

He shook his head, a gesture of defiance, but complied with her demand. He led Abby down the path, and they disappeared around a bend concealed by swaying marsh grass. I wasn't surprised. He wouldn't do anything further with a witness around.

I started after him. Max blocked my way.

"What are you doing here?" I asked as I tried to get around her.

"I came up to see what this village you're always talking about looks like."

"Anyway, thanks for that," I said as I again tried to get around her.

"For?" She raised her eyebrow.

"You know, for diffusing the situation."

Once again, she blocked my way. "Where are you going?"

"After him."

"For real? I just had to save your ass!"

"I could have handled it."

She glared at me. I'd seen that look many times back at the Blue Palmetto.

"Okay, you helped me," I admitted. "I just said I appreciate it. But someone in his mental state needs to be off the street."

"That's what 9-1-1 is for. Call."

Beyond the seagrass where I couldn't see, I heard his diesel engine roar to life and take off. No sense in chasing him now. "I don't have a phone. Long story."

It seemed Max suddenly decided to think she was my guardian angel. She pulled out her phone and punched in 9-1-1." Here," she said, thrusting it into my hand.

I recognized Chelsea's voice as soon as she picked up. "Chelsea, I'm reporting a situation.

"Is that you, Al? What's wrong?"

"A guy on the Trolley Trail acting irrationally; harassing people."

"Any details about the nature of the harassment?"

"He sicced his dog on me," I said.

"Oh my! Anyone hurt or still in danger?"

I looked at my torn shorts and the shirt that was hanging off me. "Only my pride. He's gone."

"Can you provide a description of the individual and their vehicle?

"Thin guy, head shaved, stubbly beard. He has a snake tattooed on his neck. He drives a black dual rear-wheeled truck with Colorado plates."

"Are you sure no one is hurt?"

"Like I said."

"Good. Stay on the line in case we need more information."

Max was looking at me as if she wanted to tell me something.

"What is it?"

"I saw that truck on the wharf yesterday. It had a funny slipper-shaped kayak in the back of it."

"Yellow and red?"

Max nodded her head.

Chelsea came back to the phone. "Stay there," she said. Doris will be right down."

I gave the phone back, and within minutes, Doris was pulling up. "That was quick," I said as I turned to Max. She was gone.

* * *

I barely had time to process Max's sudden disappearance before Doris pulled into the ball field in a sleek black-and-white SUV.

"That was fast," I said, eyeing her ride.

She stepped out and gave me a once-over—shirtless, bloodied, and looking worse for wear. "I'd just finished my talk at the library when I got the call. Do you need medical attention?"

"No, just a few scratches from climbing the bridge."

Her eyes narrowed. "You climbed the bridge?"

"Yeah," I said, trying not to sound defensive.

She raised an eyebrow. "With a dog snapping at your butt the whole time?"

"You saw my ripped shorts. Look, Doris, this guy is dangerous. This isn't a joke."

"See me laughing?" she replied, deadpan.

She wasn't laughing, but she wasn't throwing any sympathy my way, either. Still, she was listening, and that was something.

I took a deep breath and laid it out. "And then I found out he's the same guy who was out near the islands with the rodeo kayak around the time I discovered Ginny Lawson's body."

"Did I tell you her name?" Doris asked, her tone sharp. She already knew the answer.

"I found out by accident."

She shook her head, her expression grim. "Sure, you did."

I pressed on. "Look, given what just happened, it's not a stretch to think this guy is somehow connected to her death. He's violent—his stunt with the dog proves that. I think this Colorado Kayaker and the guy on the Boston Whaler are both solid suspects. Just like Abe."

Doris paused, weighing my words. "You want a job on the force?"

"Are you serious?"

"No! So let me do my job. And all I need from you is to stay out of trouble."

"I get it," I said, though we both knew I didn't mean it.

She climbed back into the SUV and gestured for me to follow. As we drove, I couldn't help but notice how luxurious the interior was. "When did Sachem Creek start buying high-end electric SUVs for the police force?" I asked.

She smirked. "This? It's a forfeiture from a drug case that started in town. We got it from the Federal Marshal's Office the other day."

"Not bad."

"Yeah, all we had to do was get it painted. I even paid out of pocket to speed it up. Didn't you see the sign on the back fender? 'This vehicle was acquired in a drug raid at no cost to the taxpayer.'"

"I must've missed that."

She chuckled. "Figures. You've got other things on your mind. But admit it—it looks way better as a black-and-white than in that goofy pearl color."

"Whatever you say, Doris," I muttered. But in my head, the case—and the danger—was far from over.

Chapter Eleven

After another quick trip to the police station, where Doris returned my phone, I went back to the wharf. I was surprised to see Max casually propped against my car.

"Why the sudden disappearance?" I asked, my cop instincts kicking in.

With a nonchalant shrug, she responded, "No particular reason."

"Every move has a reason," I said. I'm sure my voice sent her the message that I wanted a serious answer.

"Fine, if you must know, I just wasn't in the mood for a chat with the local cops right then."

It dawned on me that she had her eyes fixed on me, assessing the situation.

"New haircut, huh?" she said.

"You noticed?"

"Oh yeah, first thing when I saw you," she said, her fingers reaching out to play with the hair on both sides of my head, pulling them slightly as if to inspect the symmetry. "Bit uneven, though."

"Tell me something I don't already know. I think my barber is losing it."

She studied me with a blend of scrutiny and something else I couldn't quite put my finger on.

"I can't let you walk around with that haircut disaster. I could fix that up for you.

The last thing I needed was an amateur toying with my hair, making the situation worse. "You're an awesome detective, but cut my hair? Thanks, but I'll pass."

"Don't think I can do it? I'm a hairstylist."

"You never mentioned it all the time we've been working and going out together."

"It was another life. I worked in a mortuary making dead people look good. Most people get turned off by that, so I keep it to myself.

"If you think I'm going to let you touch my head, you're dreaming." I moved away from her to make my point.

"Fine. Walk around looking like someone put a bowl on your head."

She made me smile even though I was skeptical. "Right. Is that all?"

"I'm renting a cottage here in the village where we can get it done. All I need are my scissors. Let's fix that hair."

* * *

The "cottage" turned out to be a year-round Victorian located on Sound View Road, up the hill from Charlie's place. The newcomers who had bought homes on that dead-end stretch along the water had established an association and placed a sign at the entrance. The message "Turn Around Here" implied that the road was private. It was not.

I remembered the house had belonged to old Martin Clapp before he passed away. Whoever bought it had done an amazing job fixing it up. Max led me to the secluded back porch, where the nearby islands were beginning to come alive one lamplight at a time as twilight came. She sat me in a chair and put a towel around my neck. Her touch, gentle in the warm evening air, and the porch light's soft glow eased my tension bit by bit.

She looked at my hair once more. "It's not as bad as I thought. I'll get you back to turning heads again," she said with a gentle undercurrent in her voice.

"What if I'm not ready for the attention?"

A knowing smile curved her lips. "You're always ready. Let's rock this," she replied. She played with my hair, tugging at it with her fingers as she had done earlier, and despite the mild night, I shivered. It was a good shiver.

As she worked, we talked about everything—from Big Al and Greenleaf to the goings-on back in Savannah. I filled her in on Sachem Creek and how the town's dynamics were changing thanks to Amanda. We both avoided the unspoken question, the one we'd danced around since the moment we had that video call: what would happen between us now that she was thinking of going back with Phil? It had been a year since she saved me from that alligator in Georgia, but something about that moment had always lingered between us. Back then, I'd never imagined I'd be standing here, wondering how we'd navigate the space between us now. In no time, she was brushing the hair off my neck, and I felt a bit less on the defensive. Her touch gave me a rush.

"Done?"

She pulled the towel from around my shoulders. "Done." She passed me a small mirror.

"It's nice. Thanks. Guess, I'll be going now."

I got up and handed the mirror back to her. We both held on to it for longer than necessary.

"You're welcome, she said."

"Well, I'll be going."

"You already said that."

"Well, okay then. How much for the haircut?" I reached toward the wallet in my back pocket, hoping that she wasn't going to charge me New York salon prices.

"No charge. I enjoyed the company."

I eyed the gas grill on the porch. "Hey, I'm good at grilling."

She snickered. She knew I'd had more than my share of problems cooking dinner for her. "Like the time you forgot to turn on the oven?"

"That was a one-off. You have hamburgers?"

"Do you like Veggie burgers?"

"Love 'em!" In truth, I'd rather eat sawdust. "I guess we're having dinner together," I said with genuine cheerfulness, but not because of the menu.

Max went inside to make a salad while I barbecued. I heard the phone ring but couldn't make out what she was saying.

As the food was ready, it started to rain. We ate at a small table protected from the elements by the porch. The company was excellent, the view was great, and the burgers weren't half bad. It was as if the Phil problem didn't exist.

We moved from the table to the porch swing. The air smelled cleansed and sweet. Darkness had settled in; we watched the lights twinkle on the islands. I stopped the swing and inched closer to her. She didn't move away.

"Tell me more about your brother," she said.

That caught me off guard. But okay, she wanted to slow it down a bit. I got it.

"The guy's got more problems than a math book. He thinks we're brothers. I don't."

"Tell me more."

"Not much more to tell other than he lost his farm to a mortgage shark."

"Tell me about that," she said as she sat back and crossed her legs.

"He took a mortgage to pay his taxes but ended up signing over his house to the mortgage company. That's it."

"Do you think the murder and the mortgage fraud are connected?" Max asked as she watched my face.

"Not the way Chief Page does. She's assuming Abe killed attorney Lawson over losing his farm. I think there's a connection, but I'm not convinced that Abe is at fault."

I leaned in closer again. She pulled back.

"What?"

"That's enough for tonight. That call— I'm meeting an old friend in New York tomorrow. I need to leave early. I'll be back. Give Big Al a hug for me," she said.

We said our goodnights and I went down the stairs. As I got to the car, she leaned over the railing and called out. "I had a good evening!"

I touched my forefinger to my forehead in salute and drove off, wondering if Max's old friend was Phil.

Chapter Twelve

Early Sunday, June 26

The rain had stopped, and I drove around thinking of the almost perfect evening with Max and wondering if it had come to an abrupt halt due to something I had said. After a while, I decided I wasn't going to worry about it and concentrated on enjoying the night air.

My drive brought me past the Lobster Pot on Rt. 1, the place where Abe said the bartender had given him a DNA test kit. I decided to stop in and see if she was there. I pulled into the parking lot at 1:45 p.m., fifteen minutes before last call.

Back in the day, I was a regular despite the place's identity crisis. Noontime—packed with summer tourists, no entry. Late afternoons and early evenings boomers' territory. As night fell and the elder crowd dispersed—it turned into a den for desperate prowlers.

At this time, the parking lot was almost empty. Abe had said the bartender's name was Doreen. There was only one person behind the bar. She looked like a Doreen to me.

"Sam Adams," I said.

"You cut it close. It took long enough for you to get here."

"I just got thirsty."

"I mean to come in to talk to me."

"You Doreen?"

"Yeah, and I know who you are. Abe's brother Al. He described you. Said you looked like a cheap nerdy detective."

I snickered."Gotta love him, even if he isn't family."

"But he is," Doreen said. I had him do the test a second time. Different company. Same result."

"Tell me something," I said. "Are you and Abe...you know?"

"Involved? No, just friends. And I'm not looking for anything if that's what you're thinking."

"I'm not thinking anything. I'm asking questions. That's what cheap nerdy detectives do."

"You know, you two got the same sense of humor. I kind of like you."

"It's nice to be liked. Do you know where Abe is?"

"Not a clue."

I nodded. "I see."

I pushed some money across the bar for the drink.

She waved her hand. "Forget it, it's on me."

"Put it in the tip jar," I said.

"See, I knew Abe was wrong about you."

"Be careful. Most people are."

As I turned to leave, she said, "Honey, when you find him, let me know. I'm as worried about him as you are."

* * *

It was about 2:30 a.m. I pulled into Phoebe's driveway of crushed oyster shells. The whole house was dark. The previous day had been a long one, and despite my disappointment, I fell right to sleep; no Grey Goose needed.

* * *

In the morning, I climbed out of bed at 7:30 a.m. and checked in the mirror. Less than five hours of sleep had taken its toll. I picked up my shirt from the floor and noticed a stain, probably from when I had dinner at Max's. I threw it in the hamper. Veggie burgers suck.

Still, I was happy that the second haircut wasn't a dream. Max had done an excellent job. She was going to New York City later, but I wanted to see her to say goodbye before she left and try to get a feel of what there was between us.

Then I would paddle to Long Island in the afternoon to get a base time to prepare for the race.

The main house was quiet when I went downstairs to get the kayak from the backyard. Despite the early hour, Phoebe came to the window the minute I walked onto her crushed shells. I wasn't surprised; Phoebe rarely missed a trick.

"You got in pretty late again. Were you out drowning your sorrows or something?"

"Nope...don't have any sorrows," I said as I lashed the kayak to the roof of the Mercedes.

"So, you were with a woman." She gave a knowing nod. I let her think what she wanted.

"Gotta run," I said. With that, I put the paddles through the open window of the car and sped away to see if I could catch Abe at Tide and Griddle before I hit the water. I wanted to see if he was back and what his intentions were. Right now, he was only a person of interest. Had he gotten a lawyer? Furthermore, I was eager to confirm whether the boat fender Doris had discovered did indeed belong to him. If it did, in my view, it would only confirm he was in the vicinity. And if he was around, he might have witnessed something that could help his case.

* * *

When I got to Tide and Griddle, I found Captain Bruce and the usual regulars, but Abe was nowhere to be seen.

Buster looked at me like he had seen a ghost.

"I heard you were in the hospital."

Walter searched my face for tell-tale damage. "They let you out already? Let's see the stitches."

"I didn't get any stitches."

"Of course you did, your face was ripped off. We heard it at the barbershop. Did they use those invisible stitches?"

"That guy must be nuts to make his pit bull do something like that. I like dogs, but pit bulls are another matter," Buster said.

"The dog was an American Bulldog. They're two different breeds, and they both get bad raps. The dog was simply following her owner's commands. Don't worry, I'm going to get even with that guy. Anybody see Abe around?"

Captain Bruce looked like a chipmunk with a mouth full of food. He took a sip of coffee to help him swallow before speaking up.

"Haven't seen him since he left with y'all the other day."

"Walter and I took a ride over to his place early on today. The House kid was taking care of the livestock. He hasn't seen him since Friday either," Buster said.

Walter gestured at me with a fork. "Doris said Abe's a person of interest. I'd watch my step and keep away from Abe before Doris finds you interesting, too."

"That's crazy! I have nothing to do with it."

"Okay. Don't say I didn't tell you so. But if you lie with dogs, you're gonna start chasing cats sooner or later, and Doris knows that."

Buster stood about a foot from me and looked me straight in the eye. He must have had a garlic pizza the night before.

"Love or money. Those are the only two reasons someone commits murder. I figure you didn't know the girl, so it wasn't for love."

"So, you're saying I did it for money?"

"Of course not! She was in a bikini and on the water. She wouldn't have any money for you to rob. But your Abe's a different story. His disappearance certainly doesn't look good, and people might think you're hiding him if indeed he is your brother."

I attributed that remark to Amanda's innuendos about me. Well, there was nothing I could do about it. I left Tide and Griddle, sorry I had ever gone in. I. Just. Don't. Learn.

* * *

With the town hall closed since it was Sunday, I called Chelsea at home. She confirmed what I had heard at the restaurant. Doris was indeed looking for Abe as a person of interest in the case, although she wasn't calling it murder. Yet. Suddenly, Chelsea began to whisper into the phone. A bit dramatic I thought since she lived alone but it underscored the seriousness of the situation.

"I'm afraid it doesn't look good for Abe, Al. Doris is officially listing him as a person of interest out of respect for him, but between you and me, she considers Abe to be a prime suspect."

"Prime suspect! Why?"

"I'm sure she has her reasons," Chelsea said."

"I wish I knew what those reasons were."

"For one thing, Paul Hartt at Island Marine Services confirmed the bumper belonged to Abe. He sold him a set last week."

"So what? I'm sure Abe isn't the only one who uses that type of bumper. It could belong to anybody."

"Each bumper has a small serial number on its lower edge, and according to Paul's records, this number perfectly matches the one on the bumper he sold to Abe."

That wasn't what I wanted to hear, but at least I knew, thanks to Chelsea. I hung up more determined than ever to help Abe. I still wasn't convinced we were brothers, but I couldn't turn my back on him either. I needed to clear my head and think everything out. Abe was going to need money for a good defense, and I reminded myself that the race meant more than just defeating the cheater Donahue; the twenty-five thousand dollar prize could greatly help Abe. Paddling over to Long Island, approximating the course that the race would take next Sunday, would give me time to think and to get a base time as well. At the moment, that was the best, no, make that the only, strategy I had.

* * *

It was already getting hot, and a haze blocked out the distant New York coastline. I had to get started soon, but I had to say goodbye to Max first. I could still catch her before she left for the city. I didn't want to wait until she returned to propose rekindling our connection. However, deep down, I wondered if I had unwittingly set the stage for disappointment. My breakup with Kim and Max's recent proposed return to her ex-husband had made me somewhat wary of diving back into the dating scene. Nevertheless, the idea of spending my downtime with Max sounded good to me. In addition to her skillful haircut fix, we had been drawn to each other, and I believed we still had something worth saving.

I followed Nutmeg Island Road to where it intersects with Sound View Road at the shore. Ignoring the Turn Around Here sign, I drove up the hill.

When I got to her place, Tyler House, the same kid who was helping out Abe, was mowing the lawn. He nodded above the noise of the mower.

I went up to the porch and knocked at the door like a love-sick teenager.

Nobody answered. I walked around the back to see if the car was there. Nothing.

I walked back out to the front lawn and, after several idiotic hand gestures, got Tyler to turn off the lawnmower.

"Tyler, have you seen the woman who rents here?"

When he told me that a car service had picked her up about a half hour before, my morning suddenly went from bad to worse.

"By the way, Tyler, who owns this place now?"

"Ms. Kittle."

My face must have dropped a foot. I should have known that Amanda would grab the property as soon as old man Clapp died.

* * *

It was way too hot to be paddling across the Sound; under such conditions, sunstroke and disorientation are a real possibility. But I wasn't going to waste the day, no matter how disappointed I was that I had missed Max, so I took the chance and went out. I packed my water bottles, loaded up with sunblock, and protected my head with a floppy hat. I shoved off at 2:00, working on pace and endurance. I wasn't trying to break any records. I followed the path that the race would take. I headed southeast to the mid-sound buoy and then southwest to an area on Long Island's North Shore called Friars Head before returning north. I didn't return until late in the evening, having paddled a total distance of about forty miles.

Chapter Thirteen

Monday, June 27

I was up by 5:30 a.m., a habit I got into when I was on the force. Back then, I hated when the alarm went off; now I feel like early morning is the best part of the day. Over at Phoebe's, the house was quiet. Good. When I got to the harbor, I took in deep breaths of the refreshing morning air. The village was deserted, except for a jogger following the middle line on the road and an old man on the sidewalk, determined to keep pace with his wife, who relied on a three-wheeled walker. I peeked in Tide and Griddle's window, hopeful that Gabe would be there. He wasn't.

Proving Abe's innocence was still a priority. After all, what are brothers for? I smiled at the irony of the thought. Still, I had the 4th of July race looming over my head in exactly one week, and settling a score or two would be sweet.

Despite being in decent shape, I had to get back on course with training for the race. Soon, I was on the water doing four sets each of 1,000, 500, and 250-meter sprints in the harbor.

I was the only one out there except for four boats filled with Amanda's work crews and a barge carrying a small backhoe headed toward Kittle Island, presumably to do some last-minute landscaping before the wedding.

Amanda must have been pulling out all the stops to get the place ready for the big event. About ten minutes into my sprints, I noticed another kayaker about three-quarters of a mile out by the innermost islands. It was too far away to see any detail, and their lack of movement made me think they were fishing.

With the grueling sprints finished, I turned my attention to fine-tuning my pacing before the sun could become too intense. As I headed up the channel, the kayaker left the mouth of the harbor and disappeared amongst the islands.

I headed toward Bear Island, one of the Nutmegs closer to the shoreline.

Every so often, I'd glance back, and saw that the same kayak had reappeared and was now heading in the same direction as me. I wished I had a GPS to check my speed, but I figured I was going at a decent six miles per hour, and the other kayaker was keeping up with me. I was trained to be observant as well as cautious, but I was also disciplined enough not to assume the worst in people. Long Island Sound was a big body of water, and that paddler was free to go where they wanted. As long as they didn't cross into my personal space, that is.

I slowed my pace and changed my direction. When I glanced over my shoulder the next time, the other kayaker had maintained the same gap between us. My willingness to give them the benefit of the doubt was dwindling.

As I approached Bear Island, I noticed a young guy aboard a small power boat had dropped anchor near the island, in a cluster of lobster traps. These traps were marked with makeshift buoys made from plastic bottles fastened to the pots resting on the bottom. Normally, the buoys are snagged with a gaff hook, and the pot is pulled up. Clearly, he wasn't a professional. He had tied the pot's ground line to the boat and was revving his engine, obviously trying to free a stuck trap. I paddled over to help, and he cut the engine.

"Are you working alone today?" I asked, trying not to sound accusatory. Lobster pot poaching was common and a serious offense, but I didn't have reason to suspect this kid.

"Are you with DEEP? I'll show my license. The orange jugs are ours," the kid nervously replied, holding up an orange-painted milk jug. According to the law, each license holder paints their buoys with unique colors to identify their traps.

"I'm just offering help. This is tough work to do alone," I said.

"My brother has a college interview today. You can't leave lobsters in the traps too long. They start eating each other," the kid explained.

"I hear ya," I said. "Let me lend a hand with those pots."

The kid seemed distracted. "There's that funny-looking kayak again."

I turned to see the Colorado Kayaker approaching from the far side of the island. He stopped about two hundred feet behind me.

"You've been following me. Why?" I demanded.

He made the "I'm watching you" sign, pointing at his eyes and then at me. Then he sped away in his kayak like a rocket.

I chased after him.

"I'll be back to help you. Don't continue what you're doing; it's dangerous," I yelled to the kid on the power boat. But before I could react, I heard the engine revving and a crack. I turned to see the line had snapped, whipping around the kid's arm and pulling him into the water. Luckily, the kid had his kill switch lanyard on, causing the boat to jerk forward and then stop abruptly.

I watched the Colorado Kayaker go. Confident he wouldn't get away the next time we crossed paths, I paddled as close as I could to the spot where the young guy disappeared into the water and then plunged in. He struggled in the water, desperately attempting to free himself from the tangled rope. Despite the bubbles and turbulent water caused by his frantic movements, I could see fear in his eyes. I swam up to him, placing my hands on his shoulders to reassure him of my presence. Using one hand, I pointed to my head and made a slow downward motion, hoping he'd understand my signal to stay calm.

Examining the situation, I noticed the rope was tightly entangled around his arm. Working as fast as I could, I untangled the rope and let it fall free. Giving him a thumbs-up, I let him know that he would be alright and signaled for him to swim upward. We both broke the surface, hungry for air, coughing and gasping. I helped him back into the boat.

Chapter Fourteen

I strapped the kayak to the car roof. I was wiped out, but relieved the kid was safe and promised not to check his lobster pots alone again. At the same time, I was pissed that the Colorado Kayaker was stalking me. I wished I knew what his beef was. As far as I knew, I had never laid eyes on him before he set his dog on me. But one thing was for sure: if he was looking for trouble, I had no problem giving it to him.

As I double-checked the kayak, I noticed Max pull onto the wharf. She parked, got out, hair pulled back, looking determined.

"Been keeping out of trouble?" she asked.

"You're back," I said. "Where were you when I needed you?"

"You knew I was going to The City."

"Kidding. But I could've used you earlier. A kid almost drowned because the Colorado Kayaker distracted me. All good now, though."

"You can stop calling him that," Max said. "His name is Harry Carter."

"How do you know?"

I got a picture of his plates, and my New York contact ran them. They're registered to a Harry Carter. Used to be an outdoor adventure guide. No criminal record, but the guy's got a history of being... intense."

"Intense enough to stalk me in a kayak?" I asked.

Max raised an eyebrow. "I'd say so."

I processed that, trying to fit it into the bigger picture. "Why would Doris keep this quiet? She must have run his plates, too."

"Because it's Doris," Max said. "She has her own agenda, and if Carter's a suspect, she won't let either of us mess with her investigation."

I shook my head, annoyed but not surprised. "So, what's Carter doing here?"

"That's the million-dollar question," Max said. "Maybe he knows something you don't."

"Yeah, well," I said, my mind racing. "Next time I see him, things are going to be different."

* * *

When I got back to the house, Aunt Phoebe and my father were having coffee on the porch. They had been spending a lot of time getting reacquainted and enjoying each other's company.

Aunt Phoebe looked a lot like my mom, which made sense because they were twins. I couldn't help but wonder if Big Al was seeing her as his mom, his sister-in-law, or maybe just a new friend.

"Here he is!" Big Al said as I came up the steps. One thing was clear: he wasn't seeing me as his son at that moment.

He had gotten very skillful in disguising his memory problems. Plus, I suspect he was also skillful at faking them when it was to his advantage.

"Sit down and have some zucchini bread," Phoebe said. She was already cutting me a thick slice before I could respond.

"I'm good," I said.

"Don't make my wife feel bad. She just made it this morning, and it's good."

"Sister-in-law," I said. "Phoebe is your sister-in-law." I had to give him a pass on that one. But it bugged me that I was back to being his detective friend right then.

Phoebe gave me a shrug. "It's okay. It comes with the territory. Old age is a bitch."

"Yeah, I suppose. He's not always like this, you know. It's more of an on-and-off thing," I mentioned.

Phoebe flashed a knowing smile, and Big Al busied himself with his coffee. Regardless of the situation, his getting along with her relieved a significant burden from my shoulders. It was also good for him. He had lost his second wife, a nice woman I'd only recently got to know, a few months before.

"What's with you?" he said as I sat down. I tried to overlook his less-than-charming personality by taking into consideration that he can't always find the right words to express himself.

"You do seem a bit preoccupied," Phoebe said. She must have seen a reaction from me and was trying to be a peacemaker.

I cast a quick gaze down the hill, taking in the view of the harbor and the islands. Despite the changes in the village, Sachem Creek remained a slice of paradise, or so it seemed.

"This place has changed in more ways than one. The people deserve better. I used to be a cop, and I still can't get used to the idea of murder. I can only imagine how it affects regular folks," I admitted.

Big Al set his coffee mug down and fixed his gaze on me. "You were a cop?"

My stomach twisted. "Yeah, I was," I replied, a touch of frustration in my voice. How many times had I mentioned it?

Big Al leaned in, his coffee forgotten. "Nobody becomes a cop because they love murder. They become a cop because they love justice. A cop who gets used to murder is useless."

For all his flaws, the old man must have been a hell of a good cop back in the day.

Phoebe smiled."Pretty profound, if you ask me. I guess the sense of justice is the last to go."

Big Al went back to his coffee.

"And then there's Abe," I said. "Doris seems to think he's a suspect, but I say she should be looking at the guy whose dog attacked me."

I didn't want to upset Phoebe any more than she was, so I didn't mention that Harry Carter, a.k.a. the Colorado Kayaker, was stalking me. Besides, that would make me sound paranoid.

Phoebe looked sorrowful. "I'm sure when the facts come out, Abe will be cleared," she said. It was clear she had a soft spot for the guy. Maybe she knew him better than I did. But like him or not, in this case, I had a feeling he was innocent.

"Right, and I'm going to dig for those facts, starting with talking to Jamila about all of the activity on Outer Island. Are you coming with me, Dad?"

Big Al looked from me to Phoebe.

"There he goes with that Dad shit. Cut it out. That joke is getting old."

I rephrased the question rather than start an argument. "Are you coming with me?"

Phoebe answered for him. "We had talked about doing some things this afternoon. I mean, unless you need him."

Did I need another hole in my head? "No-no, no-no. You two have plans. We'll catch up later."

I beat a hasty retreat to my apartment to call Jamila.

I found my phone after a pocket search of a pair of pants balled up under the bed that netted me a gas receipt, some gum, a pencil stub, lint, and a Maya Angelou quarter I was saving for my collection.

"Call Jamila," I said into the phone. She was in charge of the Outer Island Wildlife Refuge, and maybe she could shed some light on why the Colorado Kayaker, as well as the guy who crashed the speedboat, were so interested in the island.

"Do you want to call Charlie?" The phone's artificial intelligence answered.

"No!"

"You want to call Charlie?"

"No! Damn it."

"Who do you want to call?"

"Já-mil-a."

The phone rang three times. Finally, but then it went to voicemail.

"This is Charlie. Leave a message."

I hit end and punched in Jamila's number by hand.

I asked Jamila if she'd meet me for lunch at The Lobster Pot. Unlike the other night, today I'd be part of the tourist crowd. She agreed.

The Lobster Pot had the best whole-bellied fried clams in the area, and a great lunchtime jazz combo to boot. By some miracle, I found a parking spot. However, I would have preferred to save my miracles to find Abe and clear him of murder.

CHAPTER FOURTEEN

Jamila was a little late, so I put my name in for lunch and waited at the outdoor bar nursing a Sam Adams. I asked for Doreen but was told she only worked nights.

After about a half-hour and another beer, I decided that something had come up and Jamila wasn't going to show. I was getting up to leave when I saw her little Miata convertible circle the parking lot. After several minutes, she found a space.

She and I used to go out long ago before I met Kim, but somewhere along the line, we became friends. Jamila stepped out of the car, looking as sharp as ever, her braided hair pulled back and gold earrings catching the light. A colorful scarf was tied loosely around her neck.

"Sorry, I'm late. I was busy." Jamila has a high-context personality. She's happiest when she's doing twelve things at once. She kissed me on the cheek.

I ordered fried clams, and Jamila ordered a soft-shell crab sandwich. After the usual small talk, I segued into the subject of Outer Island.

"Seems like there's a lot of interest in Outer Island lately," I said. "Any idea why?"

"Interest? How so?"

"I've seen two people out there in two days. Why would anyone want to land on the island when it's posted?"

"People, especially the tourists, ignore signs when they think no one is around. I had to kick a kayaker from Colorado off a couple of days ago."

"Colorado? A guy with a shaved head and a reddish beard?"

"Yes, he said he kayaks the white water back home. He wanted to try sea kayaking while he was on the east coast, but he was disappointed to find out that Long Island Sound doesn't have big waves."

The food arrived in record time. I eyed the claws sticking out between the two pieces of toast of her soft-shell crab sandwich.

"Seafood down south is good, but different from what we get up here," I hinted.

She grabbed a knife and cut the sandwich in half. "Here! Now let me eat in peace."

Between mouthfuls of whole-bellied clams and juicy softshell crab, I asked her more about the kayaker. "If he was looking for waves, why didn't he go to Rhode Island or the Cape?"

"I don't think he came here for the kayaking. I got the sense he was out on the island on other business. Do you think he's the one who murdered Ginny Lawson?" she asked.

That caught me off guard. I hadn't mentioned Lawson." It seems like murder, to me, but that hasn't been confirmed," I said.

"Doris went up to Farmington to pick up the autopsy report. She had no intention of waiting around for it. The coroner is classifying it as a murder case. Trust me. Ginny Lawson was keelhauled. She had scrapes and cuts consistent with what one might expect from barnacles on a boat's hull."

That explained the rope burns, too—a cruel practice of ancient pirates called keelhauling. The victim was bound to a rope and dragged from one side to the other until they revealed information. It wasn't usually intended to be fatal. The perpetrator likely wanted information from Lawson, or they were totally unhinged. Possibly both.

"How do you know what's in the autopsy?" I asked.

"I'm not revealing my sources."

"Well, something is going on, and I know that it isn't something good for Sachem Creek. And now we have murder thrown into the equation. What else do you know?"

"Did you call me out here for lunch or to pump me for information?"

I frowned. "Well, a little of each," I admitted.

"Lighten up," Jamila chuckled, her smile reminding me of what had drawn me to her. "I was just joking." She leaned in. "I've got something else to tell you. At the time, I had no clue who Ginny Lawson was, but about a week ago, I found myself at Tide and Griddle, standing behind her as she ordered her breakfast. She was a bit short on cash, left with only a fifty-dollar bill, which Ernie refused to accept. I covered the difference, and we ended up sharing a table. She introduced herself and mentioned that she is leasing a place nearby."

"Did she say where?"

"We didn't get that far."

"Now, if only I could find a connection to the guy from Colorado," I said.

Jamila's eyes lit up with interest. "I can't say for sure if there's a connection to him," she replied. "But I do know something about someone else."

I let out a frustrated sigh. "What else do you know?"

She paused, carefully selecting her words. "I don't have concrete evidence, but Ginny mentioned that she was working for Amanda. It seemed to involve title searches, if I recall correctly."

"That's correct. I already knew that."

"Did you know this?" Later, as I was leaving, Amanda approached Ginny on the deck, and I overheard Amanda saying, 'Not while you're on my payroll.' That's when I decided to make my exit."

I knew Ginny Lawson was working on title searches for Amanda, but I didn't know there was any bad blood between her and Amanda. "Well, that's interesting," I said. I wonder how serious the problem between them was."

"Jamila's voice was filled with doubt, like she couldn't wrap her head around the idea. "Are you thinking that Amanda killed Ginny Lawson?"

"I'm thinking the guy from Colorado was in the vicinity of the murder. And now you're telling me Amanda had some kind of problem with the victim? If there's a connection between Amanda and the guy from Colorado, she might be behind it all."

"I still have a million things to do this afternoon." Jamila pushed back her chair. "I'm out of here."

Before she stood, I hesitated, then said, "We were good, you know."

She paused, her hand resting lightly on the table. "Yeah. Here's to good friends." A small smile tugged at her lips before she added, "Your friends define half of you."

I thought of Max. She'd been more than a friend, but lately, she seemed to be slipping back toward Phil. What did that make me? The other half? Or just a placeholder?

Jamila leaned in, kissed me on the cheek—quick, soft, but unmistakably final—and left before I could find an answer.

Chapter Fifteen

As I watched Jamila drive away, I decided I'd check out Ginny Lawson's place. I had another beer as I looked through her social media profiles on my phone to find her address. But, like a smart lawyer, she didn't have it listed there. So, I dug a bit deeper, scanning her posts for any clues about where she lived. I saw she'd checked into the MOMA in Manhattan, a pizza place in New Haven, The Beinecke Rare Book & Manuscript Library at Yale, and a new restaurant in Whitfield Green. Then, I noticed she'd asked for birthday donations to the Whitfield Green Public Library.

Whitfield Green appeared to be a good bet as to where she was living, but I needed to narrow down the precise spot. As I scrolled through her photos, I came across a selfie of her on a deck by the water, with the unmistakable Faulkner's Island Lighthouse in the offshore background. The photo's caption provided some clues: "Playing hooky to stay home and read a good book."

Faulkner's can be seen from the shorelines of Madison, Whitfield Green, or Sachem Creek, which made the shoreline a bit lengthy to pinpoint.

Then, there was a photo of her beside her new electric Mustang, and I noted the license plate and called Lenny Rodriguez, hoping he would run it for me.

"Sorry, no can do. I'm too close to retirement," Lenny said.

This from the guy who dragged me back to Connecticut in the first place to investigate Abe's problems with the police.

After that dead end, I went back to her photos. There was one posted by a friend showing a party at Ginny's house. The friend, obviously not as cautious as the lawyer, did have a geotag on the photo—32 Longshore Drive in Whitfield Green. I decided to check the place out.

I hopped in the Mercedes bound for Whitfield Green. I headed east on Route 147. As much as I love the village, driving through the marshes north of the Amtrak underpass renews me mentally. I put the Mercedes through its paces, the road winding around ledge outcroppings as it made its way across the swampy grasslands. It was made for a road like 147, and it shifted curves as smooth as it must have the day my father bought it.

The sulfur smell of the marsh at low tide, tempered with the smell of salt air, cord grass, and mudflats, brought me back to the pleasant part of my childhood. I loved playing near the marsh, listening to the rustle of the grass and the calls of the birds.

The rumor around town was that Amanda had some grand plans for the salt marsh on the other side of the village, the one where the Trolley Trail meanders through and butts up against Abe's farm. If it was true, another fight was brewing. With Connecticut's salt marshes already suffering from the mysterious "dieback," the notion of people trying to "develop" the land was nothing short of criminal.

As I mulled it over, a theory started to take shape in my mind. Could Amanda's intentions involve pushing Abe off his land? Did she have some bone to pick with her employee, Ginny Lawson? Jamila had mentioned something about Amanda making threats regarding Ginny's job. It'd be rather convenient for Amanda if she could somehow implicate Abe in whatever.

The change in the character of the village was connected to Amanda. The rumored destruction of the marshland ecosystem was connected to Amanda. And the murder may be connected to Amanda. I felt like every major issue in my life was tangled in a web spun by Amanda, and I knew for sure that these distractions were standing in the way of my one goal: winning that race across Long Island Sound and earning the twenty-five thousand dollars to help Abe.

I passed a dirt access road to the granite quarry that was hidden deep in the woods. In my great-grandfather's day, huge blocks of granite were moved on wagons down that path to the rail line. From there, the granite ended up on barges to become part of the fabric of America. I could still see my grandfather puff up with pride as he told the story of how his father quarried stone that was used to build the base of the Statue of Liberty.

After downshifting for a blind curve through the granite base of an Amtrak trestle, I entered Whitfield Green at Leete's Island. Leete's Island isn't an island. It's more of a peninsula with Long Island Sound to the south and a tidal marsh on the north.

A while later, I passed the deteriorating sandstone slab that marked the roadside grave of a colonist killed during a British raid in the Revolution. His descendants still live nearby.

Although Whitfield Green shares the same shoreline as the village of Sachem Creek, it is everything the village doesn't want to be. The chemical-green yards, hacked out of West Woods, are separated by borders of forest trees that create a barrier between properties. As a result, you get no sense of community or neighborhood as you drive down the gently winding streets, designed to bring old-time carriage drives to mind.

I noticed a few "fat ass" pick-ups hauling landscaping equipment in the area. The only people who enjoy these properties during the daytime seem to be the maintenance men and remodeling contractors who make tons of money there. As I drove, I made sure that I kept an eye out for the Colorado Kayaker's dual rear axle truck.

After a few passes through the neighborhood, I found Ginny Lawson's house. It was a large modern structure that looked like stacked boxes of concrete and glass sitting in a pine grove with water as a backdrop. Not my kind of place, but I knew a place like that wasn't cheap to lease. Ms. Lawson must have been doing very well working for Amanda.

I was going to stop to investigate the house on the next pass-by when I noticed Phoebe's car pull out from a side street. Big Al was with her. I wondered if they were out for an innocent joy ride or if something more nefarious was going on. I tried to catch up to them. As Phoebe rounded a curve on the narrow road, I spotted a large SUV on my tail. Suddenly, red and blue lights flashed in the fancy vehicle's grill.

I was about to meet one of Whitfield Green's Finest. I pulled over and watched the officer get out. I shut off my playlist and took off my sunglasses. Just common courtesy and what I would expect from someone I had stopped back in the day.

"Afternoon, Officer."

"License and registration."

"Yes, sir."

He watched as I fished the license from my wallet and got the registration out of the glove box. I handed them to him.

"Is there a problem?"

He looked at the license again.

"Do you realize your license plate is hanging?"

"Hanging?"

"Hanging. You might lose it. What's your business in the neighborhood?"

Ah, so there it was. I was being profiled because my car didn't fit into the neighborhood. While landscapers' diesel trucks with dual rear axles were common there, a 1979 Mercedes wasn't exactly this year's car of choice in tony Whitfield Green.

"I'm just taking a ride. Did I do anything wrong?"

He went to his SUV to run the registration.

I turned my playlist back on, laced my hands behind my head, and leaned back with my eyes closed, letting the music take over. I didn't open them until I heard him by the window again.

"You into Phish?" the officer said, returning to my car.

"Yeah, I'm a Phishhead," I said, a little sharper than I meant. "Why, you a fan?"

I watched him slowly take off his shades. Then I detected what just about could pass for a smile crossing his face.

"I saw them in Burlington."

"No kidding. That must have been awesome."

"Absolutely, the vibe there and the energy at the show were amazing."

He laughed, and then his smile dissolved.

"Listen, I could give you a ticket for improperly displaying your plate and speeding, but that isn't going to serve any purpose for either one of us."

"But?"

"You know how it is. The people around here get nervous when strangers cruise the neighborhood. That's why this association pays for extra police protection."

"So, you're asking me to leave?"

"I'm asking you not to make things difficult for me. One cop to another."

"Ah, so you found that out when you ran my plate?"

"I checked it out because I saw your New Haven union card when you took out your license. I was wondering what was up, considering you have Georgia plates. I also wondered why you didn't flash it off the bat."

"Because I've been on the other side of the door. I don't look for favors."

"Right."

"So, I'm free to go?"

He nodded. "Do me a favor. Get a screw for that plate, Detective."

Chapter Sixteen

I got a steak sandwich and fries to go from Tide and Griddle and headed to a bench at the far end of the wharf where the tour boat was docked. This way, I could enjoy my meal in peace. Throughout my dinner, all I could think about was searching Ginny Lawson's house at Whitfield Green in the morning. This time, I planned to paddle over and make it a successful trip.

After dinner, it felt too early to call it a night. On a whim, I swung by the house Max rented, hoping for some company. But her car wasn't in the driveway, and the windows were dark. Spending time with her would've been nice, I thought as I drove away. I was already on Charlie's street, so I went to his place. When I arrived, I had to wait for a silver Benz to leave his driveway before I could park. The car had its high beams on, briefly blinding me as it drove away. I found Charlie on his front porch, standing behind the gingerbread railing.

"My accountant," he explained as I walked up the steps.

I never made enough money to file quarterly reports, which is what I assumed the visit was about. I didn't ask, and Charlie didn't elaborate.

He handed me a Corona with a slice of lime. The porch was dim, lit only by the glow from the living room window. We sat in wicker rockers, sipping our drinks and watching the islands and the occasional boat passing between them and the mainland. A soft breeze drifted in from the water, carrying the salty tang of the sea mixed with the sweet scent of blooming beach roses. We chatted about the weather and the Yankees' 10-3 win over the Red Sox. Eventually, he brought up the subject we'd both been avoiding.

"How's the case going?" he asked.

"I'm sure you heard the woman's name was Ginny Lawson, and she was an attorney doing title searches for Amanda. I found out where she lived in Whitfield Green, so I drove over, but I got kicked out.

"I wouldn't expect less from a detective. Oh, right, it's P.I. now. You're going to tell Doris, of course," he said.

"She probably already knows. If she doesn't, she'll find out soon enough. And get this, the coroner thinks Lawson was keelhauled."

"Keelhauled? Literally?"

"Yup. Just like the pirates used to do to make someone talk. Only in this case, she drowned."

"Unimaginable," Charlie said.

"The evidence seems to point to Abe, but I have a different theory."

"It's obvious that you want me to ask you what it is." Charlie doesn't beat around the bush.

"Since you asked, I'll tell you. I think Amanda hired the Colorado Kayaker to kill Ginny Lawson."

"You have proof?"

"I'll let you know after I search Lawson's house tomorrow."

"Search, as in breaking and entering?"

"Entering, anyway. Somebody must get to the bottom of this, and it looks like it's going to have to be me. Right?"

"Absolutely. But let me play devil's advocate here. Suppose someone catches you breaking into her house. What happens then?"

"I don't intend to get caught, Charlie. Doris probably won't find out until long after I'm out of there."

"I don't understand why you'd want to get involved. Abe has been a thorn in your side since your school days."

"Because as bad as Abe is, I don't think he killed Lawson."

"He seems to have had a motive."

"Such as?" I asked.

"Such as he lost his house. Maybe he assumed this woman was doing a title search on his property so that Amanda could buy it. He might have transferred blame to Attorney Lawson. Everyone knows they were arguing, and from what I hear, Doris has evidence that Abe was out there where the body was found."

"Well, I don't believe Abe could do something like that. Besides, the guy from Colorado was out on the islands just before I found the body. Then, when he saw me on the Trolley Trail, he had his dog attack me. I'll put my money on him rather than Abe. And I'll also bet that Amanda hired him, hoping that Abe would be blamed so she could get his property for her project, whatever it is."

"That's all highly speculative. You can take this warning for what it's worth. If I were you, I'd keep out of it, my friend."

The moon was up now, laying down a silver path over the water between the mainland and the islands. I left Charlie sitting on his porch. When we were young, I could always rely on his being the voice of reason, and I'd listen to him. But I wasn't going to listen this time.

Chapter Seventeen

Tuesday, June 28

I needed a break from people. Thinking about what Big Al and Phoebe were doing, or what the guys at the barbershop were saying, was making it hard for me to focus on finding the killer. So, I went for a run on the Trolley Trail to clear my mind. I secretly hoped I'd bump into the Colorado Kayaker, but no such luck. In fact, I had the whole beautiful path to myself.

I was itching to get a look at Ginny Lawson's place, but hopping in my car just wasn't an option. Hell, even strolling down that private road would be like waving a red flag at that Phish Head cop.

I watched an osprey feeding her young in a nest on a pole platform erected in the marsh. The big bird took off, flying over the trail to the Sound, where it took a nosedive into the calm water for another fish. Like all kids, hers must have liked to eat.

As I watched the bird flit between the marshland and the ocean, I realized what I had to do. I went home, grabbed my kayak from the garage beneath my apartment, and brought it to the postage-stamp-sized beach Doris had designated as a kayak launch.

As I was about to shove off, I noticed Doris standing on the seawall, arms crossed.

"Keeping out of trouble?" she called. Bart the Barometer stood beside her.

"Yeah, keeping out of trouble?" Bart echoed, his voice wheezing.

I flashed them a grin. "Just getting in some training for the race. You know

100

me, Doris."

"That's the problem."

I winked. "Like they say, one by land, two by sea." I gave her a quick salute and paddled into the harbor.

"What does he mean by that?" I heard Bart mutter as I pulled away.

I didn't look back to see if Doris answered. Whether she guessed or not, I had my cover: a grueling series of sprints in full view of anyone onshore. After all, it was the truth—just not the whole truth.

By the time I had finished the sprints, I felt Doris and Bart were no longer concerned with what I was doing, and not seeing them around, I headed east in open water toward Whitfield Green and Ginny Lawson's house to see if there was anything that could lead me to Abe. Who says men can't multitask?

Following Faulkner's, a lone island near Whitfield Green, as my visual guide, I steered my course eastward. At first, the island located approximately six miles from Sachem Creek appeared as a mere distant smudge on the horizon. Yet, as I drew nearer, it expanded in size until its silhouette, crowned with a two-hundred-year-old lighthouse, resembled that of a surfaced submarine.

Without warning, the roar of an approaching powerboat pierced the air. I swiveled my head, but my eyes met only open waters. Then, from around the island, a boat came into view, hurtling toward me with the speed of a runaway Acela. I clenched my paddle, my heart racing as I prayed for the boat's operator to notice my kayak and veer away. As the boat closed to within a mere twenty feet of my kayak, I braced myself. Its spray showered me, causing my kayak to rock violently like a rubber duck in a baby's bathtub. This time, I wasn't swamped. As the Boston Whaler swung away, retreating around the island's far side and disappearing, I caught a glimpse of its flag— the Jolly Roger.

Someone was trying to send me a message, but who and what were they trying to tell me? They always say to trust your gut, and right from the get-go, my instincts were screaming that the Colorado Kayaker was the prime suspect in Ginny Lawson's murder. But let's face it, you can't keelhaul someone using a kayak. True, this guy from Colorado sicced his dog on me, trailed me, and warned me he was keeping an eye on me, but I'd never seen him behind the wheel of a powerboat.

So, who the hell was piloting that Boston Whaler that capsized my kayak just before I stumbled upon Ginny's lifeless body? And who just buzzed me? It had crossed my mind that Abe might be the culprit. But he'd been desperate for my help, even going so far as to claim we were brothers. He knew I'd promised to help him sort out his legal troubles and deal with the eviction. Trying to bump me off just didn't add up.

If this most recent incident was meant to scare me off, someone miscalculated. I don't scare easy. I continued on. From Faulkner's Island, it was an easy paddle to Ginny Lawson's house in Whitfield Green. I had a feeling deep down that I'd find something in her house that would put Abe in the clear.

Sure, I knew that it was breaking and entering, and that bothered me. But I wasn't going to steal anything. And not being a cop anymore, there was no chance of getting a warrant. I was looking for something, anything, to move this investigation along.

* * *

I spotted the Lawson house from offshore and noticed that almost the whole back of the place was glass. I shouldn't have been surprised. The posh homes in the neighborhood were built there for the view of the water.

Lucky for me, there were trees on each side of the home that separated it from the houses on either side. Instead of landing on the beach directly behind the house, I pulled the kayak up on the sand near some trees by the edge of the property. I walked through the woods until I was close to the building, then I made my way to the side. With my back to the wall of the house, I inched toward the front and I peeked around the corner to see if there was a car parked out front, just in case a housekeeper still came by. No car. Good.

Next, I looked for a sticker on the windows that might indicate her security system and discovered that it was the same company that Aunt Phoebe used. As with most systems, it dialed a central office if a sensor went off. Such a waste of money. All I had to do was cut the phone line where it entered the house, and the system couldn't call in. If anything, all the security company would do is notify the phone company of trouble on the line. I figured I'd have a good hour or more before I had to worry about anyone coming around to check out a problem. I'd notify the phone company anonymously later so they could go out and get the alarm working again. If I found anything that solved the murder, I figured that the end would justify the means.

When I got to the phone box, I was taken aback to find that the line had already been cut. An adrenaline rush sent me flat against the concrete wall of the house. Could there have been a robbery? When? I inched my way to a large plate glass window and peeked in. It was a bedroom. Nothing seemed out of place. As I noted that it was a whole lot neater than my room back at Aunt Phoebe's, I felt something poke at my butt.

I must have jumped two feet. I instantly recognized Abby, the same dog that had attacked me on the trail. She stood with her front legs spread and her hind end sticking in the air. With my back against the wall and a bush on each side of the window, I had no escape.

"Abby," I whispered. "Sit, Abby!"

She didn't sit. Instead, she hopped from side to side, wagging her tail playfully. She was so different from the way she acted on the Trolley Trail that I wondered if a dog could be bipolar.

"Sit, Abby. Don't bark."

It didn't take a genius to figure out that Abby's irrational master had broken into the house. I still might have a chance to catch him off guard if I could calm down his playful dog. I tentatively put out my hand. The dog let me scratch her head.

"Good dog. But I'm still pissed at you for what you did."

I heard something inside the house, and I turned to glance in the window. I caught sight of the kayaker walking out of the bedroom. I don't think he saw me.

As I sprinted toward the front yard, the sharp slam of a door pierced the air. Rounding the corner, I spotted the Colorado Kayaker bolting from the house, clutching a laptop in his hands. "Here, Abby!" he called.

Abby dashed from behind me and through my legs. I fell flat on the ground, hitting my nose in the process. I was stunned just long enough for them to get into his fat ass truck that was parked a little down the street. I had seen it but thought it belonged to someone working in the neighborhood. No time to worry if I was losing my edge now. Before I knew it, they were gone.

I didn't know how long the phone wires had been cut, but I decided to chance it and go inside.

The air was filled with the smells of cedar and lavender. The place felt peaceful and refined, like it belonged to someone who appreciated simple classiness. The living room seemed untouched, decorated with watercolors of ships and a few old compasses. On the bookshelf, I noticed two books I was familiar with, one was *Legends of the Colonial Connecticut Shoreline*, a collection of stories about the region's past, while the other, *The History of Sachem Creek*, was written by a local author and offered a more detailed account of the area's history.

* * *

I found a room set up as an office. A desk with a tooled leather top sat under a window overlooking Long Island Sound. An empty docking station told me this was where the Colorado Kayaker had found the laptop. The room hadn't been ransacked, which made it clear the laptop was all he was after. I'd give anything to know what was on it.

Next to the docking station was a pile of receipts held in place by a brass nautical chart weight. I thumbed through them, hoping to get a sense of what Ginny was like.

A gas station receipt for a tank of premium fuel. I could relate, my Mercedes only takes high-test. A grocery store receipt for milk, bread, and eggs. Maybe she was planning to make French toast. A coffee shop receipt for a double espresso and a muffin. A woman after my own heart.

Then, a hardware store receipt for duct tape, nails, and a flashlight. I get it—hardware stores are my happy place. And I used duct tape for everything.

A movie theater receipt for a ticket to an action movie. Not one I cared for, but to each their own. Another hardware store receipt caught my eye, this one for a metal detector. That made sense. She lived on a beach.

Finally, a dry cleaner receipt for two shirts and a pair of slacks. That's where she lost me. I don't wear anything that can't be tossed in the washer, including suits.

I set the receipts back down. Nothing here gave me a clue about what was on that laptop—or why someone wanted it so badly.

There were a few photographs on a desk. In one, I recognized Ginny with a small group of people, drink in hand and mugging it up for the camera. Ginny had a beautiful smile and red hair. I was trying to replace the image in my head of her dead on the beach with this one when I was taken aback with the realization that one in the group was the guy from Colorado. He was off to the side of the gang with his arm around another woman. It was all the proof I needed that he knew Ginny Lawson. I took the picture out of the frame to see if there was an inscription on the back. There wasn't. I copied the picture with my phone and sent it in a text to Max.

Me: Looks like the guy from Colorado knew Lawson.

Max: Got it. Meet at your place at two? We need to talk.

I heard someone in the driveway and looked out to see the Phish Head cop's Lexus SUV. It made me think of Doris and how proud she was of her shiny new cruiser, finally on par with the luxury rides of Whitfield Green's private force. Back in New Haven, I'd only ever driven the beat-up clunkers from the motor pool.

I wondered if he was there in response to the phone line being cut. I doubted that he would believe that I didn't cut the wire, so I shoved the picture back into the frame and rushed toward the back door.

I bolted for my kayak. Once he found things amiss in the house, the Parrot Head cop was going to tell Doris that he had sent a former New Haven Police Detective, namely me, away from the area just the day before. I'd have to handle that one later.

Chapter Eighteen

There are only two reasons someone commits murder: "It's either love or money," Buster had said. I kept thinking about that as I paddled away from Whitfield Green. My suspicions were confirmed: the Colorado Kayaker had some connection to Ginny Lawson. But was it love? Or money?

As my paddle sliced through the water, my mind kept returning to Ginny. Her life had ended brutally, and now I was tangled up in it. Buster's words echoed in my mind. Especially now that I knew Lawson had ties to the man I suspected was behind her murder. And Abe's future—hell, his life—might depend on what I found out.

I had digging to do. I needed to figure out how deep Ginny Lawson's connection to the Colorado Kayaker ran—and whether it was love, money, or something else that had led to her death.

Dark clouds were building to the southwest, hanging heavy over Port Jefferson on Long Island. Thunderstorms on the Sound were fast and nasty, and I needed to get back to Sachem Creek before this one hit. As I paddled, my mind drifted to another stormy day—back in Savannah, when Max and I got caught out on the water.

I hadn't wanted to go that day, but Max had talked me into it. The skies were clear when we set out, no plan in mind—just two people who couldn't get enough of being together. Max teased me about my paddling. "You're all splash and no stroke, Al," she said, laughing. I grinned and "accidentally" sent a wave of water her way with my paddle.

Then the storm came out of nowhere.

It hit hard—fast, mean, and unrelenting. The wind knocked us around, and the rain turned everything into a curtain of gray. I yelled for Max to stay close, but when her kayak flipped, fear hit me like a punch. I could still hear her shocked gasp, still see her pale face in the flashes of lightning.

I pulled her out of the water, holding on so tight I was afraid I might hurt her. By the time we made it to the dock, we were soaked and shivering—but alive. Max, still catching her breath, managed to laugh. "You surprised me, DeLuca," she said, grinning. "Maybe I should listen to you more. Or...maybe not."

That night, I thought we had all the time in the world to figure out what we were to each other. But now that Phil was back in the picture, things between us were uncertain.

I shook my head, grip tightening on the paddle. I hated how that guy still got under my skin, even from hundreds of miles away. Worse, I hated how much Max still mattered to me.

The low rumble of a motorboat snapped me back to the moment. Focus, Al. There's a job to do.

I turned, my pulse kicking up as the engine got louder. A police boat. Great. I'd just broken into the murder victim's house, trying to find anything to tie this case together. All I'd come away with was a photograph of the Colorado Kayaker and Ginny Lawson. What it meant, I wasn't sure yet. I thought I'd slipped out clean, but now the roar of the motor cut through the calm of the Sound.

The boat closed in, red and blue lights spinning in the midday sun. My gut said to paddle faster, to put as much distance as I could between me and the house. But they'd already spotted me.

"Hey! You, in the kayak!"

I eased off the paddle, forcing my breathing to slow. Running wasn't an option. Better to play it cool.

Doris stood at the bow, arms crossed, her glare sharp enough to cut glass.

"Afternoon, Chief," I called, keeping my tone casual as I paddled closer.

Her expression didn't budge. "Afternoon. Care to explain why someone saw you at the Lawson house?"

I smiled like I didn't have a care in the world. "Just passing through. Figured I'd take a look around, see if there was anything helpful."

"Helpful?" Her voice was flat. "You're not a cop anymore, DeLuca. You can't just go poking around other people's property."

"Old habits die hard," I said, shrugging. "I didn't think anyone would mind me lending a hand."

"Lending a hand," she repeated, like the words left a bad taste. "Witnesses said someone matching your description was hanging around the house. You break into places often?"

I gave a low chuckle, even though it felt like sandpaper in my throat. "Breaking and entering? That's not my style, Chief."

"Uh-huh. So, you're saying you weren't there?"

"Were they sure it was me?" I asked, keeping my paddle steady.

"No. But they saw a guy with a kayak on the beach."

"Did anyone see me inside?"

"No."

"Was anything stolen?"

"Not yet."

I nodded toward the dark clouds rolling in. "Storm's coming fast. If you want to search me or my kayak, go for it. Let's just get it over with."

Her eyes flicked to the sky, jaw tightening. After a long pause, she sighed. "You're lucky I've got bigger problems today, DeLuca. Get out of here before I change my mind."

"Glad we're on the same page," I said, my voice lighter than I felt. I dipped my paddle into the water and started to move off.

"Wait," Doris called. "Give me your hand."

My heart sank. "You're arresting me?"

She rolled her eyes. "I'm giving you a ride. I'm not leaving you out here with that storm coming."

With her help, my kayak was hoisted onto the dock. The boat sped back toward Sachem Creek, but her words stuck with me, heavy as the gathering clouds.

She wasn't just watching me. She was waiting. And she wasn't going to wait long.

* * *

On the way to the dock, the conversation with Max about how I got the photo of Lawson and Carter already forming in my head. I knew she wouldn't approve of breaking and entering any more than Doris. Unlike Doris, though, Max wasn't just my boss, or my ex, or whatever the hell she was now. She was also the person who knew me better than anyone else. And she'd see right through me if I wasn't careful.

I glanced at my watch. It was already two o'clock, and I still had to haul my kayak to my car and tie it down. As I headed to bring my vehicle over, my mind churned with possibilities. Love or money? Maybe both. But there was only one way to find out for sure.

And I wasn't about to let Doris, Max, or anyone else, stand in my way.

Chapter Nineteen

I had promised Max that I'd be at my apartment by two o'clock, but because of being delayed by Doris, I didn't get back until two-thirty. The storm had blown through as quickly as it had popped up, and the sun was out again.

Max's car sat parked on the street in front of my place. I raced up the stairs, hoping Phoebe had let her in my apartment.

She wasn't there.

I changed my wet clothes and then thundered back down the stairs and checked out her car, hoping for a note. Nothing. I scoured the backyard but didn't see her there either. Reluctant as I was to involve Phoebe, I stood on the porch and peered through her wooden screen door. I knocked with enough force to make it tremble on its hinges.

"Phoebe?"

Leaning against the screen, my hands cupped to my brow, I strained to see inside. A computer monitor displaying garden scenes as its screensaver sat atop an antique table with lion-clawed feet. Aunt Phoebe was nowhere in sight. It seemed improbable that she would leave her house unattended.

"Phoebe?" Uncertain about barging in, I called out once more. "Phoebe? Aunt Phoebe? Are you there?"

Finally, I heard a response. "Come in, I'm in the kitchen."

Entering the living room, I met Phoebe emerging from the kitchen.

"I was just pouring myself a glass of lemonade. Here, I got one for you."

As she thrust a glass into my hand, the computer sprang to life.

"You have an instant message," the synthetic voice announced.

Aunt Phoebe hurried over to the computer, attempting to shut it down, but not before I caught a glimpse of the bold text box on her IM catcher: "Instant message for Lady-in-lace from Nine-Plus-Guy. Are you willing to accept?"

My face grew warm, and I chugged the lemonade to suppress laughter.

"Oh, that," she dismissed, waving her hand. "It's just a diversion. A woman can only watch so much Kelly Clarkson, you know."

My mother enjoyed crocheting, while her twin sister immersed herself in chat rooms. Good for Phoebe.

"Nice to see you embracing the digital world," I commented, struggling to erase the image of my aunt in a naughty nightie from my mind.

Phoebe laughed it off. "You didn't come here to discuss my online habits."

"A friend was supposed to meet me here. Her car is outside. Do you know where she is?"

"You mean Max? She was chatting with Big Al and me on the porch. Nice girl. Seems interested in local history."

"She is?"

"Oh, yes. She bombarded us with questions."

Max's interest in local history was news to me.

"Do you know where she went? Her car is still here."

"We chatted about the old quarry for a bit, and when you didn't arrive, she and Big Al decided to check it out."

Given Big Al's cognitive troubles, it wasn't the wisest choice. However, I had faith that Max would look after him.

"Did she mention why she wanted to go there?"

"I didn't ask. You know, I have a life of my own."

I suppose she did. Glancing at the computer, I added, "I didn't mean to imply…"

"That I'm nosy? Of course, you did. But don't worry about it. I know I am."

She dismissed the notion with a wave and chuckled.

My eyes shifted toward a photograph in an ornate gold frame beside the computer. The small black-and-white image depicted a young couple standing next to a fancy roadster. The woman was undoubtedly Phoebe, and she hadn't changed much since her youth. I also recognized the man: Oliver Welles, although when he was young, he looked nothing like he did in his later years.

"Your friend Max was quite intrigued by that picture. "I told her about Oliver's fascination with pirates. He even had an old treasure map he obtained from who knows where."

"A stage prop," I assured her. "Don't forget he was an actor, and quite the braggart, I heard."

"No, it was a genuine map, an ancient one."

This revelation caught me off guard.

"How old?"

"Oh, very old. He showed it to my father once. Dad seemed troubled when he saw the map. I noticed his reaction, but Oliver seemed oblivious. You never met him, but my father, your grandfather, feared nothing. That's what made it so peculiar."

"Why would Oliver Welles share a supposedly genuine treasure map?" I asked.

"Because there were inconsistencies," Phoebe replied. "The islands and landmarks didn't match. Whoever drew it didn't do a good job. Oliver thought my father could help identify some of the places."

"And did he?" I pressed for more information.

"No," she said with a serious tone. "Father told him the map was completely wrong, like a lot of old maps were. But you know how people are—they believe what they want to believe. Your grandfather dismissed it, but Oliver was convinced it might still lead to something valuable."

I leaned back in my chair, intrigued. "What happened to the map?"

"Your friend Max asked the same question," Phoebe shared, "Oliver decided to donate it to Yale for its historical collection. It may not have been a treasure map, but it was still a piece of history."

I took a thoughtful sip of my drink, the gears of my mind turning. "Speaking of Max, I'd better go see what she and Big Al are up to," I said, wondering what her interest in ancient maps might be.

Chapter Twenty

I knew the quarry pit was dangerous, especially after the thunderstorm. Even though the sun was out now, the trail might still be slippery. I hurried up the steep street toward the woods. The last time I'd been here was the fall before I left for Savannah. Back then, sunlight streaming through yellow and orange leaves made the place feel like a jewel box. Now it was a different forest, its cool dampness and earthy scent sharp after the rain.

It was quiet except for a chipmunk scurrying into a patch of waxy mountain laurel. The stillness underscored my desperation to find them. Max had promised help, but instead, she brought my father here. Now neither of them was in sight.

Beyond a stand of solemn pines, I came upon a pile of massive boulders—ancient debris left by the last glacier. Locals called the heap Fat Man's Squeeze. Climbing the rocks, I scanned the quarry below. The semi-circular blasting cap channels etched into the sheer walls were the only signs of its bustling past. Now abandoned, the quarry floor was a graveyard of massive stone blocks, some stranded in a pool of foul green water. A decaying derrick loomed over the abyss, its towering wooden pole anchored precariously by rusty guy wires. The iron hook on its frayed cable swung slightly in the breeze. This was no place for an old man with dementia. Panic gripped me as I imagined my father falling into the deep pit.

If anything happened to either of them, I'd blame myself. If I hadn't been late, they wouldn't have come here.

"Big Al! Max!" I called. No response. From the top of the rocks, my eyes searched the quarry floor. Nothing. Then, near the edge of the woods, I spotted them lying on a sunlit block of granite. Neither of them moving.

"Max! Al!" My voice cracked. My imagination spiraled: had they fallen? In my frantic state, I lost my footing on the mossy boulders and slipped, almost landing in Fat Man's Squeeze.

I ran down into the pit and stood at the base of the granite block. "Big Al! Max!" My yells echoed until a gruff voice answered.

"What the hell are you yelling about?" Big Al was staring down at me from the top of the slab.

"Are you okay?" I called.

"Why wouldn't I be?"

"I thought you fell!"

Max appeared beside him, brushing off her jeans. "We were sunning and communing with nature. There's an energy in places like this."

I stared at her. "Is Wiccan another side of you I don't know about?"

"I have a spiritual connection with nature," she said with a shrug.

Despite working with Max for a year—and even dating her—I learned something new about her every day. It was unnerving. "How are you going to get down from there?"

"Abracadabra!"

"There you go again with the Wiccan stuff! Now you're putting a spell on me." I made the horns, an Italian hand gesture with the pinky and index finger extended, thought to ward off the evil eye.

"You wanted to know where Harry Carter is, didn't you?" she asked, unfazed.

"Yeah, but I don't want to turn into a frog in the process." I was only half kidding. Lately, I was beginning to wonder about Max. There was something going on that I couldn't put a finger on.

"Well, I'm telling you. Carter works at Abracadabra, a restaurant in New Haven. And I only turn people I like into frogs."

I raised an eyebrow. "Abracadabra? Really? What's a guy from Colorado doing working there?"

She shook her head in disbelief. "Yale? You know? He's from Colorado, but he's going to start grad school at Yale. Ever hear of it?"

"More information from your friend?"

"Didn't need him after I had Carter's name. A few searches told me he's in grad school at Yale and works at Abracadabra. You were going to follow the same lead, right?"

"Of course I was."

"I handled the legwork for you," she said, smirking.

"Damn, you're good," I admitted. "I wanna swing by Abracadabra and have a few words with Harry Carter."

She shook her head with a knowing look. "He's not working tonight. I checked. But I made us a reservation for the day after tomorrow when he will be. Figured you'd want to catch him while he's on the clock—and in his element."

I had no choice but to wait until Thursday. That was okay, I had other leads to follow in the meantime. "You don't miss a beat, do you?"

"Not when it counts," she said, a faint smile tugging at the corner of her mouth.

I let out a low whistle. "Remind me never to underestimate you."

"Smartest thing you've said all day," she said.

Before I could respond, Big Al appeared beside me.

"How did you get down?" I asked.

"There're stairs carved into the other side. How'd you think we got up there?"

Max came down, and we headed back to Phoebe's place. Al ambled ahead, his steps steady for someone his age. As we left the shade of the trees and stepped onto the open street, he picked up his pace and grumbled, "I'm starving. I'm going ahead."

I watched him trudge up Phoebe's porch steps and go in the door. Knowing him, it wasn't just about food. He enjoyed Phoebe's company.

Max and I walked slowly, each with our own thoughts. As we got to the yard, I finally broke the silence. "Care to come up for something cold?" The words escaped before I could stop them. I regretted it immediately—I didn't even have anything cold in the fridge. Though I still would have liked some alone time with her.

"Thanks. That would be nice."

I blinked. "Really?"

She shook her head, her smile fading into something sad. "It would be nice, but I can't. I've got unpacking to do. Besides…" She tilted her head toward Phoebe's house. "I see Big Al and your aunt watching us from behind the curtain. After the way she grilled me earlier, I can only imagine what she'd say if I went up to your apartment."

"Grilled you? Are you sure you weren't grilling her?"

Max shrugged, her lips twitching into a faint smirk. "Maybe a little of both. But her story about a treasure map was interesting. I wanted to know more."

I groaned. "Phoebe loves a good story. She was telling that one to me, too—claiming Oliver Welles showed my grandfather a map. It turned out to be junk. He donated it to Yale anyway. For all I know, it's sitting in the Beinecke Rare Book Library next to the Gutenberg Bible."

"This town and its treasure obsession," she said, shaking her head. "It's exhausting."

"It sells souvenirs," I said. "What can I tell you? Want to sit on the porch?"

We walked up the stairs and sat on the swing. She was quiet for a moment, her gaze distant.

"I'm thinking," she said.

"That's dangerous." I tried to make a joke of it, but her serious expression told me she wasn't in the mood.

She shot me a sidelong glare. "I'm trying to figure out what Amanda's angle is. Buying up all that land—it doesn't make sense."

"You sure it's Amanda you're thinking about?" I asked, lowering my voice to a teasing tone.

Her head snapped toward me; her voice sharp. "What's that supposed to mean?"

"You've been different since Phil came back into the picture," I said. "Distracted."

"You want to psychoanalyze me now?" she snapped.

"Just making an observation. We've been through enough for me to know when something's eating at you."

She sighed and turned her gaze back toward Phoebe's window. "It's not as simple as you think."

"Maybe not, but that doesn't mean you have to figure it out alone."

Her head turned, and for a moment, her eyes softened. "Phil... Maybe part of me feels like I never really closed that door. I don't know."

I clenched my jaw, forcing my voice to stay even. "So what? You're thinking about giving him another shot? After he took credit for your work and stole your Emmy?"

Her shoulders sagged. "I don't know what I'm thinking, okay? But this isn't the time to sort out my personal life."

"Maybe it is," I said.

She stood, crossing her arms. "Look, I know you want to help your maybe-brother and figure out what happened to Ginny Lawson."

"But?"

"But neither of those are on the Blue Palmetto's case load. I know it's your agency, but my job is to keep it running smoothly."

"And I appreciate that. I know Big Al would, too, if he were completely himself. Is that why you came up to Connecticut out of the blue?"

"Yes."

"What are you saying?"

"I need to know if you're planning to take an extended leave or if I should hire someone temporarily," she said.

"You've already thought of someone, haven't you?"

"Yes. Phil."

The words hit me like a sucker punch. "You want to hire your ex-husband to work at my agency?"

"It's not about Phil. It's about keeping things running."

"And you think hiring him is the answer?"

Her jaw tightened, but her tone stayed calm. "He's a good investigator. And it would only be temporary. But I won't do it without your input."

I stared at her, frustration rising. "I need time to think about this."

"Fine," she said, her voice softening. "But don't take too long."

She walked to her car, the tension still thick in the air. Before getting in, she gave me a kiss on the cheek. It felt like a punctuation mark—a period, not a comma.

"You know," she said, pausing with her hand on the car door. "You never told me where you got that photo with Ginny and Harry. At this point, I'm not sure I want to know."

As she drove off, I climbed the stairs to my apartment, my chest heavy. This wasn't how I'd hoped the afternoon would go. By the time I stretched out for a nap, the frown on my face refused to budge.

Chapter Twenty-One

I f I remember this correctly, I needed a haircut bad. My unruly locks tumbled over my ears and lapped over my collar. It was high time to pay a visit to Neal's barbershop. I figured a bit of jogging on the way wouldn't hurt; it had always been my way of dealing with the stress that haunted my time on the force. Kim, ever observant of my faults, never held back her dislike for my jogging habit when job stress turned me into a ball of pent-up nerves. She believed it was a feeble attempt to evade my problems, but the way I saw it, jogging was my version of, when the going gets tough, the tough get going. I needed to be tough if I was going to win the cross-sound race.

I must've been tired because it felt like I'd never reach that fountain where Wharf Street splits off from Main. I checked my watch; it had only taken me four minutes to get from my place to the wharf. But it felt like an eternity.

Finally, I arrived at Neal's and stopped dead in my tracks. The familiar gold letters spelling "Neal's Barber Shop" were gone, replaced by a sleek new sign: "Neal's Hair and Nail Spa." First, they tore down the old cottages to make way for those pretentious weekend mansions, and now this. Neal had gone full Southampton posh, just as he'd hinted he might, thanks to Amanda's relentless gentrification of the village. I opened the door, and the familiar bell tinkled, but the smell of nail polish in the place almost took my breath away. If it were not for the bell, I wouldn't have known where I was. I found myself at a curved glass desk behind which a young lady, with jet-black shoulder-length hair, had her eyes glued to her mobile. She was short and wore a smock as black as her hair. Her lip was pierced with a small gold ring, and her face was vaguely familiar, like Max's maybe.

I stood at the desk waiting for her to acknowledge that I was there. Finally, she finished doing what she was doing on her device.

"Yes," she said as if I was intruding.

"I'm a…that is…I want to get a haircut. Where's Neal?"

"Hold on." She turned to a large screen, and after a few pokes with her finger, an appointment book came up. "You've been here before?"

"Yes. Of course. Unless I'm dreaming or something."

"Name?"

"Al."

"Mr. Al, you're not in the computer."

"Not Mr. Al. Mr. DeLucia."

She looked at me like I didn't know my own name. "Sorry, no DeLucia in here either. New customer….let's see. I can fit you in for an appointment with Mr. Neal next Wednesday at 10:00 AM. Cut and blow dry? Or you need a color and nails too?"

"Wednesday? What about now?"

"Now? I'm afraid that wouldn't be possible."

"But the dump is open!"

"Then I suggest you go to the dump and…"

With that, Neal came from behind a partition. He, too, was wearing a black smock. I almost wished that his lip had been pierced because then I'd know I was dreaming."

"What's the racket?" he said. Then he spied me. "Al! How do you like the place?"

"Neal, man, what's with all this chrome and glass, and these black leather chairs?"

"Stations. They're stations," he said.

"Whatever. What's going on?"

"The flow, Al. The flow. I'm just going with the flow. The Creek is changing, and I'm going with the flow."

"What the hell are you talking about?"

"Look." He led me to the window, which now had gold lettering that said

Neal's Hair and Nail Spa in reverse. "Look out there." He pointed across the green and beyond the water to the gigantic house on West Point. "The Creek is changing, and either I change to meet the needs of the new clientele or I'm going to be left behind.

"But Oliver Welles. Remember, if it was good enough for him...?"

"Look, Oliver Welles was what you call a liar. He made things up. I don't know why. It must be something we creative people do. Anyway, I never cut his hair."

"But the picture. I saw you and him."

"Right. That was us all right. He used to come here, even did some filming at the dock once. I think that's when the picture was taken. We went drinking at the Lobster Pot, it was called the Phoenix Tavern back then because it had burned down and was rebuilt several times. We got drunk a few times. I didn't cut his hair, though."

"Damn."

"Hey, don't look like the world is coming to an end," Neal said. "You need a haircut?"

"Well, yeah."

"Talk to Kylie here. I may have an opening about Wednesday or so."

Kylie pulled up the appointment book on her computer.

"Let's see...Wednesday...it looks like there's an opening..."

"Forget it."

"Forget it? Why? Wednesday isn't good?"

"No day is good. I can't get my hair cut here. I can't stand the smell. This place reeks of nail polish!"

"Acetone. The nail technician uses it." She twitched her nose. "I can hardly smell it."

"Whatever. I can't stand that smell. I hate it. Forget the appointment."

She reached for a candle in a round jar and struck a match to light it as she screamed, "Get out! Get out!"

But her voice sounded like Aunt Phoebe's. The flame from the match blinded me, and the smoke made my eyes water. Neal's fire alarm went off. The sound split my ears.

Aunt Phoebe was shaking me. Big Al was spraying a smoldering upholstered chair by the window. The smoke detector was wailing. The danger was over, but everyone coughed.

"That thing can start up again. Call the fire department," I said as we went down the stairs to the yard.

"You damned fool you've set my place on fire!" I think it was the first time Aunt Phoebe yelled at me.

"Not unless he was painting his nails," Big Al said. "The place reeked of Acetone. Someone used it to set the chair on fire."

By the time the Sachem Creek volunteer fire department arrived, there was nothing to do but remove the burned chair from my room and vent the place with fans.

Half of the town was in Aunt Phoebe's yard, gawking and giving their opinion on how the fire started, and how they would have handled it.

"I would have thrown the chair out of the window. You have to get rid of the fuel. No fuel, no fire." Walter said.

Buster waved off the comment. "That's ridiculous. How would you lift a burning chair? You have to smother it with a blanket! It's the only way."

"Actually, the correct thing to do would be to get out and call 9-1-1. Our friend's attempt at being a hero could have backfired." Good old Charlie, always the practical one, but I knew he was there out of genuine concern rather than curiosity.

"It took the fire department long enough to get here," Neal said. "I heard it on the scanner and got here from the shop in a minute thirty for seconds flat."

Maybe if they all stayed where they were and didn't clog the narrow street the fire department would have gotten here faster, I thought. About that time, I spotted Doris marching toward me. She didn't look happy.

"I'm thinking of locking you up."

"Why, what have I done?"

"I didn't say you did anything, but every time I turn around, I've got more paperwork to do involving you. I may have to lock you up so I get some rest."

"Well, thanks for your concern. Did you ever think of picking up that guy from Colorado? I learned his name is Harry Carter, and I'll bet you dollars to Danishes he's the one who just tried to barbecue me."

The minute I said it, I knew it was a mistake to question Doris's ability as a police officer, especially in front of the others.

Doris glared at me. If she were a thermometer, I would see grey stuff popping out of the top of her head at any moment.

"I'm aware of his name. I ran the plates, thank you. You think this fire is arson, I take it."

"Any fool can smell the acetone. Acetone is an accelerant. Ask Lou."

Lou LaValle, the fire chief, was ambling toward us. He's an easy-going guy who knows his stuff when it comes to fires. "It's not the most efficient way to start a fire, but it does the job," he said.

Doris examined my face, which left me feeling quite uneasy. "What reason would Carter have to target you?"

"I believe he might be responsible for Ginny Lawson's murder. He knows I saw him in the area where she died. Maybe he suspects I witnessed something."

"What exactly did you see?"

"I don't know! But he clearly thinks I saw something. Why don't you track him down and ask him yourself?" I could've mentioned that he was likely at Abracadabra in New Haven, but now that I was on the other side of the badge, I knew better. No investigator worth their salt would just hand over information like that to the police.

* * *

Sachem Creek doesn't have an arson squad, but I knew Lou would have a team down from the state before the end of the day. The bad news was that I couldn't get back into the house until the investigation was over.

Aunt Phoebe approached me, and as soon as I saw her expression with squinted eyes and a tight-set mouth, I knew I was in trouble.

She bluntly stated, "Don't expect to get your deposit back."

Subtlety was clearly not her strong suit. Ignoring her comment, I tried to calm the situation by expressing concern for her.

"I'm glad to see you're okay. Did you happen to see anyone near the house?"

Phoebe remained sullen. "No."

It was hard to believe that anyone could get up to my room without her seeing.

"But you see everything. It was 4:30 in the afternoon. You didn't see anyone?"

"Did you?"

"I was sleeping," I said.

"Well, I was on the computer."

She sees everything, night or day, and the one time someone comes around and sets a fire in my room, she's on the computer. Probably talking to Nine-Plus-Guy.

Chapter Twenty-Two

I looked for Charlie, who was still milling about with the gawking villagers. When I told him I couldn't get back into the apartment, he said I could crash at his place for the night. Later that evening, from his front porch, we watched the lights of small fishing boats quietly bobbing at anchor between his beach and Cut-in-Two Island. The flats were running.

"It doesn't seem worth it to go out for only three flatfish," I said. "Remember when we were kids and used to bring them home by the bucketful?"

"Precisely the reason for the limit."

"Simpler times when we were kids…" My voice trailed off. "Charlie, I don't know how Aunt Phoebe couldn't have seen someone go up to my room. She sees everything."

"You said the chair was by the open back window?"

"Right."

"Well, maybe the person responsible for the fire entered and exited through the window. It would be easy enough to get onto the back-garage roof without her seeing."

"True."

In the yellow light of his porch, I could see he was studying my face, trying to read my thoughts. "There's something else on your mind. What is it that you're not saying?"

"Max dug up the Colorado Kayaker's real name—it's Harry Carter, and he works at a restaurant in New Haven called Abracadabra. I still think he's the killer, but as far as setting my apartment on fire, I have to agree with Lou. It's not the most efficient way of doing it. Why didn't he use gasoline?"

"It is an odd choice. Unless the arsonist works with it." Charlie let that hang for a minute before going on. "Everyone from chemists to nail technicians and artists uses acetone as a solvent."

Charlie had a voice-activated device on the porch. I called out to it, "Hey, Clara, is acetone used in restaurants?"

"According to a Clara contributor: One of the most common solvents used to clean restaurant kitchens is acetone because of its ability to cut oil and grease," the virtual assistant answered.

"Grease. Well, there you go. Carter works in a restaurant," I said.

Charlie nodded slowly, then glanced out toward the darkened horizon. "It does make you wonder, though. Why go through all the trouble? Starting a fire like that—it's not random. Someone wanted something, or maybe they thought you had it."

The idea landed like a cold stone in my stomach.

* * *

The bed in Charlie's spare room was about as comfortable as sleeping on a granite slab. With all the money the guy had, you'd think he would spring for some new furniture. I had plenty to think about besides the mattress as I lay there, gazing at the island lights through the window. The race was just around the corner on Monday, and when I woke up, it would already be Thursday. I'd been training hard, and I didn't want to lose my edge at the last minute.

Abe also crossed my mind. I needed to figure out why he vanished. I decided I should look into the antique dealer who got him involved with Big Apple Mortgage and see if that could help me track down my alleged brother.

Then there was Harry Carter. I needed to track him down at Abracadabra in two days. I already had questions, but now he was looking like the prime suspect in the fire, too.

It was clear that the next couple of days were going to be jam-packed. I also thought of Kim's wedding. She was tying the knot on Saturday. I wondered if I should send her a gift to signal there were no hard feelings, even though there definitely were. What would be an appropriate wedding gift for the happy couple from the ex-husband? She already got everything I own.

Between the murder, the race, the wedding, the fire, and Abe, I couldn't totally blame my lack of sleep on the mattress, though.

Before I fell asleep, I formulated a plan. I would paddle over to Meigs Point in Madison bright and early, about twenty-four miles round trip, just to keep on top of my game. Once that was out of the way, I didn't mind spending the rest of the day trying to find the antique dealer. Maybe that would lead me to Abe. Then, later in the day, when Abracadabra opened, I would pay a visit to Harry Carter.

It would be a full day, but as long as I got in that early morning training, it worked for me.

Chapter Twenty-Three

A t 5:45 a.m., I left Charlie a note on his kitchen counter telling him breakfast at Tide and Griddle was on me at about 8:00, when I returned from my paddle to Meigs Point. It was the least I could do after he put me up for the night. I carefully closed the wooden screen door so as not to wake him. As I stood on his front porch, the morning sun streaming through a mist that surrounded Cut-in-two and Bear Islands gave them a dreamy quality that made me wish I had time to take a picture.

When I got down to his driveway, I noticed Charlie's car was gone. I didn't expect that at such an early hour, although I knew he had mentioned he had to run to Yale in the morning. Hopefully, he would be back early, see the note, and still make it for breakfast.

To save time and to avoid going home to get my kayak, where I'd probably see my aunt and get an earful, I borrowed Charlie's kayak. I had no doubt that if he had been home, he would have told me to do so.

The trip over to Meigs Point was uneventful, although I was mindful of my surroundings. I got there and back without so much as having to ride the wake of a powerboat, let alone getting buzzed, swamped, or followed. By eight, I was at Tide and Griddle. Charlie wasn't around. Either he missed the note, or he was still in New Haven. I spotted Max on the deck eating as she worked on her laptop. I hadn't seen her since she left my apartment the day before. I stopped at her table, hoping my guilty conscience wouldn't show.

"Mind if I sit?"

She looked up with a puzzled look on her face. When she realized it was me, she gave me an encouraging smile. I didn't know how to tell her the latest other than by jumping right in.

"I had an incident at my apartment after you left yesterday."

"Incident?"

"A fire. No big deal, even though half of the village showed up. The news spread faster than the fire."

"I didn't know. Are you all right?"

Talk about asking the obvious. She could see I was all right, but I guess it's one of those things people feel obligated to ask.

"Sure. Fine. Just a small fire. It might have been arson."

"Arson? What makes you say that?"

"It was started with acetone. But arson is only a theory at this point. I changed the subject and told her I intended to track down the antique dealer who hooked Abe up with Big Apple. "My apartment is cordoned off with crime scene tape. I was going to break in to get to my computer. Mind if I use your laptop instead? I want to see what I can find out about the antique dealer who visited Abe."

She turned it toward me.

I pulled up the browser and entered *antiques, Litchfield* because Abe had said that the frame on the guy's license plate said Litchfield Mercedes. "I'm assuming that his antique shop is in the same area where he bought his car. It's a long shot, but it's all I've got."

The search came up with Results of over seven thousand references to antiques, and Litchfield.

I looked at Max. "You in a hurry? This may take a while."

Max came around the table and leaned over my shoulder. "That's because there's more than one Litchfield—from England to the Midwest, plus it's a county here in Connecticut. Change that to antiques, Litchfield, CT."

That brought the list way down. I clicked on Antiques Dealers of Litchfield County and found a listing of seventy-one dealers in the county.

"Now let's see if we can find Mr. D. W."

"There it is," Max said. "David Warner Antiques!"

We gave each other a high-five. I clicked the hyperlink, and his webpage came up.

"There he is," she said, pointing to a picture of a man of about forty in a shop with expensive-looking antiques.

"That's interesting. It seems he specializes in rare maps as well as antique furniture and tools," I said.

The website was quite detailed. There was even an interactive map showing how to get to the store, which was not in the town of Litchfield, but in the Village of West Cornwall, in Litchfield County.

I was proud of us. We made a great team. "We know where he works, now let's see where this Warner character lives."

I put his name in the White Pages search engine and found one who lived in Danielson, which is in the eastern part of the state, too far. Another lived in Hamden in the southern part of the state, still too far from the antique business. Then I found one in Litchfield, age twenty-six. Close proximity, but too young, and then finally another aged sixty-one, whose address was the same as the antique store in West Cornwall. That was definitely the guy. So, I was a little off when I guessed his age. Either he looks young for his age, or he put up an old picture on his website. It also listed five previous addresses for this person, all in New York State.

"Bingo!" Max said.

"We're on a roll, now we know where he lives and that he works from at his antique store in West Cornwall. That's something."

"Here, let me see if I can find out anything else about him," Max said. She pulled the computer toward her and did a general search on David Warner.

Her findings netted an actor, a literary agent, and a guy who translated the bible into an obscure dialect of a tribe in Thailand. Then she hit upon an interesting entry about a David Warner who served time in New York several years back for dealing in rare stolen maps.

"This is our antiques dealer. Nice job," I said. "You deserve a raise."

She laughed and then, without thinking, I gave Max a quick hug, which didn't seem to bother her. "I guess I should go pay David Warner a call."

"Excuse me?" Max asked, her voice dripping with sarcasm.

Oops. It was foolish of me not to invite her along. "We. I meant *we* should pay Warner a call."

"That's better. But sorry, I can't go. I need to meet with a friend."

"Really?"

"Yes, she's a well-known hairstylist in New York. You go, and we'll compare notes later."

"I wasn't about to question Max's priorities, but I certainly wasn't following her reasoning."

"I'll fill you in," I said.

ᛝ ᛝ ᛝ

There's no easy way to get to the Village of West Cornwall up in Connecticut's northwest corner. I punched the address of Warner Antiques into my GPS. The digital female voice directed me to head to the southbound entrance of I-95 toward New Haven. As usual, because of road construction, the traffic on 95 was ridiculous.

As I drove over the Pearl Harbor Memorial Bridge in New Haven, my mind couldn't help but drift back to the day that my life had changed. A head-on collision there and an insane shootout with a drug dealer resulted in me tossing my badge in front of the chief and opting for early retirement. Then an even crazier chain of events led me to rediscover my long-lost father and embark on a new career as a private investigator in Savannah.

Passing the very spot where the drug dealer met his demise in a gruesome encounter with a tractor-trailer, my grip tightened on the steering wheel, and I tapped the brake pedal. My heart raced, and I felt the familiar surge of anxiety creeping in. To regain composure, I rolled down the window and took a few deep breaths.

"I can do this," I reassured myself. "I have the skills. I've been in worse situations before." I recited my personal mantra for dealing with PTSD and proceeded to cross the bridge without any further incident. I was proud of the remarkable progress I'd made in my mental and emotional well-being over the past months, and I continued my ride through the evolving landscape of New Haven.

In the short time since my departure, I noticed significant changes in the city. New buildings seemed to sprout up everywhere, and the inner city was undergoing a process of gentrification. I couldn't say that I particularly cared for these changes any more than I did for the transformation occurring in Sachem Creek.

Leaving the Yale fields behind in Westville, I headed through the countryside toward the hilly town of Derby. The terrain gradually gained elevation with each passing mile. Despite the influx of people and urban sprawl, Connecticut remained predominantly a lush forest. Under different circumstances, I might have considered this a scenic drive, but today was different.

Chapter Twenty-Four

After eighty-five miles and an hour and a half, I found myself following the Sharon-Goshen Turnpike, a two-lane country road, into the hamlet of West Cornwall. Cornwall is known for two things: being the birthplace of Ethan Allan, and its red covered bridge that spans the Housatonic River. With only a handful of buildings, including one named the Cool Moose Café and another colonial structure that had served as a toll booth when the road was actually a turnpike, it reminded me of Sachem Creek before the Amanda era. I hoped it would never have to suffer the same growing pains that Sachem Creek was experiencing.

As I approached the one-lane covered bridge, I stopped to allow a car to enter from the other direction. When it was my turn to cross, I drove slowly not only for safety but also to admire the intricate wooden beams that formed the lattice truss framework of the barn-like bridge.

After crossing, I reached David Warner Antiques situated on the riverbank. The store occupied the ground floor of a colonial house, and a sign on the front read "Jacob Stone, 1737." An assortment of vintage items, including a little tricycle, a red Radio Flyer wagon, and a metal Taylor Tot baby stroller, was displayed on the lawn. I looked at the high price tags. The guy wasn't giving the stuff away.

I entered the store. Every inch of floor space was packed with antiques that looked like old-fashioned junk. Besides the expected somewhat comforting smell of dust, mildew, and furniture polish, there was an underlying chemical odor. Not spotting anyone immediately, I peeked into the back room, where I found a man in a tweed sports jacket hunched over a worktable covered with tools and cans of stain. I recognized him as David Warner, even though he appeared considerably older in person. A stuffed owl perched nearby, seemingly overseeing his work on the back of a mirror. He didn't look up as I entered.

"You can leave the keys and the bill on the counter out front."

"Keys?"

Warner turned to look at me with a puzzled expression. "I thought you were here to deliver my car from the garage. I'll be right with you. Feel free to look around."

He stood, and I could see a small monitor on the table, showing a view of the shop. Now that I was playing the role of a "customer," he considered me worth his attention. He didn't suspect that I might be anything more than a casual visitor.

I sniffed the air. "Is that acetone?"

"Yes. I'm fixing the backing on that mirror. We can't use mercury anymore, so I'm putting on some silver leaf." He rushed to open the back door and turned on a large box fan that sat on the floor. "That should take care of the smell. I'm so accustomed to it that I forget it might be bothersome to some people."

I suspected Warner had something to do with Abe losing his house. I also suspected that he was working on behalf of Amanda. Now that I knew he worked with acetone, I wondered if he had anything to do with the fire.

"That stuff could dissolve your liver," I said.

He nodded his insincere agreement. "Now, what can I help you with?"

Deciding to continue my pretense as a tourist, I pointed at a dark painting and said, "This is interesting."

"Indeed. It's American, Joshua Shaw."

"American? It looks like an English scene," I said.

"He immigrated from England in the early 1800s and drew on his memories. He became an important American landscape artist. I can offer you a good price on it."

Thanks to my mother instilling an appreciation of art in me, I could have told him it was a copy, but I wanted to get out while I still had some brain

134

cells left, so I moved on.

"What I'm really interested in is a seascape. Something for my aunt's place in Sachem Creek."

I thought his body stiffened a bit. "I don't have a seascape at the moment, perhaps you'd be interested in this riverscape; Hudson River School."

"Are you familiar with Sachem Creek?"

I studied his face for a reaction. He looked straight at me, hesitated a moment, then blinked.

"I know it's on the shoreline."

"Yes, east of New Haven."

"Yes, yes. Of course. East of New Haven. I can't recall having been there, but I understand it's quite quaint."

"Would the name Abe Cromwell refresh your memory?"

David Warner's eyes shifted from me to the back door.

"Cromwell? I can't say that rings a bell."

"Abe Cromwell. About my age. He sold you some old tools a month or so ago."

"I travel all over New England acquiring inventory. It's difficult to remember everyone."

I studied him carefully. "True enough. But some items tend to stand out—especially the ones with history… maybe even a bit of legend attached."

Warner's hand twitched toward the worktable, his voice tightening. "Collectors love a good story, sure. Doesn't mean there's any truth to it."

"Maybe not. But stories sometimes end with someone cheated out of what's theirs—or worse, up in flames."

His jaw clenched, lips thinning into a hard line. His eyes darted toward the back door. "This conversation is over."

I took a couple of steps closer to Warner. "Abe is about to lose his house."

"I'm sorry to hear that, but I don't see how that's my concern. It had nothing to do with me."

Warner bolted for the door, knocking over a shelf full of paint cans in the process. I threw the shelf aside and jumped over the cans before going after him. Warner had already hopped a porch railing. He ran to the river, where he dragged a small river kayak into the water and jumped in. By the time I got to the riverbank, Warner had shoved off and was headed downstream. My most promising lead was slipping away.

"Don't just stand there. Help me carry this!" Big Al was making his way toward the river, dragging a bright orange and yellow tandem Kayak.

I took the stern end and we dashed toward the river with the boat. "Where did this come from? And more importantly, where did you come from?"

"One, I found it behind the store. And two, I Ubered," he said as he hopped into the stern seat.

"That's my seat," I said.

"Dumb jocks in the bow," he said. "You want to catch him or not?"

There was no time to argue. Besides, he was right. The paddler in the stern controls the direction of a tandem kayak. But the stronger paddler needed to be in front for speed. At least he was giving me that.

The river boiled over the rocks thanks to the recent heavy rains. Warner's small river kayak handled the rapids much better than the seventeen-foot tandem kayak. Although Big Al managed to avoid most rocks, with a craft of that length striking boulders with teeth, a jolting impact was inevitable.

"Ubered isn't even a word," I said as I dug the paddle into the water.

"Who gives a shit?"

We were both shouting to be heard above the roar of the rapids.

"I do. I could have handled this myself."

Big Al scoffed. "Some detective you are. You didn't even know we were following you."

My father was still a good P.I. despite his memory problems. I'm sure he taught that driver every trick in the book to keep them out of sight.

"The fare must have cost a fortune,"

"Don't worry about it. I charged it to the Blue Palmetto."

"The agency account?"

"Yeah, your account. Keep paddling."

Warner kept a constant one hundred yards ahead of us. Despite the handicap of not having a river kayak, we stood on his tail as the river twisted through woods and farms. Eventually, we got to the Kent Dead Water where we gained on him. But soon the river narrowed and we were swept by the stream. Then I could hear the roar of the waterfall at Bulls Bridge ahead. Warner stopped dead in the water.

"It looks like he's had enough," I said.

"Bull shit. They never have enough."

Big Al was right. As we got closer, Warner leaned to the right, turning his boat on edge. He dipped his paddle toward the bow and, with a right sweep-stroke, he started to turn. Then a reverse stroke on the left completed the turn.

But Warner sat there in the water. I saw the glint of the sun off something in Warner's hand.

"Gun!" I yelled to Big Al.

As I braced, I had a flashback of the drug dealer who had spun his car the ensuing shootout on the New Haven bridge.

My father maneuvered the kayak, putting the stern end, his end, between Warner and me. A brave gesture if I were in a sentimental mood.

"Get down," I yelled.

A bullet grazed the deck of the kayak just behind the cockpit, snapping one of the bungee deck lines.

"Where's your gun?" I could hear the sarcasm in Big Al's voice. He knew it was locked in the compartment of my car. I'd had enough of carrying a gun when I was with the force, and usually didn't keep one on me during routine investigations. For one thing, it intimidates people, and they tend to clam up.

"Who knew this wasn't going to be routine?"

"Ya damned fool!"

One minute, he was putting himself between me and a bullet, and the next, he was criticizing me. Typical Big Al.

Warner seemed to be taking his chances with the falls ahead. But we were in bigger trouble. There was no way that our seventeen-foot kayak was going to make it over those falls. Warner, on the other hand, had a much better chance in his smaller river kayak that was meant for doing stunts.

I fought to keep the current from sweeping us downstream as we maneuvered the kayak close to shore.

"Get on shore. I'll keep it steady. Then pull me in."

Big Al hopped onto shore using his paddle as a support so the kayak didn't turn over. Steady on shore, he held it out to me.

Seconds before disappearing over the falls, Warner took a parting shot. The bullet knocked my father's paddle out of my hands. I was caught in the current and headed for the falls.

I remembered something that my grandfather used to say. *Don't give up five minutes before the miracle.* If I survived the plunge over the falls and caught Warner, it would be a miracle for sure.

A tour guide might tell you that Bull's Bridge isn't as long as the covered bridge at West Cornwall, and it's unpainted and has a slight sag in the middle. But at the moment, I didn't care what the hell the bridge looked like. All I knew was that just before the gorge that the bridge spans, the river falls several feet and crashes on huge boulders before it surges under the bridge.

The roar of plunging water told me what was in store as the rush caught my kayak. I reached the brink and then sat in midair for a second. If I was lucky, they would find my mangled body in a few days, miles downstream at Milford Point, where the Housatonic empties into Long Island Sound.

When the bow struck the riverbed below, the long sea kayak stood upright for what seemed like forever. I fully expected I would land on the boulders in the torrent below and break my back. But after standing up like a totem pole in the water, bow down in the riverbed, the stern fell forward and jammed in the branch of a pine tree that hung over the cascade, and I was suspended sideways in the cockpit several feet above the tumultuous base of the falls. Using every ounce of upper body strength, I held on to the sides of the deck and pushed off with my arms. I pulled my legs from the cockpit and then lowered myself into the water. The force of the torrent immediately knocked me over, scraping my arms and knees. My head crashed forward, but I missed the rocks and landed on Warner in the plunge pool. His eye was already swelling, and he had cuts and bruises all over his face from his nosedive over the falls.

* * *

I dragged Warner to the bank. He wasn't in as bad shape as I figured because he swung at me. We both ended up in the river. We duked it out. He was tough. But not tough enough. He was down, and I was up. He pulled the gun out of his pocket, but I kicked it out of his hand. He got up and lunged toward me. I hit him in the jaw, and he bounced against the rock wall. He let out a long sigh as he slid into a sitting position, the water splashing down on him from above.

"Had enough?"

"No." He worked himself up and swung one more time, but slipped on the wet rocks before he was able to connect. Once more, I pulled him from the river.

"I'm not doing this a third time."

He didn't answer, but I could see that if he had a chance, he'd start all over again.

I grabbed him by the front of the shirt and lifted him to his feet.

"I need some answers, or you're going back in head first."

"This is an assault. I didn't do anything but paddle down the river." Had he forgotten that he shot at us twice?

"I guess I'm a little hard of hearing with this waterfall. Talk, or you go back into the rapids where I found you." I shook him. "Why did you trick Abe out of his house?"

I shook him, and his head bumped into the rock ledge behind him. His eyes glazed over, and for a minute, I thought I had knocked him out. It was enough to convince him that I was indeed a madman, or at least angry enough to do him some real harm.

"I had to."

I was holding on to the front of his shirt with my two hands, and in my anger, lifted him off the ground.

"What does that mean, you had to?"

"I was in debt, and a customer bailed me out. He told me if I did a couple of favors for him, he'd forgive the loan."

"Why didn't you get another loan and pay him back?"

"Because he had sold me an old map. I didn't know it was stolen, and I resold it to a guy who came in the next day. A few days later, they both come back to tell me they're going to turn me in for selling stolen maps. The guy I sold it to has proof he bought it from me, but I had no proof of who I got it from. I was in prison for stealing rare maps once. This time I'd go away for a long time."

"So, he made you defraud Abe? Why?"

"Whoever he worked for wanted the property. I couldn't afford to ask questions."

"Who'd he work for?"

"I don't know."

"A woman?"

"I told you I don't know."

"You set my place on fire. Didn't you?"

"I don't know what you're talking about."

"My apartment; you set a chair on fire in my apartment while I was sleeping."

"No!"

I shook him again.

"I want the truth!" I shook him, and his head bumped into the rock wall again. I swear I didn't mean for that to happen.

"That is the truth."

I tended to believe that he was working for someone else. He couldn't have a personal grudge against me. He didn't even know who I was when I entered his shop. He admitted to duping Abe but not to setting the fire. My gut told me he was telling the truth. So, if he didn't do it, who did? I held him by the collar, contemplating what to do next.

I tried to meet him halfway. "Okay, maybe you didn't start the fire, but you ran away for a reason."

"Don't you get it? This isn't just about maps. You're missing the big picture here. This is bigger than you think."

Then a sound so loud that it hurt reverberated through the gorge. I was aware of blood, a lot of it, just before my head struck a rock in the turbulent water.

Chapter Twenty-Five

I woke up in an unfamiliar bed with my head throbbing. I can't say it was the first time that happened. But this time, I was surrounded by beeping monitors.

A doctor came in and introduced himself. I didn't pay attention to his name. I was trying to figure out what was going on.

"Do you know where you are?"

I looked around.

"Hospital."

"Memorial in Torrington," the doctor said.

"Where am I shot, anyway, Doc?"

"You're not shot, Mr. DeLucia. But you've had some head trauma."

"Okay then." I started to get out of bed.

"Not so fast." He put a blood pressure cuff on my arm and asked who the president was.

I wasn't in the mood for quizzes.

"I'm fine. We don't have to do this."

The doctor drew his brows together. "Try."

I huffed, "George Washington, 1789-1797; John Adams, 1797-1801; Thomas Jefferson, 1801-1809; James Madison, 1809-1817; James Monroe, 1817-1825. Let me know when I get to the one you want.

The doctor grabbed my forearms. "Open your fingers."

142

"Mr. DeLucia. Can you count backward from one hundred, please?"

"One hundred, ninety-nine, ninety-eight, ninety-seven. I have to get out of here."

"Not until we're sure you're not concussed. You hit your head hard, and you have lacerations. I want you to get a CT scan to rule out a bleed. You should stay overnight. Make a fist."

"Are you sure you want me to do that, Doc?"

The doctor shook his head. "I wouldn't have asked if I didn't."

"I'll check myself out. I'm not staying overnight."

He started giving me a warning about the insurance consequences of checking myself out. I didn't want to hear his spiel.

"Where's my father?" I asked.

"In good hands. You were mumbling something about your father. The police found him nearby and managed to piece together enough of what he told them to locate his wife," I was told.

"It's actually his sister-in-law; he occasionally confuses things," I attempted to explain, despite the throbbing ache in my head.

"I can see he can be a handful. He left with her. We promised to inform her once we're done evaluating you. The other woman stayed behind."

"What other woman?"

"Ms. Brophy. I understand the two women came up here after we contacted your father's sister-in-law." The doctor pulled the drape aside, and I saw Max on the other side of the window talking to two cops. Max waved to me and mouthed something I couldn't make out.

"I have to talk to her."

"I'm afraid the police want to talk to you first."

A cop with sandy hair and of medium height, with a build that made him look like he lived at the gym, came in.

"Mr. DeLucia, I'm Lieutenant Porter of the Kent Police Dept." He gave a slight nod and smiled like he'd known me all his life.

That was a red flag for me. It was an interrogation technique I'd used myself. Build trust. Make the suspect feel comfortable talking to you, no matter how you felt about him inside. I was going to tell him of my service with NHPD but decided to hell with it. I wanted a feeling for where things were going.

Porter went on. "I have to ask you a few questions. I understand you were on the job in New Haven until recently, so you get it about formalities and paperwork and all that. But what's more important right now is I want to make sure you're doing okay. Are you up to this? I could come back. Say tomorrow?"

"I intend to be long gone from here tomorrow. Let's get on with this."

"Listen, I know how it is. I hate these places too. Tell me what happened concerning..." He made a show of checking his notes on his laptop. "Concerning Mr. Warner. Yes, David Warner."

He knew the antique dealer's name just as well as I did. I played these games myself, and I hate them. "Is Warner dead?" I asked.

The smile disappeared from the cop's face. He gave a deep sigh.

"I'm afraid he is."

Dead. My prime suspect. I remembered all of the blood just before the lights went out.

"Am I being questioned as a witness or a suspect?"

His facial expression was neither accusatory nor affirming, but neutral. He was well-trained.

"Good question. That's a really good question. I wouldn't expect anything less from a brother."

I realized I was rubbing my hand on my forehead. "You're not answering the question."

Porter could have shut me up by saying he was the one asking the questions, but he didn't. Instead, he chuckled. "Okay. No more bullshit from either one of us. Tell me in your own words what happened, and we're done. Does that work for you?

I tried to use my professional cop voice. After all, Porter had called me brother. "It does. So, this guy, Warner, was heading toward the falls. I tried to step in, but we both went over. My kayak got hung up, and I ended up taking fewer hits, so I managed to get out on my own. Warner, though, he took a nasty fall. I pulled him out of the water, but he was in bad shape. Then, outta nowhere, he gets shot, and that's the last thing I remember before I went out cold."

He entered notes in his pad.

"You were both headed toward the falls. Were the two of you in a race?"

I had the impression Porter was asking questions he already knew the answers to. I told him the truth without telling him too much."

"I followed him from Cornwall. He seemed distraught, and I was concerned about him on white water."

"Did you know Warner?"

"Nope, I never saw him before I went into his shop."

Porter looked at his notes again. "That would be an antique shop in Cornwall."

"Right. I'm sure you've been there already and seen the mess in the back room. He made it."

"How did he end up on the river?"

"He ran from the shop and jumped into a kayak. He didn't seem rational. That's why I followed him."

"Do you know why he ran?"

Not at all.

"Did anyone else see what happened?"

"My father was in the kayak with me until I let him out."

"His name?"

"Same as mine. They call him Big Al. He's got a bit of dementia. But I think you know all of this."

He didn't look up from his computer. I don't know if not making eye contact was part of his grilling technique or if he just wasn't didn't know how to relate to people.

I looked out the window and noticed Max was on her phone. She saw me watching, and she walked away.

"Why were you and your father in the antique store?"

"I was there looking for a painting to give to my aunt. I didn't know my father was in. Town." I knew that the police would eventually get an order to see the shop's CCTV. I had to keep as close to the script as possible without telling too much.

"So, your father, who has dementia, got there how?"

"Uber." I saw the cop's eyebrows raise. "What can I tell you? The old man is a hipster. He Ubers."

I looked out the window, and Max was back. She tapped at the window.

"She can come in Porter said."

When Max came in, she grabbed my hand.

Porter stood up. "Before I go, do you have anything you want to say that I haven't asked you?"

"I didn't kill him," I said.

"We know that. An EnCon officer saw someone with a rifle on the bridge."

I couldn't ask for a better witness. Environmental Conservation Police Officers are part of the Department of Energy and Environmental Protection. They work everything from wildlife management to homeland security.

"You didn't bother to tell me?"

"The officer was down below, headed to break up your fight. You didn't bother to tell me that. So, we're even. But yeah, you're in the clear as far as the murder."

So, the shooter's in custody."

"The guy did a leg bail," Porter said.

"You're lucky he didn't kill you first." Max had this really concerned look on her face.

"But he didn't." I could have and should have left it at that. But did I? Nope. I had to elaborate. "At least my father felt he had to come along for backup."

"Just what are you saying? That I shirked my responsibility?"

"I'm sorry. I misspoke. I'm sure you had a good reason to visit your hairstylist."

"That's the most sexist remark I've ever heard you say. Of course, I had a good reason."

"Like I said, I misspoke."

Porter got up to go, looking like he wanted to get out of there before things got serious.

"I'll leave you two to get on with it. I don't do domestics," he said.

I realized it was still a dumb, stupid, sexist remark even if I didn't mean it that way. "Just as well, I have some apologizing to do," I said.

* * *

As Porter was leaving, the doctor came in, and I was glad for another interruption. He glanced at Max.

"It's okay, she can stay," I said. After another round of Count Backward and who's the president, I told him I was leaving.

"I wish it was that easy, Mr. DeLucia. We're short-staffed and there's a lot of insurance paperwork. It's going to be an hour or two."

"Forget it. I'll pay the bill out of pocket. How much is it?

"My guess is you don't want to know. Trust me. Wait." He pulled out a cell phone and turned his back to us, mumbling into the phone. When he hung up, he turned with a smile. "Good news, we'll have you out of here in fifteen minutes."

"Great. Thank you," I said.

"But I want you to go home and rest for a day or two," he said. "Do you have a ride?"

I looked at Max. She nodded yes. Honestly, I don't know if I would have been so generous to someone who had just insulted them.

"Good. Do you have any questions?" The doctor asked.

"Yeah, Doc. Is there any cure for being an asshole?"

"I'm afraid not, Mr. DeLucia."

Chapter Twenty-Six

After signing the hospital paperwork and taking the required wheelchair ride to the front entrance, the hospital attendant and I waited for Max to bring her car around. The attendant helped me into the car and handed me an envelope with medical instructions I knew I'd never get around to reading. Max started driving.

"My car's over there," I said, pointing to the parking lot.

"The doctor doesn't want you driving. We can arrange to pick it up tomorrow."

"The hell we will." I reached for the door handle, but she'd already locked it.

"Stop acting like a spoiled teenager and let me drive."

"Fine, but we're stopping in New Haven on the way home."

"New Haven? Your discharge papers said to go straight home and rest, not take a detour."

"You said this Harry Carter guy works in New Haven and he'd be on tonight. Don't you want to find out if he's the one who killed Warner? If you're not interested, drop me off in Sachem Creek, and I'll get there myself."

Max sighed. "All right."

"All right, as in the Creek?"

"No, all right, as in New Haven. But I'm running the show."

"We'll see about that," I muttered.

* * *

From Kent, we headed down Route 7, about twenty-five miles to Danbury. The scenic state road didn't allow for rushing, so we had time to talk. I apologized again for being a jerk.

"I don't know what's worse," she said, "you talking without any connection between your mouth and brain, or hearing you apologize on loop. Let's focus. We've got two cases to crack: who swindled Abe and why, and who killed Ginny Lawson?"

"They're both tied to Amanda," I said.

"Maybe. But when Warner was killed, we lost our best lead. If he was telling the truth, he was pressured into pushing Abe toward Big Apple Mortgage."

"That doesn't mean he didn't start the fire," I countered.

"True. But helping Abe doesn't seem like a strong enough motive to kill you. And the fire wasn't the only attempt."

"Let's stick to what we know. Sachem Creek has a high turnover of homes that later default. That pattern screams mortgage fraud, and Abe's situation backs it up."

As we hopped on I-84 in Danbury, Max shot a glance at me. "Wanna keep your eyes on the road?"

"I know how to drive," she said, turning her attention back to the windshield. "And I know you think I should've gone with you to track down Warner."

"Weren't we moving on from that?"

"We were, but I want you to know that when I went into the city, it wasn't just for a hair appointment. I talked to some people. Big Apple Mortgage is a ghost—barely a trace of it before it started operating in Sachem Creek."

We drove for the next ten miles in silence. The narrow state road wound its way along the hillsides above the Housatonic River. As we crossed the dam at Lake Zoar and climbed into the hills of Derby, I said, "Maybe we need to work on our communication skills."

Max didn't respond, and I'd have been disappointed if she had. But I caught her holding back a smile. We listened to Pandora for the remaining half-hour drive to New Haven.

* * *

As we got to New Haven, the draining sun was already reflecting off the glass walls of the Knights of Columbus building. We drove past the ancient green to the heart of Yale.

We parked at the surface lot in the center of pedestrian-heavy Broadway and hiked around the corner from the Shops at Yale to Abracadabra. The restaurant, which rested between Toad's Place and Mory's, opened while I was in Savannah. But I knew the area well from my days on the force.

We waited a half hour before someone led us down a ramp past a crowded bar to the packed dining room. Three cooks toiled over an enormous circular grill that dominated the room and filled it with the aroma of cooking steaks and vegetables. It was easy to spot Harry Carter flipping concoctions of food on the sizzling surface. There aren't many people who have a snake slinking into their ear.

The waiter sat us at a table where we received bowls and were directed to salad bar-style stations where we filled them with our choice of vegetables, meat, seafood, and sauces. I brought my bowl to the grill and got in Harry's line. When it dawned on Max that I had positioned myself to have Carter wait on me before her, she shot me a look that could have cooked my veggies without the grill.

I placed my bowl of food on the counter, and Carter picked it up and poured its contents on the grill.

"You're B twenty-five."

"I'd like to talk to you," I said.

The snake on his neck seemed to slither as he gestured with his head toward the multiple orders he was working on. "I'm busy."

"It's about Ginny Lawson."

The mention of the murdered girl's name got his attention. I caught a flicker of recognition in his eyes as he must have remembered me from the Trolley Trail. The color drained from his face despite the heat from the grill.

"I don't know anybody by that name."

"But you did. The girl that was murdered in Sachem Creek."

The guy behind me dropped his bowl, the contents spreading across the floor.

"Look, man," Harry said, "You're going to get me fired. I get a break in fifteen minutes. We can talk then."

Max's food was ready at the next station. She picked it up and turned to Carter. "We'll be eating right over there." She motioned toward a table by the wall. "We'll wait."

Carter gave her a "who the hell are you?" look, then nodded.

When we got to our table, the food wasn't half bad. Fifteen minutes later, Harry came over to the table.

Al DeLucia." I said, reaching out my hand, but he didn't take it.

"I know who you are. Who's she?"

He eyed Max. "I saw you at the trail."

"My co-worker, Max," I said.

"Maxine Brophy, Max for short," she said. "So, we meet again."

"Seems so," he said.

"What do you want, exactly?"

"We're investigating Ms. Lawson's murder.

"You're private detectives. I don't have to talk to you. Or her, for that matter."

"You don't have to talk to us," I said. "But since the evidence points to you as the prime suspect, I thought you might want to clear your name if you're Innocent." Actually, the police considered Abe the prime suspect. I was the one who thought Carter was number one. But he didn't need to know that.

Four women at the next table were staring at us. I turned toward them and smiled. "It's a game. You know, like Clue? Role-playing and all that."

"Ah, role-playing," one of them said. They all murmured and shook their heads; then went back to their conversation.

"Look," Carter said. "Let's go out in the alley where we can talk."

I got up and Max did the same.

Carter glared at her. "Just you."

Max stepped in front of me. "I'm coming."

"Whatever you say to me can be said in front of my partner. She comes."

"Out front," I said. "We can talk in that small park across the street."

We walked out the front door, and Carter bolted, disappearing in the never-ending foot traffic.

"I'll check in here," Max yelled as she ran into Toad's Place, a nightclub famous for hosting acts like the Rolling Stones.

I ran around the corner to Broadway. The only other possible way that he could have disappeared so quickly is if he had ducked into the Yale Book Store. I bolted into the store and found myself surrounded by Yale typeface on sweatshirts, notebooks, mugs, and you name it. But no sight of Carter. I headed down a wide staircase, taking four steps at a time, until I got to a landing. Then spotting Carter headed toward the back of the store I vaulted over the railing landing on a display of Handsome Dan stuffed dogs. I ran through the stacks of the book department, looking up each aisle. Nothing but startled customers until I rounded a corner and spotted him.

Max came out of nowhere at the same time.

I tackled him. Max did the same. We all fell. Carter's eyes had the look of a wounded animal. He scrambled along the floor until he could support himself on a shelf. He got up and ran, crashing into a display of Yale drinking mugs and falling again. I pulled him up by the collar.

A small group of people, including several Yale Book Store employees, gathered around us. Carter struggled, and Max took him from me and put him in an armlock.

"Teamwork," we both said at the same time.

Carter looked confused. "It's him you should be hassling."

"Because you think he killed your sister, right?" Max turned to me. "Something was bothering me about that picture he was in with Ginny. I couldn't put a finger on it. Now seeing this guy in person, I see the resemblance in the eyes."

"Is she right?" I asked.

Carter nodded his head. "Yeah."

"Listen, man, I found her, that's all. I found her and tried to revive her. I wish I could have done more."

The devastated look on his face was convincing. I'm not so sure that he believed me. He didn't seem to have the energy or the will to run. Max let go but stood alert. He brushed the glass off his shirt and looked me in the eye. "I hope you have money because I'm not paying for this stuff."

The Yale Book Store employees moved in a little closer to me.

After I paid for the broken merchandise with my Blue Palmetto credit card, the store agreed not to involve the cops. As we were escorted to the door, I was relieved I wouldn't have to suffer any ribbing from my former colleagues.

Just because Carter claimed to be Lawson's brother, Max wasn't about to give up on getting to the bottom of things. "What time did you get to work at the restaurant?"

"Five o'clock."

If Carter did shoot Warner, he would have had plenty of time to get back to New Haven from Kent.

She seemed to be studying his eyes as she questioned him. "And your whereabouts before that?"

"At my other job. I work at the Yale Commons preparing food for the students. I worked from six this morning until two-thirty this afternoon. I went home, showered, relaxed, and got to Abracadabra by five. I probably don't have that job now. Thanks to you." He glared at me.

Who told him to run? I only wanted to talk to him. I kept my mouth shut and let Max continue.

"Can you prove you worked at the Yale dining hall all day?"

"You can call them and ask. The supervisor is there from 10:00 a.m. until ten at night. He saw me all day and can check my timecard to tell you I came in at six."

He gave Max the number, and she called. From the one-sided conversation I heard, Carter was there from 6:00 a.m. until two-thirty, as he had said.

"I believe you were there, Mr. Carter. Your supervisor confirmed it was you who worked, right down to the tattoo," Max said.

Carter refrained from saying I told you so. "I hope you didn't blow that job, too."

The street didn't seem like a good place to be talking about this. We agreed that we should go to Carter's nearby apartment to talk. My only regret was that I didn't get my dinner.

* * *

The Roger Sherman Apartments is an imposing 19th-century Gothic-style building. The limestone street-level walls are topped with six floors of massive brownstone, punctuated with copper-topped bay windows and faux towers. I knew from my days on the job that over the years the building had gone through a metamorphosis of a hotel, brothel, tenement, college dorm, and now luxury apartments. I wondered how Carter could afford it. He must have read my mind.

"My sister pays for it. Next month, I don't know…"

"It's haunted, you know," Max whispered to me as we followed Harry into the building.

She was a wealth of useless information. "How do you know that?" I asked.

"I lived here. When I went to Yale. Theatre studies. Yet another life." She shrugged.

Carter put the key in the lock and stopped.

"Abby is in there, but don't worry. She's protective, but she'll realize you're with me."

Protective? I seem to remember that he sicced the dog on us. The door opened, and Abby came bounding to us. Carter didn't know that the dog and I had already made peace when we met at Ginny's house.

Carter continued when we got inside. I guess he wanted to get it off his chest. "I'd just found out about Ginny, and I was out of control. The liquor didn't help. There was a lot of talk in the village. I heard you were involved…" He stopped and shook his head.

I think he was going to apologize or something. I didn't need it. Besides, I'd made some wrong assumptions myself. All I wanted to do now was get any information that could help Abe.

"Look, if the three of us work together, we can figure this out. Tell me about your sister."

154

Carter dropped into a well-worn armchair that stuck out like a sore thumb among the sleek, modern furniture in the room. It looked like something he'd rescued off the curb, the one piece his sister hadn't picked out.

"Such as?" he prompted.

I stayed on my feet. "What exactly was your sister doing for Amanda Kittle?"

"She was a real estate lawyer. Handled title searches for her."

"I know that," I said. "But what about this big secret project Amanda's been buying up land for? She already owns half of Sachem Creek."

Carter shrugged. "Sis didn't tell me what it was. Just said it was huge, something that'd change the whole area."

"A timeshare?" I guessed.

He gave me a look like I'd just sprouted a second head. "Who buys timeshares anymore?"

"An amusement park, maybe?"

"I don't know, okay?" Carter snapped. "All Ginny said was she hated the idea, but like it or not, it was the future."

"Anything else that would get her killed?" Max asked.

"Ginny was a good person. Very kindhearted. She worked many cases pro bono and saved a lot of people from being on the street. I can't imagine who would want to hurt her."

"She never talked to you about her job?"

"She was a real estate lawyer. It's not an exciting job."

Max was looking at the books on Carter's shelf. "Did she ever talk to you about mortgage fraud in connection with Amanda?" she said.

"My sister was an honest lawyer. She wouldn't be mixed up in fraud. I do know that she wasn't too enthusiastic about Amanda's partner, though."

That hit me like a paddle to the back of my head."Partner?" I asked.

"Yeah, a silent partner. Someone from the area."

"Amanda is loaded. She didn't need a partner," I said.

Carter leaned back in the chair, arms crossed and a knowing look in his eye. "Money doesn't always do the trick. Sometimes connections are just as important as money."

"You mean a local was working with her on this project?" I asked. "I can't imagine any Creeker wanting to be involved in something that would disrupt their way of life."

Carter shrugged. "You'd be surprised. I've seen it happen back in Colorado, places like Vail, Talleyrand, and a dozen other resort towns. Locals see a chance to cash in on the beauty of the land, so they team up with developers. At first, it's small stuff, but before you know it, the place is overrun with development. The ones who run businesses? They're living large, happy as pigs in shit. But the folks who just want peace and quiet? They get fed up and move out."

I thought he said that he didn't talk to his sister about what she does. I wasn't going to call him on it while he was spilling the information.

"What were you doing on Outer Island when you took off in the kayak?"

"I was supposed to meet Ginny there." His face grew pale, and I thought for a minute that he might lose it. "She never showed."

That was an understatement, I thought. "Any idea why she wanted to meet you there?"

Max lost interest in the bookshelf and sat down on the sofa. Abby immediately hopped up and nuzzled next to her. "She found something while she was doing the title searches. Didn't she?" Max asked.

"Yes. She wanted to keep it secret, but she said she could show us what she was talking about from Outer Island."

Max and I both picked up on it and spoke at the same time.

"Us?" I asked.

"Yes, me and a local. A guy named Cromwell. He never showed either."

My heart sank. Doris had the proof that Abe's boat was out there from the bumper we found, but now Carter was placing him out on the islands at the time of the murder.

"Abe Cromwell? Did you see him out there?"

"I wouldn't know him if he walked through that door. I questioned why I should meet someone I didn't know out on the island, but Ginny only said it would be clear to both of us once we were there."

Max leaned forward and spoke in a soft voice.

"Harry, do you know that Abe Cromwell is a suspect in your sister's murder?"

Harry's face turned red with anger.

"Where do they have him? I'd like to see him."

His voice showed that he was fighting to control his emotions.

"He's missing," I said. "I was…we were hoping that you could give us some information that would lead us to him. We want to find him before the local police do."

"Why should I help you let this guy get away with killing Ginny?"

"Because we don't believe he did it," I said. "Don't you want the real killer caught?"

I could see Max was getting annoyed, so I let her take over the questioning. Harry never answered my question.

"Where did you go when you paddled away from Outer Island?"

"I headed out into the sound until I felt I was safe, and then I paddled east and headed back to Ginny's place at Whitfield Green. I got in my truck and came home. I tried calling her until about 11:00 p.m. but couldn't get her."

"You didn't call the police?" I asked.

"I was worried, but I didn't see any reason to get the cops involved. Whatever she wanted to show me and the local, she wanted to be secret. The next morning, when I couldn't get her on the phone, I figured she was working. Meanwhile, I went back out to Outer Island in a Boston Whaler I rented at a marina in New Haven. I didn't know the waters and hit a rock. Now I'm on the hook for fixing the boat."

Max looked like she didn't believe him. "You hit a rock and the boat didn't sink?"

"I grazed it and damaged the port side."

I explained to Max about the "unsinkable" reputation of the Boston Whaler. "He was just lucky that the motor didn't hit the rock." I turned to Carter. "So, the Boston Whaler Doris and I saw that morning was the one you rented, and the one that swamped me the night before must have been Abe's. It's hard enough to imagine that Abe would swamp me and even harder to imagine he would harm someone."

Max ignored my comment and continued with the questioning. "What does Outer Island have to do with Amanda's project?"

Outer Island was about two miles offshore from Abe's property and the marsh where Amanda wanted to build her new project. For the life of me, I couldn't understand what the island had to do with anything either.

Carter nodded toward a laptop computer on the table. "I wanted to know the same thing. I went to her house to see if I could find out. I had to bypass the alarm to get in, but as her brother, I feel I had the right."

He certainly had more of a right to be there than I did, I thought. "True."

"I got her laptop and a few other things I didn't want to get stolen. I got them just in time. I think the police almost caught me."

Carter didn't realize it was me outside of the house. I was just about to tell him when he handed me a manila folder. "Most of the files on the laptop have passwords. I'm trying to figure them out. There was this, too."

Inside were several satellite survey maps of Sachem Creek and the islands. "What are these for?" I asked.

Carter glanced around the room as if he would find the answer written on the walls. "I don't know. They're professional quality, not something you'd get off the internet. I wondered why they would interest Ginny, so I took them."

Max shuffled through the images. "They're used for all kinds of things—government, military, agriculture, mineral exploration, even environmental monitoring." She spoke with the confidence of someone who knew her stuff. I wondered if this was yet another tidbit from one of her many past lives she had yet to tell me about.

Carter said we could have the maps. I wanted to study them, maybe I'd figure out what I was looking for later. Max must have thought they were insignificant because she handed the maps to me. "I'll take the laptop, though," she said.

Carter seemed taken aback by her request. It took him a few seconds to recover.

"No. I have a right to it."

"It's evidence in an investigation."

"Neither one of you are cops, so I don't understand what you're doing here. Either of you."

The guy was sharp and unafraid to stand up for his rights. I respected that. Max, however, didn't seem to share my sentiment. "This can become an official investigation. I can hand it over to Doris, and she'll get a warrant," she said, her tone hard-edged.

It was a bluff if I'd ever heard one, and Carter wasn't buying it. "You said if the three of us put our heads together, we could figure this out," he countered, unimpressed.

"I didn't say that. DeLucia said it."

Carter persisted. "Look, I have a better chance of figuring out what passwords my sister used than anybody. I'll work on it. In the meantime, you do what you think you have to do. Cromwell or not, I want the bastard who killed my sister found. If you let me work on it, I could save you time."

I could see Max assessing the possibilities in her head. "Two days. That's all. Then we have to tell Doris."

We left Carter, who promised to keep letting us know what he found if he got into the files on Ginny's laptop.

It was after midnight, and both Max and I were exhausted from the long day. So much happened since I left Charlie's house two days ago that it seemed like two weeks. We headed back to Sachem Creek. When we got to Aunt Phoebe's, the house was dark and the police tape was still up on my apartment over the garage. It was too late to go knocking at Charlie's door, so Max let me crash at her place. On the couch.

Chapter Twenty-Seven

Friday, July 1

We enjoyed breakfast on Max's porch, where the sun danced on the water, casting a million diamond-like sparkles across Long Island Sound. Water views are always impressive, but the Nutmeg Islands nestled a stone's throw from the Sachem Creek mainland added a touch of magic that made the view from the porch even more impressive.

As we talked about what it was like here when I was going up, I learned more things about Max that surprised me. For one, her childhood in Georgia wasn't so different from mine in Sachem Creek—filled with swimming, sailing, fishing, and what she called "treasure hunting."

"I never thought I could love someplace as much as Savannah," she said. "But this is perfect."

"You better enjoy it while you still can," I said. "If Amanda really is thinking about reviving or even expanding the quarry, this place will be set back a hundred fifty years."

Max waved it off. "I think the rumors are just that. There's no way they'll make it profitable. I'll believe it when I see it."

She shifted gears without missing a beat. "But here's something you can believe. I meant what I told Carter. If he doesn't crack that laptop's password, we have to bring it to Doris tomorrow."

"Tomorrow's Saturday, and Monday's the Fourth. Much won't be done until Tuesday. Give him a few more days—I trust the guy." I left it at that, and not wanting to overstay my welcome, I called Doris, who told me I could go back to my apartment.

As I was leaving, Max had one parting shot.

"Tomorrow." The word was final as I walked down the stairs, my car waiting where Triple A had left it.

* * *

On the drive home, my cell phone erupted with "Stars and Stripes Forever," my ringtone for unknown callers—a fitting tune, considering it's what circus bands play to signal a disaster. Calls from strangers usually bring news I can do without. This time, I was wrong.

"It's Carter. Ever heard of something called the Sachem Creek Allotments Map?"

"What am I, your lifeline? Are you on a quiz show or something?" I replied.

"I finally got into some of the files on Ginny's laptop. Cracking her password took some time—it was our childhood dog's name, spelled backward."

That was a relief. "I'm still not following." I couldn't see what 17th-century local history had to do with her murder, but I played along. "The first colonists drew up a document called The Sachem Creek Covenant as soon as they got off the ship. Basically, it pledged that each of them would help and look out for the other."

"But this is a map that she was looking for, if I'm not mistaken," Carter said.

"Right, I was getting to that. It's said that they also made a map showing how they divided the land, labeling each plot and its owner. As far as I know, it was lost a long time ago. Why are you asking?"

"Just curious. It was one of the things she was researching. Ginny was a history buff, so I'm not surprised. But there's a lot on this laptop; it's going to take a while to go through it all. I'm puzzled by some of the things she had on there."

"Maybe it's related to real estate. Anything else stand out?"

Either Carter was trying to throw me off, or he genuinely didn't know what to look for. "Anything on there that seems important?"

"I checked her browsing history. Ginny was curious, but she visited a wide range of sites—medicine, electronics, Chile, ceramics. They all seem like dead ends."

"Any suspicious purchases?"

"Not suspicious, just odd. She paid for access to one of those companies that provide satellite images. I didn't have time to analyze them, but I noticed several that looked like the old granite quarries around here."

That was interesting, given the rumors that Amanda was thinking about reopening the quarry. For now, I'd chalk it up to coincidence, but I'd keep it in the back of my mind.

"Remember, your sister was a real estate lawyer—maps and satellite images were her thing. I'll let Max know you cracked the passcode. Send me the satellite images and call me back if anything jumps out at you. And hurry—Max is itching to get that laptop to Doris."

* * *

With the 4th of July kayak race looming on Monday, I wanted to get in some last-minute training and then have Saturday and Sunday to rest.

Even though I couldn't see a connection between Ginny's interest in history and her murder, I decided to fit in a quick stop at the library to find out more about the Sachem Creek Allotments Map before jogging.

On the way to the library, I spotted Charlie and Summer walking down the docks with water skis. They leapt into a boat. Bart was nowhere in sight, so I double-parked and then ran down the dock to greet them.

"Going skiing?" I asked.

Charlie glanced at the skis they'd just stowed in the boat as a way of telling me to stop asking stupid questions, and then went about checking out the fuel tanks.

"Do you ski?" Summer wanted to know.

162

I nodded my head. "Watch the rocks."

Charlie looked up from the fuel tanks. "I was born here, remember?"

Summer went to the car to get her beach bag. I waited until she was out of earshot.

"I wanted to pass something by you," I said to Charlie.

"By all means. What is it?"

"Ginny Lawson was doing title searches for Amanda."

"I know. You told me about that the other night on my porch."

The image of the lights from the fishing boats bobbing on the dark waters between the shore and the silhouettes of the islands flashed through my mind.

"Right, I did, didn't I?"

"I don't think that it's any secret that Amanda is interested in buying up as much property around here as possible," Charlie said.

"True, but title searches usually only go back fifty years or so, mainly to check for liens on the property. Ginny Lawson was digging into stuff that's hundreds of years old."

"Apparently, she was very thorough at her job."

"No," I insisted. "She seems to have gotten sidetracked. Suddenly, she was more interested in old land maps."

Charlie seemed uninterested. "A cartophile, perhaps?"

A cartophile, perhaps. Who the hell talks like that other than Charlie?

"I think there's more to it than that. She was researching the Sachem Creek Allotment Map."

Charlie shrugged. "Good luck with that. If it ever existed, it's probably long gone. I'm convinced it's mostly part of the legend of Sachem Creek, like Captain Kidd's treasure buried out on the islands."

"Probably, but legends sometimes have a grain of truth. I'm headed to the library to see if I can find any copies or references. Maybe Ginny found something everyone else overlooked."

Charlie gave me a look that said I really should get a life. "You're chasing a ghost. Even if it existed, it was only supposed to show how the plots were divided and to whom they belonged. I think you're wasting your time."

"Maybe, but Ginny seemed to think it was important. There might be something more to it."

Charlie sighed but didn't argue further. As long as I already had him all in a twist, I figured I might as well tell him what else was on my mind. "There's something else I have to tell you. I'm going to the wedding."

"You weren't invited. You can't crash a wedding."

"Watch me. This is just between us—I have to get into Amanda's house to see if I can find any reason why Amanda would want Lawson dead."

Just then, Summer returned. I watched her as she hopped on the boat. Charlie was a lucky man. He was already casting off the ropes.

I dropped the subject. "So… Nice day for skiing."

Charlie gave me a look like I was missing the obvious. "Care to come along?" There was absolutely no enthusiasm in his voice as he glanced at Summer.

I called his bluff. "Okay."

He cast off the last line and pushed off from the dock just in case I was serious. Summer waved as they headed up the channel.

* * *

When I arrived at the library, Bev Taylor, the librarian, greeted me with her usual bright smile and warm, cheerful voice. It didn't take her long to locate a copy of the Sachem Creek Covenant in the history room.

"Brushing up on our local history, are we?" she asked.

"Something like that," I replied. Bev, do you know anything about the legend of the Allotment Map that supposedly accompanied the Covenant?"

"Ah, now you're getting into the real mysteries," she said. "We used to think it was just a legend, but now it seems the map was real, lost during the British Invasion."

"But surely there were copies made, right? I was hoping you might have one here."

"There certainly were," Bev replied, her enthusiasm reaffirming my appreciation for librarians.

"For a long time, those copies were dismissed as hoaxes, but modern technology has proven otherwise."

Bev headed straight for a series of flat storage map cabinets. She pulled out a shallow drawer and began sifting through the maps.

"I'm sure we had a copy of one of the copies. It might be misfiled." She rummaged through several more drawers, her brow furrowing with each empty-handed attempt. Finally, she called over her assistant librarian. "Stacy, I can't find a copy of the Allotment Map. It should be here."

Stacy looked puzzled. "I know the original was lost during the Revolution, but we should have a copy of the copy. Let me check." After a fifteen-minute search, she came back empty-handed. "No luck here. Have you tried Town Hall?"

"Already did." A lie, kind of, but I knew if there was a copy at town hall, attorney Lawson would have found it.

"What about the library in Whitfield Green? They might have a copy. Hold on, let me save you the trip."

Stacy made a few calls, but the result was the same—no one had a copy. She even reached out to surrounding towns, but all leads came up dry.

I wasn't ready to throw in the towel just yet.

"Any other ideas?"

Determined to help, Bev continued to search through the history room, hoping to stumble upon the elusive map tucked away in some forgotten tome. After more than an hour of fruitless searching, I decided we'd hit a dead end. I didn't want to waste any more of her time, or mine.

As I left the library, the Allotment Map remained a mystery, but my determination to uncover the truth was stronger than ever.

Chapter Twenty-Eight

F inally, I made it to the Trolley Trail. As I ran, questions kept surfacing in my head. Could the Sachem Creek Allotments Map show something that would put the kibosh on Amanda's project? Could Amanda have had Ginny Lawson killed to cover up something that Ginny found? Did Amanda try to frame Abe for Lawson's murder? Why were all the copies of the Allotments Map missing? Was the original still in existence?

But, instead of finding answers, more questions nagged at me like a stone in my running shoe.

* * *

I jogged from the ballpark up the trail to the trestle where Harry Carter's dog, Abby, had attacked me. I had to stop at the iron bridge so that a young couple pushing a baby jogger in front of them could come off the structure. After crossing the trestle, I was again on the nice, wide trail that followed the old trolley bed. I watched a red fox run from its den on the steep side of the trail. It ran across the marshy ground at the base of the bed and then up into the woods.

I entered the cool dampness of the trolley cut through the hill. As I approached the overpass, I negotiated around an equine-sized pile of dog droppings. So much for pooper scooper laws. I was concentrating on not stepping in the dog pile when something whizzed behind me so quickly that I felt the breeze move the hair on the back of my head. It landed with a thump that echoed off the rock walls.

A grey dust filled the air, making me cough. My eyes watered, and my nose and throat had a caustic burning sensation. It took me a moment to realize that a bag of cement had plummeted from the overpass above.

I ran out of the dust cloud before stopping to bend over with my elbows on my knees. When the coughing stopped and I got my act together, I bolted up a narrow path that branched from the main trail leading up to the overpass. I was fuming and determined to get to the bottom of what had happened. My first thought was that teenagers were playing a dangerous prank, and I had to stop them before they hurt an unsuspecting jogger.

At the end of the path, I came out of the woods near the bridge that spanned the Trolley Trail. I could see several bags of cement mix, destined for bridge repair, on a wooden skid by the side of the road. I looked in the other direction. There was no one in sight, but one thing was for certain. That bag of cement mix didn't jump off the pallet and fling itself over the side of the bridge to the trail below.

I wanted to write it off as horseplay, but if I was going to keep it real, I had to face the fact that someone was trying to kill me. I suspected that it was the same person who killed Lawson and Warner. What I couldn't figure out was why they would want to add me to the list of people they wanted out of the way. Was I getting too close to something that someone wanted to keep secret?

I decided not to tell Doris about this latest incident. I wanted to respect her wish for handling the case her way, but with an attempt on my life, I knew I had to do something. My determination to crash Kim's wedding and check out Amanda's house was stronger than ever. I now had a good reason to go where I wasn't wanted. While Abe's motive, blaming Ginny for losing his property, made sense, my gut still pointed to Amanda's involvement. I had suspected that Harry Carter might have carried out Ginny Lawson and David Warner's murders on Amanda's orders. But even after Carter was ruled out as a suspect, Amanda who'd had me in her crosshairs for a long time, remained under suspicion.

The mystery was why Amanda would benefit from Ginny's death. I needed evidence of a motive beyond the threat Chelsea overheard. Since Abe had already lost his property, there was no need to frame him. Maybe Amanda's connection to Abe was simply convenient. The next day would confirm or debunk my hunch. But I knew gaining access to the wedding would be as challenging as sneaking into a state dinner at the White House.

In the meantime, I wanted to talk to Aunt Phoebe again on the chance that the Oliver Welles map she told me about might be the same one as the Sachem Creek Allotments Map that Ginny Lawson was researching. I hurried home to talk to her. She was on the porch when I drove in and all too ready to talk about the old days. For a change, I was willing to listen.

"Phoebe, about that map you mentioned, the one Welles had that turned out to be completely inaccurate. Why'd it bother Granddad so much?"

"Because every few years, the treasure-hunting fever resurfaces. Folks start searching for pirate treasure, and it never ends well. He'd witnessed the chaos it brings, just as his father and grandfather had in their time."

"Did he actually believe there was treasure?"

"I think he was reluctant to accept that the treasure might not exist. The legend is part of the history of Sachem Creek."

As I left Aunt Phoebe's porch, her nostalgic gaze lingering in the past, I couldn't help feeling the connection between the Welles map and Ginny Lawson's research seemed increasingly likely. I couldn't wait for the wedding day to arrive, hoping for a chance to explore Amanda's mansion to find more pieces of the puzzle.

Chapter Twenty-Nine

Saturday, July 2

It was wedding day. I don't think I was as anxious when I was the one marrying Kim. I was too restless to hang around my apartment, so I decided to spend the morning paddling. I was in no mood to deal with Bart, so instead of going to the "official" launch area, I parked at the Little League field. I portaged the kayak several hundred feet up the trail. When I lived up here, I had a carrier, two wheels that strapped under the kayak, which made it easy to pull in situations like this. It was one of the things I left at the house when I moved out. One of the many things of mine that fell to Donahue.

As the iron truss over the bridge came into view above the tall saltwater cordgrass on either side of the trail, I thought of how I had to climb the rusted iron bracings to escape from Harry Carter's dog. I also thought about how Max showed up out of the blue and helped me. Where was Max anyway? She sure had been acting strange since she decided to hook up with Phil again.

When I got to the bridge, I looked out at Kittle Island hugging the shoreline like a vessel in a safe harbor. I could see boats dropping off people at the granite pier on the north side. Too early for guests, workers, and staff was my guess. I dragged the kayak down the embankment and launched from below the trestle.

A short time later, I was well into the harbor. The tour boat passed between me and the island. I steered clear. Captain Bruce recognized me and waved. Sound carries over the water, and I was near enough to hear Bruce's tour spiel complete with his southern drawl over the boat's loudspeaker.

"Y'all notice the Camelot-style tent on Kittle Island there, folks. Today, the Wedding of the Year for these parts is going to take place. Rumor has it that the event will cost over half a million dollars!"

Bruce always embellishes his stories as he gives the tour, but I wondered if he upped the cost of the wedding for my benefit. The barbershop crew had told me it would cost two hundred and fifty thousand dollars. I know he thought I was spying on the wedding. I wasn't that pathetic. I didn't have to listen to that crap. I headed in the opposite direction. Right then, my focus was on doing some sprints around the islands to build speed for the race. I set my sights on the trees that serve as a windbreak for the swimming pool on Potato Island and set a steady pace for a while. Then I slowed down a bit as I approached Governor Island, careful to avoid the shallows. Picking up my pace again as I passed between Hen Island and a group of rocks called the Chicks, I estimated I was doing a decent five mph, as I headed for the channel flanked by Pot and High Islands. I thought of Ginny Lawson. Then I thought of Abe. I knew Doris was competent, but I still wished she'd let me help.

With mid-morning rapidly approaching, I had some hard paddling ahead to make it back to my car by the trolley path before noon. In fact, it was twelve fifteen when I got to the bridge. By the time I hauled the boat up the embankment, carried it down the path, and secured it on the roof of the car, it was twelve-thirty.

I pulled onto Phoebe's oyster-shelled driveway around twenty to one and didn't see her or Big Al around. In a hurry, I dashed to my apartment over the garage. Racing up the stairs to my room, I snatched my tuxedo and stuffed it into a gym bag. I would have preferred to get dressed at home, but I didn't want to risk someone associated with the wedding spotting me in the village wearing a tuxedo. As it was, too many had already predicted that I would crash the wedding, and that was before I had even considered it. Following a quick shower, I threw on some shorts and a T-shirt and headed back out for the wharf.

As I approached the fountain in the little traffic island where Main Street meets the entrance to the wharf, I spotted Bart. He was chewing out a guy in a wetsuit who obviously had not followed his kayak launching rules.

As usual, cars from out of town occupied most of the parking spaces. I knew Bart wouldn't let me use one of the spaces he held in reserve for his friends. That meant I'd have to double park by the beach, drop off the kayak, and then park far down the road and hike back. I just didn't have the time.

I called out from the car as I got within earshot.

"Hey Bart, a guy is launching a kayak from the swimming beach."

His face got so red he looked like a lobster in a pot of boiling water.

"The hell he is." He marched off down the road to the public beach.

I parked on the wharf and took the kayak from the roof as quickly as I could. Breaking Bart's strictest rule, I lugged it down the slippery boat ramp, a major no-no, and dropped it on the "official" launching beach.

As I walked back up the concrete incline, I could see Bart headed back up the street from the swimming beach. He hadn't taken as long as I had hoped. If he noticed the car, he'd make me move it, and that would cost me time. Just then, several limos and a large party bus entered the tiny traffic circle and stopped. It didn't take a mastermind to figure out the wedding party had arrived to be ferried out to the island.

Bart rushed back from the bathing beach with his hackles up again. He screamed at the partygoers. "You can't block the circle. Move those vehicles. Now!"

The driver of the party bus explained that they had to drop off the wedding party so they could take the water taxi to Kittle Island, and he would only be parked there a little while.

"You can't block the circle. Not even for a little while," he insisted. "You'll have to park in the lot behind the Congregational Church back there. They can walk back." Bart hopped onto the bus to bring them to the parking lot.

I didn't want the water taxi to pass me as I was headed out to the island, so I'd wait until it left. I pulled the gym bag out of the Mercedes and ran into the barbershop. I must have startled Neal as I entered because he jumped out of the barber chair in which he had been napping. He eyed my shorts and T-shirt.

"I'm glad to see you came to your senses and decided not to crash the party," Neal said. His tone shifted abruptly, excitement replacing his earlier calm. "Well, I'll be! Will you look at that?" He gestured toward the window, his eyes wide with amazement. "You'll be what?"

Neal ran to the open doorway so he could get a better look. "They're doing the Conga," Neal said. "They're decked out in gowns and tuxedos and they're dancing up the street like damned fools. With the bride leading them, yet!"

I looked past him to the street. Sure enough, there was Kim in a fancy white wedding dress leading the dance line. I'd bet it was expensive. She looked great.

The dance line circled Old Man Kittel's granite fountain and snaked around Doris and Bart. She blew her whistle to try to restore order as he flapped his arms like a seagull.

To my surprise, I spotted Big Al and Phoebe in line, swaying left and right—Big Al dancing with Summer, and Phoebe with Charlie. I could hardly believe my eyes. "They got an invite!"

"You know, Phoebe, a regular party animal. And your father seems to fit right in, too," said Buster. He noticed my gym bag.

"What in Sam Hill is that?"

I could tell by the tone of his voice that he had a pretty good idea.

"My tux is in there."

By this time, the wedding party with Doris and Bart following had proceeded down the dock to the water taxi. I bolted from the shop as Neal called after me.

"Where are you headed?"

"To the wedding," I said.

"Ya damned fool!"

I hurried across the street towards the beach, where my kayak awaited. After getting in, I shoved off from the shore.

Kittle Island, unlike the bustling Doubloon and Governor Islands, hosted only Amanda's Tudor mansion and a few outbuildings. As I approached from the east, a quick five-minute journey, I got a better look at the wedding tent where the ceremony would be held, set against the backdrop of the village.

I circled the island to get a sense of the preparations. On the south beach, there was a caretaker's tool shed, while a pool house on the western side faced the Sachem Creek Yacht Club on the mainland, about half a mile away. The pool house had been the talk of the Creek since Amanda had one built the year before, only to tear it down for a larger one to grace the wedding.

As I coasted along the north shore, I spotted the landing made of Sachem Creek Granite blocks where some guests had arrived earlier in the day. Now, several boats were moored there, and more guests were disembarking.

Besides the people who came over on the water taxi, others arrived by private boats, which were valet moored. If anyone saw me, nobody called out. I decided that it would be best to land by the tool shed on the south side of the island.

A stiff breeze at my back came in off the open Sound, easily propelling me onto the shore. I beached the kayak, pulled it up over the sand, and put it behind a nearby fieldstone tool shed used by the groundskeepers. I didn't worry about being seen from the mansion on the hill above, as this side of the island was well wooded with specimen trees that old man Kittle had brought in from around the world after he came back from World War II. At the time it was looked upon as a good thing. Today, we have laws about bringing in plants that could potentially become invasive species. I left my kayak behind the trunk of a huge tree with a brass plate that identified it as a Russian Oak.

I knew that if I were spotted too early, I would be thrown out, especially since Amanda regarded me as Public Enemy Number One. However, I figured that if I showed up just as the ceremony was about to begin, they wouldn't take the chance of disrupting the solemn occasion by ejecting me. I looked at my watch: 2:30. The ceremony was scheduled to start at 3:30. If I knew Kim, she wouldn't walk down the aisle before 3:45. I was hoping for a long ceremony because that's when I planned to search the house.

Chapter Thirty

I ducked into the shed to change. The air was thick with the scent of old wood, two-cycle oil, and Malathion. I took a deep breath, enjoying the smells, which reminded me of my grandfather's shed where I fixed outboard motors as a kid. Against one wall stood a rickety tool bench on which sat a metal chest full of screws, drill bits, and rusty tools... rusty tools have a smell of their own that I always liked.

Feeling a bit like Clark Kent, I slipped off my kayak shoes, discarded my cargo shorts, and pulled my shirt over my head. Just as I was about to unzip my duffle bag to retrieve my tuxedo, voices outside caught my attention. With a quick sweeping motion, I stuffed the duffle and my clothes underneath the workbench. I wasn't going to be the best-pressed guest at the wedding, but so what, I wasn't going to be the most welcomed either.

Now only in my boxers, I scrambled into the cramped space between the bench and the wall and crouched on the damp dirt floor.

From outside the shed, I could hear voices—a female and a male.

I huddled close to the ground, taking a moment to regain control over my racing thoughts. *Don't come in. Don't come in.*

Meanwhile, the talking outside grew louder and seemed to have deteriorated into an argument.

"I'll be up in a minute," the woman said.

Where had I heard that voice before?

"Amanda's going to be pissed if you get stoned." the guy said.

"Go, Jerry!" she said.

Wishing they'd both go, I huddled closer to the workbench, my heart pounding in my chest. I made myself as small as possible, vowing to remain undetected. I couldn't afford to make a sound, not even a gasp or a whimper. The stakes were too high. Discovery would mean I'd be kicked off the island without searching Amanda's mansion. I shrank my body, willing myself to become one with the shadows.

My eyes scanned the surroundings, searching for a means to defend myself if need be. And there it was—a small red pry bar resting on the bottom shelf. As I stretched my arm to seize it in my hand, I felt a subtle movement against my fingertips. I pulled my arm back, and the pry bar fell with a loud clang.

I prayed that whoever was outside hadn't heard. But I had a more immediate problem. I peered into the depths of the shelf to see what was among the tools. And there it was—a monstrous, hairy spider, almost as big as my hand, sitting on my cargo shorts. Its eight beady eyes locked onto mine, radiating annoyance at my intrusion. It was clear that I had disturbed its resting place.

But I held my ground. The spider, as if mocking my audacity, raised its front legs in a sinister taunt, challenging me to make my move. I refused to show weakness. I studied the creature's calculated movements and its methodical approach.

It darted toward me, then stopped at the edge of the shelf, glaring at me with its many eyes. Suppressing the urge to gasp, I focused on keeping my breathing steady and controlled. I willed myself to be calm as I hoped for the creature to retreat into the shelf. But my silent plea went unanswered. The spider raised its front legs in a wicked taunt, deciding on its next move.

My breath caught in my throat. I watched it with horrified fascination as it jumped on me and began to goose-step up my bare arm. Every muscle in my body tensed at the thought that any sudden movement might provoke it to bite. My skin crawled as the spider maneuvered onto my shoulder. Then it teased me, brushing against my ear as if savoring its cruel bullying.

Enough was enough. It was time to reclaim my space. Without making a sound, I swiped at the creature, hoping to send it back to wherever the hell it came from. But the spider landed on my lap, raised its front legs in anger, then scuttled toward the leg of my boxers. My imagination kicked into overdrive.

The line crossed; I summoned every ounce of resolve. I swiped at it once again, and it landed next to me. I picked up the prybar and scooped the monster up with the flat end, sending it hurtling across the room. But my triumph was short-lived as I realized the spider had landed at someone's feet.

"It's only a Wolf Spider." The voice was mocking yet sympathetic at the same time. It was Summer.

"I knew that," I replied, slightly flustered, as I got to my feet.

Dressed for the wedding in a black gown, she was smiling. I took the smile as a good sign. She had a joint in her hand. I took that as an even better one.

"If you're crashing the party, they requested formal attire." She eyed my boxers, and I remembered I was half naked.

I held up my duffle bag. "Check." Then added, trying to sound convincing. "I was invited."

She didn't buy it. "No, you weren't. I helped with the guest list."

"You going to get me kicked out?"

"I'm thinking about it. It's kind of cool, though."

"What is?"

"You crashing your ex-wife's wedding. It's incredibly gutsy of you. And romantic."

"I saw you in the Conga line. With my father," I said.

"He's cute."

Cute? What the hell was in that joint she was smoking?

"I saw Charlie, too."

"He's my date."

"Before you have me thrown off the island, could you tell me one thing?"

"What?"

"Did they get old man Kittle a formal urn for the occasion?" I don't know where that came from, but it came out of my mouth, and it worked.

She laughed.

"Why aren't you up there with the rest of the wedding party?" I asked.

She took a drag. "I needed a break. I can take only so much of those people."

"But you are those people."

Her face hardened and lost some of its beauty. "You're making presumptions."

Damn! "I just meant…"

She offered me the joint.

"Listen, I don't exactly fit in up there." There was a sadness, yet a defiance in her voice.

"I won't exactly fit in either, being the bride's ex."

She thought a bit, and as she did so, I could see all kinds of emotions cross her face.

"You're not going to ruin the wedding or try something funny, are you?"

"No. I just want to be there."

"Why?"

I wasn't about to spill my guts to Summer. She wasn't my barber. Besides searching Amanda's house to find any evidence that linked Amanda to Lawson's murder, I wanted to see for myself that Kim was marrying Donahue. I tried to tell myself that it was to bring some closure between Kim and me.

"Damned if I know. I guess I'm worried that Kim may be getting into more than she bargained for."

She laughed. "With this family, that's definite. You sure that's all?"

"That's my story, and I'm sticking with it. I'm not going to cause any trouble."

She studied my face like she was reading a polygraph tape.

"I believe you."

"But you're going to make me leave."

"No, you're going to sit with me. Now get dressed."

I did as she said. Then, after helping me with my tie, she grabbed my arm and led me up the hill toward the tent.

I was always one to look a gift horse in the mouth. "Why are you doing this?"

"Because if you go up there alone, you are going to be kicked out in five minutes. You have a better chance of getting away with crashing this shindig if you're with me."

"That's not what I mean."

"I think you're entitled to be here, that's why. And I told you, I don't really fit in, so they're not going to be all that surprised that I brought the bride's ex as a date. Come on. We're going to miss the wedding."

"Aren't you here with Charlie?"

"I have two dates. Big deal."

We strolled up the path toward the lawn, where several dozen guests mingled, their laughter drifting through the warm evening air. It felt like stepping into one of Gatsby's parties. Waiters in crisp white jackets glided with trays balanced between clusters of conversation.

Summer picked up a cracker topped with a dollop of tan paste, examining it with a curious tilt of her head before taking a bite."Foie gras?" She tried to get me to take a bite.

"I'll pass."

Thinking of her claim of not fitting in, I wondered if she saw the irony of her choice of finger food.

Another waiter came by and I opted for a couple of strawberries decked out in what looked like chocolate tuxedoes. We both took a glass of champagne from yet another tray.

We were standing a little too close to the chamber musicians, so I put my hand on her elbow and guided her away. Black seemed to be the color of the day, women in black gowns, men in tuxedos. In my world, it was bad luck to wear black to a wedding. But my world and this world were two different places.

I stopped to peek inside the huge, air-conditioned tent where several people were putting last-minute touches on the formally set tables. A larger orchestra was setting up on a stage behind the dance floor. It was Summer's turn to guide me away by the elbow.

"Just stick by me."

A short, slim woman approached us. At first, I took her to be much younger than she was. Her tight face gave me the impression that it would be an effort for her to talk. She eyed me as she spoke to Summer.

"We must do lunch."

Summer smiled and told her to call. Then pulled me toward the nearby bar.

My blood ran a little cold from the encounter.

"I think she wanted to know who I was."

Summer laughed. "She's just nosy."

"Lunch isn't going to happen, right?

"Not even if she had meant it."

Where I come from, a whole half mile away in the village, people say what they mean. I needed another drink; something with a little more kick.

Summer had a waiter bring her a Cosmo. I ordered a Jack Daniels neat. I normally would have taken a Sam Adams, but what the hell; my ex was getting married.

"That woman talking to my father looks like J. Lo," I said.

I caught the amused look on Summer's face. "It is. And that's your aunt talking to Billy Joel and Tom Hanks. Half of Southampton is here."

I was beginning to feel sorry for Kim. These people were big-time players. I worried that she had bitten off more than she could chew. The waiter came with our drinks. I looked at my watch. It was 3:09, and people were heading toward their seats. A woman with dark hair and wearing a veiled hat stopped by us.

"Really, Summer. A cosmo. How last year!" She gave Summer a peck on the check and then looked me up and down like she was inspecting a polo pony. "I don't believe I've met your friend."

"Dianne, I'd like you to meet my date, Al."

I took her hand. "DeLucia. Al DeLucia."

Summer didn't miss a beat. "Of the Newport DeLucias. He just arrived on his boat."

Summer put on a haughty face. Even though I knew she was goofing on the woman, it gave me insight into another side of her. She was enjoying this. I enjoyed it too.

Dianne couldn't have sounded more disinterested. "The DeLucias.... Of course."

As she headed to the seats, I called after her. "Uh, nice to meet you."

She didn't answer.

I turned back to Summer. "Shouldn't we find Charlie?"

She pointed to one of the bars. "He's over there."

We were about to head over when a guy in his mid-fifties with a red, bulldog-face approached us, drink in hand. He gave Summer a hug and a big, wet smooch on the lips. That alone was enough to make me dislike him. He gave me a questioning look.

"Oscar Rondell, this is Al DeLucia,"

"DeLucia." His voice couldn't have been more condescending.

I didn't like Oscar. It's a fault of mine; sometimes I decide I dislike someone at first sight. The thing is, I'm usually right on. "It's Al DeLucia."

He offered a clammy hand."DeLucia?"

"Right. Of the Newport DeLucias"

"Certainly." He turned to Summer. "Have you caught up with Estelle?"

When Summer told him she hadn't, Rondell said, "You absolutely must! Ask her to show you her latest trinket. I ended up buying her another diamond bracelet because she was feeling a bit down about the kids leaving for boarding school this week." He turned to me with a chuckle and added, "Yes, we're that kind of parents who ship their kids away."

Lucky kids, I thought, as he yammered about how money was no good unless you spent it.

I glanced past Rondell and spotted an attractive woman approaching. She wore a black and white floral dress with a tie behind her neck, big sunglasses, and a white hat so wide it could double as shade for a small picnic. I realized it was Max. She offered a subtle nod as she passed by.

Leaving Summer with her rather annoying friend, I hurried to catch up with Max, and together, we slipped into the concealment of the nearby bushes.

"What are you doing here?" I asked.

"I might ask you the same thing."

"I got an invite," I said. It was the truth—Summer sort of gave me one. "And you? Couldn't pass up a wedding?"

"DeLucia, you realize you're sounding like a chauvinist pig again, right? Assuming I'd be here just for the chance to play dress-up."

"No, I figured you're here because of the investigation."

"Whatever. I'm working as a hairstylist to touch up hairdo malfunctions," she said.

"How did you manage that?"

"The stylist who was supposed to be here 'mysteriously' got a call to work a Taylor Swift gig in Rhode Island."

"Mysteriously?"

"Okay, I asked my friend with the New York Salon to arrange that. Then she arranged my last-minute substitution here. I see you met Rondell," she whispered. "I styled his wife's hair this morning."

"You mean Estelle?"

"That's the one. She's quite talkative when she gets her hair done. She even showed me his photo and revealed that he's, brace yourself, the president of Big Apple Mortgage."

Chapter Thirty-One

Max and I agreed to split up. I found Charlie at the bar, sipping on Remy Martin. He looked surprised to see me, even though I'd warned him about crashing the wedding.

I thought about ordering some Remy, just because I could never afford it if I had to pay, but ended up with another Jack Daniels neat. I told the bartender to leave the bottle.

Charlie took another sip of his Remy. "So, you really meant it…"

I couldn't help but think he could've just said, "Glad to see you." Sometimes the way he says things gets on my nerves. This was one of those times.

"I told you I'd be here. Did I mention that we're both Summer's dates today?"

Charlie let out a sigh. "Not that I recall."

I glanced around at the crowd. "I'm surprised at how many folks from the Creek are here."

"It's only natural that some villagers would show up as friends of Kim's family, regardless of what they think of the summer people," Charlie said.

He pointed across the lawn to Doris and Bart the Barometer as an example.

"They invited themselves and hitched a ride on the water taxi," I said. "And look, there's Jamila over there! Geez, does anybody tell me anything?"

"In her defense, she told me she got an invitation and trashed it, but then her editor assigned her to cover the wedding," Charlie said.

"With half the Creek here, I guess my presence at this wedding isn't that big of a deal. It looks like I won't run into any issues after all."

Charlie shook his head. "I don't think being the bride's ex-husband, not to mention your history with Amanda, makes you the most sought-after guest."

"As long as I don't cause any trouble, nobody's going to start a scene and risk ruining the wedding by throwing me out."

Wrong. The words hardly left my lips before I found Amanda in my face. Next to her was a guy who could be a poster boy for steroids.

"What are you doing here?" Amanda's voice was soft but tinged with hatred.

"Having a drink. You want one?" I held out the bottle of Jack Daniels.

"I want you to get out. You're not invited."

"But I'm family. Or at least I used to be." I had no sooner said that, and a group of about ten people arrived on the lawn: Kim's family. As they took their seats on the bride's side of the aisle, they noticed me. Her mother's jaw dropped. Her father had one of those smiles that say "Cause any problems and I'm going to kill you!"

Amanda spoke to the steroid guy in a quiet but firm voice. "Jerry! Throw this party crasher out of here. Now!"

Then she walked over to greet Kim's parents.

Looking up at the brute, I extended my hand. "You must be Jerry."

He ignored my hand. His voice was too small for such a big guy. "Sir, come with me."

Summer suddenly appeared at my side and grabbed Jerry by the arm. "It's all right, Jerry, he's with me."

"He wasn't invited, Summer," he said.

"He was invited. He's my guest."

Charlie looked dismayed but said nothing.

Summer was adamant. "There's already been enough of a scene as it is. Now go, Jerry."

I stared him down. "Yes, go, Jerry."

Jerry walked away mumbling. "Fine! You deal with Amanda."

Summer took Charlie on one arm and me on the other. "Don't worry about him. He's my brother. I can handle him. Come on, we should get a seat."

Before we took a few steps, Jerry returned. Summer looked annoyed. "I told you, Jerry..."

Sometimes I say stupid things when I'm with my friend Jack Daniels. "Yes, we told you, Jerry."

He ignored me and addressed Summer. "Kim won't come down. Come and talk to her."

Summer was really annoyed now. "Can't Amanda do that?"

"She's busy running around here. Amanda says you should talk to her."

Summer turned to Charlie and me and said she would be right back. She stomped off.

I called to her as she walked away. "Tom should take this as a sign!"

Charlie and I stayed at the bar. He waited until Summer was out of earshot. "Is it that important to you that you see the ceremony?"

"Not at all."

"Then why?"

"Look, Charlie, I'm going to tell you this in confidence. I'm going to search Amanda's house to find why she wants Abe's property and how it relates to the Lawson murder.

Charlie signaled the bartender for another Remy. "Preposterous. She doesn't need the money. Besides, I heard this scenario before when you broke into the Lawson house. Where did that get you?"

"I didn't break in. Someone else did. Now listen..." I put my hand over my glass when the bartender picked up the bottle and started to pour me another Jack. "I have it all figured out. I just learned that one of the guests here, Rondell, is the president of Apple Mortgage. Amanda is behind the locals getting into bad mortgages and then forcing them to sell their property to get out of debt. It's all for the land, and like Neal says, for the killer view."

"You're sure of that?"

"Pretty sure."

Charlie stared at me, his expression one of disbelief and concern. "First, you were raving about the Allotments Map, and now you're bringing up mortgage fraud and even murder!"

"I know it sounds crazy," I replied, attempting to gather my thoughts. "But I suspect they're all connected, forming part of her grand scheme to dismantle Sachem Creek as we know it."

Charlie bit his lower lip. "I'm worried about you."

"Then help me find out if I'm right or wrong."

"How?"

"Help me search her house and see what we can find."

"You are mad."

"Then this will prove it."

The conversation ended when Summer returned and said Kim was ready. "She heard you were here and wanted to be sure that you weren't intending to make a scene. I guaranteed her that you wouldn't. You won't, right?"

"No, of course not. In fact, Charlie and I are going to stay at the bar during the ceremony so as not to cause any distractions."

Charlie started to protest, but I cut him off. "Go ahead. We'll be fine. No scene. Promise."

Summer went to take her place with the wedding party. All eyes were on the bride and her father, who stood at the beginning of the aisle.

"Come on, Charlie. Now's our chance. We have to hurry."

"I'm not in the habit of breaking into people's homes."

"We're not breaking in. The house is wide open, and we're invited guests. At least you are. You've been here before. I want you to show me where Amanda's office is. That's all."

"You're not going to steal anything?"

"I'm not a thief, man. You know that. I just want to look around."

It was a hard sell, but Charlie finally came along, muttering the whole way.

The house was a mansion in every sense of the word. I peeked into the first room off the entryway and saw walls covered in fine wood panels and a massive fireplace of polished Sachem Creek pink granite.

"Where do we start?" I knew Charlie had been here many times and would have a better sense of where to begin.

"This way," Charlie said.

As he led me up a wide oak staircase, I looked down and noticed Max with her unmistakable hat, sneaking out of the door. I wondered if she had been searching too. Calling out to her wasn't an option. I caught up with Charlie at the top of the landing.

"Come on. Let's get this over with," Charlie said. I knew if I told him about Max, he'd freak out altogether.

He led me to a room dominated by an imposing, large leather-topped desk. On one wall was a portrait in a gold leaf frame of old man Kittle with one of his dogs. He looked every bit like the robber baron he once was. The wood-paneled room boasted comfortable, fine furnishings and display shelves with vintage photos that chronicled the quarry's early days. An end table held a large urn, and I wondered if it contained the remains of the old guy himself.

Through the large window, I could see Kim and her father awaiting their procession down the aisle. Nervous glances were exchanged with the guests as the wedding march started. I turned away from the scene below.

"Something's off, Charlie. This seems to be a staged space—a showcase to present what Amanda wants people to see. I want to find her working office."

Charlie grew antsy. "This is the only office I know of. We should leave before we're caught."

"You can go. I'm going to keep looking."

Despite his apprehension, he trailed me down a corridor as I explored every room. Finally, I stumbled upon another office nestled at the back of the house—a modern office adorned with glass and chrome furniture. On the wall hung a portrait of Amanda with a stern expression that reminded me of the Queen of Hearts.

"We're going to get caught," Charlie cautioned once more. His Goody-Two-Shoes nature had always been apparent, but this situation really had him on edge.

I had had enough of his distraction. "Leave. I'll meet you outside."

His anxiety surfaced. "You don't understand. I'm friends with both you and Amanda. I don't want to be caught in the middle of your feud. To his credit, he stuck around. One thing Charlie could be counted on for was loyalty. Another was an eye for cool stuff.

"Now this is something," Charlie said as he picked up a fist-sized rock from the desktop.

I paused my search of the drawers to glance at the rock embedded with pink and purple crystals.

"It's a rock," I said, and continued to look through the drawers.

Charlie wouldn't give up. "I've seen fragments of this stuff in the granite, but never such a substantial piece on its own. Leave it to Amanda to rescue and repurpose such a beautiful specimen."

If *"never bring a nerd to a burglary"* isn't a saying, it should be.

I could kick myself for getting sidetracked over something so useless. I had no right to complain about Charlie not being able to focus when I was distracted by a paperweight.

I had to focus. I booted up the computer on her desk and began searching. "We came this far. Just a few more minutes," I said to Charlie again, urging me to leave.

Charlie sighed and looked through a filing cabinet. "A few minutes. That's all."

Most of the files on the computer were password protected. I noted the names of the files, though. They included Big Apple Mortgage and Loan, and Ginny Lawson. There was even a file with my name on it. I tried several possible passwords, but it was useless.

"Let me try something," Charlie said, nudging me away.

Giving him space, I watched as he opened the trash icon. "Just as I thought. Amanda doesn't empty her trash." I think he was trying to make a joke. Nerds.

I got back on the computer and looked at each trashed but not deleted file. Bingo! I came across a document titled 'Legal Review and Expressing Concerns' and returned it to the desktop before opening it. It was an email from Ginny Lawson to Amanda.

Subject: Mining Project Legal Review and Concerns

Dear Amanda,
Having recently become privy to the upcoming mining

project, I find it necessary to express my concerns regarding potential environmental impacts.

Regrettably, without comprehensive details concerning the strategies in place to alleviate long-term consequences on our ecosystem, I cannot currently support or contribute to the project.

Your prompt thoughts on this legal matter are appreciated.

Best,
Virginia Lawson
Attorney at Law

I read it and then reread it. "According to this, Ginny seemed to be saying that if a certain mining project went through without environmental issues being addressed, she would quit."

"The word is that Amanda might reopen the granite quarry. If Ginny wanted to put the kibosh on Amanda's project. That sounds like motive for murder to me," Charlie said. "Now let's go."

"I just want a picture of this first," I said, taking my phone from my pocket. When he didn't answer, I realized Charlie had already bailed.

I snapped a photo of the screen, then took two more for good measure. As I captured the third shot, the *Search with Your Camera* feature zeroed in on the rock paperweight beside the computer. It reminded me of the stones Becky had lining her sidewalk—pinkish, with tiny sparkly flecks like mica, and smooth, shiny surfaces.

I brought the camera in closer and clicked. The search engine came up with several pictures of various minerals. The rock on the desk was a perfect match for Spodumene. Knowing how curious he was about the stone, I'd have to fill Charlie in when I found him.

I looked outside, and the wedding ceremony was just ending. Time to go. Where the hell was Charlie?

I heard voices downstairs. I recognized one as Jerry's voice. "He's not on the first floor. I'll check upstairs, you check the basement."

Three guesses who they were looking for. I slipped the phone into my pocket.

Amanda's office ran the full length of the second floor on the south side of the house, with windows on three sides. I had kept an eye on the wedding from the east window. With no time to warn Charlie, I opened a window on the west side and slipped onto a porch roof. I carefully closed the window. With the entire wedding party assembled on the east lawn for the reception line, I hung off the roof on the west side where nobody could see me. My feet dangling, I let go and dropped to the ground, narrowly missing a bush in front of the porch.

"Are you determined to ruin that tux?"

I righted myself and found I was looking at Summer, who was sitting in a wicker chair on the porch.

I brushed off my battle-worn duds. "I'll probably have to pay for it anyway."

"Did you ever hear of stairs?"

"I can explain."

Just then, Jerry burst onto the porch from the house, pointing a finger at me. "Where've you been?"

Summer got up from the wicker chair. "He's been with me."

"Amanda didn't see him around."

"It's okay, Jerry. Go back to the wedding. I'm keeping an eye on Mr. DeLucia."

Once again, Jerry left mumbling that Summer would have to answer to Amanda. Summer didn't seem concerned. She waited until he was out of earshot to address me. "Why were you on the roof, Mr. DeLucia?"

"I was getting my Frisbee. Why were you on the porch?"

Summer extended her hand toward me. She had another joint cupped in it.

I was tempted but didn't go for it. "I'm good. But don't let me stop you."

"Whatever," she said. "Anyway, we've got to make an appearance at the reception line. Where's Charlie?"

It was a good question. I could only guess that he heard Jerry coming and had to book before he could warn me. Summer and I were standing in line, ready to congratulate the bride and groom, when Charlie popped up behind me.

"Where were you?" I said under my breath.

"I heard someone coming and I decided that it would be easier to explain if I was caught somewhere other than in Amanda's private office."

"Thanks for tipping me off."

"There wasn't time. I figured you would just say you came in to use the facilities and got lost. Nobody would accept that story if I were caught in Amanda's office as well."

Summer was next in line to greet Kim. I didn't have time to chew Charlie out for literally leaving me hanging.

Chapter Thirty-Two

I stood between Charlie and Summer, capturing Kim's fleeting glances while she spoke to Summer. I wanted to feel sorry for her because I knew she wouldn't fit in with these bores. But the truth was that the couple really looked happy. What choice did I have? I was happy for them. When my turn came, I kissed the bride. She stiffened."

"Thanks for not making a scene," she whispered.

"Wouldn't dream of it. But I hope it won't put a damper on your honeymoon when I beat his ass in the race," I said in a serious tone as I motioned toward her new husband.

She took a minute, trying to figure out if I was serious.

"Joke, just a joke."

Kim tittered and blushed as she looked toward Tom.

"Glad you came," Tom said. He actually sounded like he meant it.

"Yeah. Me too." I meant it, too, but because I now had proof as to what Amanda was up to.

While pictures were taken, the guests were treated to more champagne and entertained by a rock band. I truly hoped for Kim's sake that the marriage would outlast the photos.

Eventually, the photo session was finished and the band was replaced by a dinner ensemble. Summer had the staff set up an extra place, and she sat with me on one side and Charlie on the other.

The appetizer, Lobster Rockefeller, sat on blue rock salt and was covered in sauce, which I tried to scrape away to get to the lobster tail. I couldn't understand why anyone would want lobster to taste like licorice; I preferred melted butter. The salad had goat cheese, red oak, arugula, and edible orchids, but I focused on the candied walnuts. Charlie recommended the Horseradish Crusted Chilean Sea Bass, but I went with the Porcini-dusted Filet Mignon to avoid ordering an endangered species. It was alright.

After dinner, the rock band returned. I was keyed up about the e-mail that Charlie helped me find and couldn't wait to get off the island, but I thought it would be conspicuous for me to leave right away. I mingled with the crowd, and everything seemed fine. I even talked to my ex-father-in-law, who, to my surprise, didn't have any great objection to my being there as long as I didn't ruin his daughter's day. I got the impression that he wasn't all that happy with Kim's choice to hitch up with one of the summer people.

Boyle Crawford, the guy giving the toast, raised his glass with some classy Yale vibes.

"Tom and I first crossed paths at prep school. Then, at Yale, we became roommates. While I was diligently hitting the books, he was the quintessential partygoer. Casually glancing at the material as we strolled to class, he'd effortlessly ace the tests. Even in those college days, he exuded the unmistakable essence of a man who knew precisely what he wanted. Now, at the helm of three companies, with hospital wings bearing his name, he's put on a few pounds since our Yale days. Yet, he remains a robust athlete and a passionate big game hunter, his trophy-adorned wall a testament to his pursuits. But today, he's truly outdone himself by marrying this stunning woman, Kim."

Nice. Kim was just an afterthought, another trophy. I wondered how she felt about that.

Then it was Tom's turn. He stood and made a toast of his own.

"I want to take this opportunity to thank our guests." He went on to mention and thank several distinguished people, his business associates, God, country, Yale, and finally, Kim. When he finished, the band started to play, and he quickly stopped them.

"I have a little gift for my lovely wife," he announced. He sat at the piano and played as he sang "You Are the Sunshine of My Life."

"Cute gesture," I said to Charlie.

"It would be, if he stopped there."

"What do you mean?"

"You'll see. I'm going for a drink."

It wasn't long before I found out what he meant. The tribute turned into a sing-along, with Tom as the center of attention. Kim stood off to the side with Amanda, pretending to enjoy it. I noticed Max not far from them. She still had on the huge sunglasses even though they were no longer needed.

Then I realized Jerry was standing beside me.

"Summer said to come." He escorted me to off to the edge of the lawn. Instead of meeting Summer, we found two other thugs in monkey suits. They grabbed me and pulled me behind the bushes.

"Time to go," Jerry said.

They escorted, more like half-dragged, me down an embankment to the beach with him leading the way. The two I didn't know tried to pitch me into the water, but I was taught not to swim alone. They had me by the arms, and I managed to lift both feet off the ground and catch Jerry in the stomach. He went backwards and landed in the water on his ass. My dead weight brought the three of us down, so we all ended up in the drink. I took a couple of solid belts to the stomach, but I was able to get in a few good punches. I was proud that I was able to hold my own against the three gorillas, at least for a little while. Eventually, the two goons pulled me back to the beach and held my arms so Jerry could get his best shot. I refused to let him see that it hurt.

I was saved when one of them saw Max standing at the tree line. "Who's that?"

"That's enough," Jerry said when he spotted her. Then, with the admonition that I had better leave the island the same way that I got there, they stumbled back up the hill to the house.

Max, my new guardian angel, stood at a distance, motioning for me to leave. Angry voices echoed in the background, and not one to defy a guardian angel, I sprinted along the shore, circling about a quarter of the way around the island to reach the spot where I had left the kayak near the stone shed.

Good luck to Kim, I thought, she's going to need it. When the time was right, I'd get even with Jerry.

Chapter Thirty-Three

The setting sun mottled hues of pink across a quickly darkening sky as I approached the shed. I retrieved my kayaking clothes from the dry bag I had stuffed under the workbench, shed the wet tux, and put them on. I couldn't wait to get away from that godforsaken island with its phony people. I carried the kayak down to the beach, pushed it into the water, and hopped in.

It's funny the things that go through your mind when you're kayaking. Like, why do couples always have sex after attending other people's weddings? Nothing like that was in the cards for me this evening.

The sun had set, but I had the moon and the lights on the islands and the mainland to guide me in. Suddenly, I became aware of the roar of an outboard motor closing in fast. I couldn't see any running lights, and I was well aware of the fact that I didn't have any either.

As the rumbling of the outboard got closer. I stopped paddling and, with Bart's admonition about paddling at night without running lights in mind, I rummaged through my dry bag for a flashlight and fastened it under the bungee cords on the deck.

The sound grew louder. Finally, I made out the shape of a Boston Whaler. It buzzed by within feet of me, and even in the dim light, I could see it was flying the Jolly Roger. Another pirate wanna-be, I thought as his wake gave me a jarring ride. I braced with my paddle and managed to keep from tipping.

I shouted out a few choice words as they sped away. At first, I wrote it off as some drunken yahoo. Then, considering what had happened back on the island, I began to wonder. I didn't have time to think about it long because, much to my astonishment, they made a sharp turn and headed back toward me. To try to outrun them was absurd, so I tried some evasive tacking maneuvers. Once more, the boat buzzed the kayak, but this time they threw a grappling hook at me and caught the bungee holding the flashlight just inches in front of me.

When I read Moby Dick as a kid, I imagined a Nantucket Sleigh Ride would be a lot of fun. But in this particular instance, instead of encountering a majestic whale, I encountered a deranged individual. To my astonishment, the kayak gained such incredible speed that it barely contacted the water's surface. We were headed back toward Kittle Island, and it became evident that the intent was to smash me against the rocky shore. I had just seconds before those boulders and I were up close and personal.

Bracing myself with my arms on both sides of the cockpit, I pushed myself up and out of the kayak. It flipped as it was pulled along and crashed on the rocks with a loud hollow thud.

The Boston Whaler took off, and I swam toward the rocks, my mind filled with questions. Had Jerry come out to finish me off? Was it he who had killed Ginny Lawson and Warner at Amanda's bidding?

The kayak was pretty banged up with creases and dents, but the Kevlar did its job and held together once again. Any rational person would have gotten into the kayak and headed back to the village. But I wasn't rational, I was pissed; and even though I couldn't see who had been operating the Whaler, I intended to settle a score with Jerry.

The party had grown rowdy. The way drinks had been flowing since the afternoon, I wasn't surprised. I could have used a couple of shots myself after that experience. As I started up the path, I almost stumbled on something sticking out from under a bush of sea roses.

Then, when I realized that it was a body, I swore, thinking I had stumbled over a drunk. When I realized it was Amanda, my blood ran cold because she looked more dead than drunk.

Crashing this wedding was like hitting dog shit with a weed whacker. Common sense told me it would end up in my face, but I did it anyway. I should have listened to Neal. How was I going to explain this?

I bent over Amanda and felt for a pulse. I could still hear the beat of the music up the hill. I wished I could have said the same for Amanda's heart. I was about to give her CPR when Summer came down the path to the beach with a flashlight. When she saw me bent over Amanda's lifeless body, she screamed. It seemed like she stood there forever, her hands over her mouth and gasping. Then she turned and ran up the path.

"Summer!"

I started to administer CPR, but the next few moments were filled with pandemonium as most of the wedding guests piled down onto the beach. Someone who identified himself as a doctor pushed me aside and began to work on Amanda. Normally, I'd be ticked off, but this time I was relieved to have him take over.

Summer returned with Charlie and stood at the edge of the crowd. When I walked over to them, she buried her face in his shoulder.

Even Charlie, my oldest friend, barely looked at me. "What happened here, Al?" I wish he had been more supportive.

"You two don't think I did this?"

Summer kept her face buried as she spoke. "I don't know what to think. When I heard that Jerry escorted you from the party, I came to see if you were okay. Then I find you over Amanda…" She gasped again.

I turned toward my old, no make that my oldest, friend. A person I could count on from childhood. "Charlie?"

"If you did it, I don't think you would have stayed on the island."

Jerry and his friends approached, throwing accusations. I was about to go after him when Doris rushed over and stood between us.

"Hold it right there. I'm in charge here, and if there's any more nonsense, I'll run you all in."

Jerry backed off.

"I'll take care of you later," he said to me.

Despite the fact that I was in no position to mouth off, I did. "Make sure you bring enough of your goons."

Doris glared at me. "That's enough out of you, too. Go stand against that shed until I can deal with you." She knew I wasn't going to take off.

Summer was extremely upset, so Charlie brought her up to the house. I stood alone, leaning against the tool shed like a kid punished on the playground. Meanwhile, Amanda was being attended to.

I was surprised when Max came over to me in her big straw hat. She spoke in a low voice.

"Looks like you got yourself into some trouble."

"Seems every time I turn around today, you're there."

"Someone had to look after you."

I looked toward the people trying to help Amanda. "It seems my guardian angel is on a coffee break. Listen, I have an email. Proof that Amanda is planning to reopen the granite quarry, and Ginny Lawson was against it." I pulled my phone from my pocket, happy that I had invested in a waterproof case.

She looked like she didn't believe me. "I'll handle this. You could be in a lot of trouble. What you've got to do now is keep your mouth shut. Oh yeah, and send me that e-mail, then delete it from your phone."

"No."

"It's not going to help you to have that on you." She glanced toward the people working on Amanda.

"I didn't do it." It seems like that phrase was becoming a mantra for me.

"I believe you. But I shouldn't after the way you were so chummy with that Summer chick."

I sent her the picture of the email, and then deleted it from my phone. I looked toward the beach where the Sachem Creek rescue boat was landing. When I turned around, Max was gone. Again.

* * *

I was getting to know Doris' office at the police station better than I wanted to. Chelsea wasn't at the Town Hall since it was late, but I was told to wait in her workspace while Doris prepared for another round of interviewing me in her own department office.

As I waited, various fragments of information, conversations, and events pinged through my mind like a malfunctioning computer. After finally calming down, I focused on verifying something. Typing "spodumene" into my device confirmed my suspicion: Spodumene serves as a significant lithium source. I recalled how Amanda prominently showcased the mineral on her otherwise clear desk.

Next, curiosity led me to search for "Spodumene mine images," and I was floored to discover that it comes from strip mines, bearing a striking resemblance to granite quarries. I found Spodumene is found in Connecticut, but usually not in great amounts. I was trying to wrap my head around the possibility that Amanda's crews might have stumbled upon a substantial Spodumene reservoir, and she could be contemplating quarrying it.

"You can come in now," Doris bellowed, causing me to startle from my deep thoughts. She didn't have to direct me to sit down. I just plopped into the seat opposite her desk as if I were at home.

"I didn't do it, Doris. In fact, someone tried to kill me."

"Seems like it was Mrs. Kittle who pretty near got killed there, Al."

So now it was Mrs. Kittle instead of Amanda. Funny how becoming a crime victim elevated Amada's respect quotient when it didn't do a damned thing for mine.

"So, she's not dead then?"

"Far as I know, she was alive when they put her on the Life Star chopper. You better hope she stays that way."

"And what about me? I already told you that a boat hooked my kayak and then crashed it on the rocks."

"Any reason why someone might want to kill you?"

"Good question, and not the first time either. I was shot at up in Kent, remember? And I didn't even tell you about the bag of cement that was thrown at me."

"You ain't getting paranoid. Are you? 'Cuz they have help for that."

"Funny, Doris. You should really be on television. You know? Now you tell me. Who would want to kill me?"

"Have to admit sometimes I've thought about doing it myself. But that's neither here nor there. What were you doing out on Kittle Island?"

"I crashed Kim's wedding. You know that." I wasn't about to tell her about the evidence that incriminated Amanda in the Lawson death. I didn't need to deal with burglarizing Amanda's private office right now."

Doris pulled open her desk drawer and took out something wrapped in plastic. Her voice suddenly took on the tone of one of those TV crime investigators as she placed it on the table. "Do you know what this is?"

"It's a pry bar."

"It's also the weapon that was used to assault Mrs. Kittle. And if things go south, it may become a murder weapon. We found it under the sea rose bushes."

I felt the blood drain from my face as I studied the small red iron bar. "I have to tell you something, Doris."

"That being?"

"That being, they'll probably find my fingerprints on it."

Doris raised her eyebrows. "Because?"

"Because I used it to deal with a giant spider when I changed into my tux in Amanda's tool shed before the wedding."

"You killed a spider. Really?"

"I didn't kill it. Maybe if I had, you'd be able to find it so I could prove my story."

"You know what your problem is, DeLucia? You can't leave well enough alone. When you found the lawyer's body, I told you to leave the investigation up to me. But no. You had to go put your two cents' worth in. Now you're connected to two murders. Maybe three. How is that supposed to make what you say credible?"

"I didn't kill anyone, Doris."

"I'm not saying you did. But I'm not saying you didn't. Yet. Stick around."

"So, you're not charging me?"

"Let's say right now you're a person of interest. I want to see the fingerprint report first." She reached in her desk drawer and pulled out a roll of antacids. "And until then, if you aggravate my ulcer in any way, I'm going to throw the book at ya."

Doris comes off as being as nasty as a famished bluefish in a school of bunkers, but I have to say she's fair. Where the Kent police had come on like the NYPD and detained me when I obviously couldn't have killed Warner, Doris allowed me to go free on my promise not to leave town, even though, as she said, I was a person of interest. My worry was that only my fingerprints might turn up on the weapon.

Chapter Thirty-Four

Sunday, July 3

A t 4:30 the next morning, I woke up starving. I hadn't eaten anything since I picked at that frilly meal at the wedding reception, which I didn't care for. Tide and Griddle Tavern wasn't open for breakfast yet, so I had to be content for now with a cup of instant coffee and a peanut butter and apple sandwich on whole wheat, since that's all I found in the small snack fridge in my apartment.

Jamila was on the island covering the wedding, although I didn't notice her in the crowd that gathered on the beach. Still, I'm sure she had time to phone in the story of the assault on Amanda, and it would make the front page of the Sunday edition of The Sachem Creek Gazette. Even if it didn't make the paper on time, that didn't mean that the whole village wasn't talking about it.

As I ate, I kept thinking how just when I had proof that Amanda had motive to get rid of Ginny Lawson before she put the kibosh on the lithium mining project, Amanda goes and gets beaten to a pulp. It all made sense now that I realized those weren't photos of granite quarries on Ginny's computer but potential lithium mines. Of course, that doesn't prove that she wasn't behind Ginny's murder. It could have been a case of revenge by someone who felt, as I did, that Amanda was behind every bad thing that was happening in Sachem Creek.

Did Amanda have someone try to put a scare into Ginny and it went too far? And who actually carried out the keelhauling? Was it Jerry? Or maybe it was Amanda's mysterious silent partner.

I went to my computer and pulled up one of Ginny's high-resolution satellite images of the area. There are two things that make me lose track of time, browsing in hardware stores and looking at maps. Those satellite maps fascinate me most of all. It's amazing what the cameras can see from several hundred miles up. I zoomed in on Sachem Creek. I zoomed in on my old house, and I could see the car that Kim took from the marriage. I checked out the wharf and the boat docks and could clearly see the rescue boat. Of course, I knew all the buildings in the village from street level, but the roof view was interesting.

Next, I checked out Charlie's place and the cottage that Max rented. I thought of Max. Where had she disappeared to after I found Amanda?

Back to the maps, I zoomed in. I zoomed out. Not knowing what I was looking for. I moved from the village to the islands to the marshes. I closed in on Abe's place. Inland from Abe's, I could clearly see the scar of the quarry set in the middle of the woods. I zoomed in and could see blocks of stone and the shadow of the old derrick. I zoomed out, concentrating on the trees. I noticed a clump of trees on Abe's property that projected into the marsh. The concrete footbridge that crossed the marsh as part of the trolley trail was clearly visible between the clump of trees and the edge of Long Island Sound.

Using the map's ruler tool, I measured the distance of the trail from the ballpark to the woods past Abe's place, a mile and a half. I measured the distance from the village to Long Island, eighteen miles across the Sound. I already knew that. I would be paddling it soon in the race.

I spent a long time amusing myself by measuring between familiar points on the map. Before I knew it, I found myself nodding off at the computer. I guess the events of the past few days had taken a lot out of me because I didn't wake up again until 8:15 a.m.

I was at the Tide and Griddle Tavern by 8:45 to get a copy of the Sachem Creek Gazette. Not a lot of newsworthy events happen in the Creek, so the unofficial motto of the Gazette is "All the News That Fits We Print." You can find anything in there from a story about a lost cat to someone finding a ten-dollar bill on the street. The assault on Amanda would be big news, even though everyone in town already knew what happened. I didn't relish seeing my name smeared in ink on the front page.

Charlie was on the deck having a cup of coffee. I mumbled, "Hi," and started inside to get a paper. To their credit, after I found Amanda, he and Summer wanted to ride back in the boat with Doris and me, but Doris said no. I wondered if he and Summer hooked up later on. None of my business, I guess. Still, I wondered.

"Have a seat. I got the last one," he said, motioning to the paper that sat neatly folded next to his cup.

"Is it bad?" I plopped myself into the seat opposite him.

"It doesn't mention you."

"Are you sure? Let me see that."

He handed me the paper.

"Jamila wrote it," he said.

Besides her regular nature column, Jamila often pulled other assignments. I lucked out when she drew this one. At least I hoped I did. I opened the paper and read.

Nutmeg Island Woman in Coma after Beating
By Jamila Cambridge
Sachem Creek Gazette Staff Writer

The Sachem Creek Police Department is investigating a "violent attack" on 55-year-old Amanda Kittle, who was found badly beaten on Kittle Island Saturday evening.

Chief Doris Page said the motive for the attack on the Nutmeg Island resident and land developer has not been determined, but investigators have found what they believe to be the weapon used in the assault.

Page is questioning a family acquaintance who directed rescuers to the woman. According to Page, the acquaintance

told police they and Kittle spoke briefly before being ejected from a wedding on the private island on Saturday night. After their discussion, the acquaintance left the island briefly by kayak and, upon returning, found her on the beach. After attempting CPR, they summoned other wedding guests for help.

Mrs. Kittle's condition is currently unknown. She is the widow of Anderson Kittle, a prominent New Haven banker and quarry owner who passed away on the private island four years ago.

E-mail to Jamila.Cambridge@scgazette.com

Jamila didn't say anything bad. But she didn't back me up either. Everyone in the village knew I was the one who found Amanda beaten to within an inch of her life. And everyone knew that she and I didn't get along. I was hoping that the article could have said something to support me. I guess that really was asking too much.

I looked out to Kittle Island, then back to Charlie. "I guess I really messed up the wedding."

"That would be a safe assumption." Charlie's voice was flat. Again, I was hoping for more support.

"I feel bad about that, especially after Kim thanked me for not making a scene. The wedding was ruined, and I couldn't prove a thing."

Charlie took a sip from his coffee mug, put it down, and then looked me directly in the eye, as if he were trying to read my thoughts. "What is it that you're trying to say?"

"What I'm trying to say is that all of the evidence we found in Amanda's house pointed to her being behind Ginny Lawson's murder. Lawson wanted her to stop her project. Lawson probably knew that Amanda was buying up property in Sachem Creek through fraud."

And your point being?" Charlie asked.

"That if Amanda is a victim herself, she may not have killed Lawson. The killer could be someone who was at that wedding. The same person who beat up Amanda."

Charlie stood abruptly, his chair scraping against the floor. He lingered for a moment, his hand resting on the back of the chair as if weighing his next words. "That narrows it down to a few hundred people," he said with a faint edge to his tone, before walking away without another glance.

I sat there and read the article again. Meanwhile, the satellite images kept playing on my mind.

Chapter Thirty-Five

When I went back to my car, I noticed people in Neal's Barbershop. It was Sunday, and I knew he wasn't open for business, so I walked over. To me, the barbershop was like a train wreck; a horrible scene, but I couldn't resist it. It was no surprise to find Buster and Walter with Neal, and I realized they were there for a bull-shitting meeting. What did surprise me was that they didn't break my balls about crashing the wedding. Not one "I told you so" was hurled at me as I walked through the door.

"Are you okay?" Buster asked, the other two shaking their heads in sympathy.

"Of course. Why wouldn't I be?"

"Finding Amanda like that. I hear she's in a coma and may die. You're lucky it wasn't you." Neal said. There was a real look of concern on his face. I almost would rather have had a rebuke.

"And I heard that someone tried to dash you against the rocks," Walter said.

He actually seemed concerned.

"I'm here. That's what counts."

"Thank God," Neal said.

I thought he was going to cry. I must have entered the Twilight Zone. This was totally not like these guys.

"It was only a matter of time for someone to try to kill Amanda, though," Buster chimed in. "We've come up with a list of suspects."

"Suspects?"

Yeah," Walter said. "Suspects. People with a motive to kill her, or at least put her in a coma. The village is full of them."

It was my turn to give them a warning for a change. "Look, that's a dangerous game you guys are getting into. Let Doris handle that stuff."

"Doris. She made the list, too!" Walter said.

He waved a sheet of paper in my face. That confirmed it. I was trapped in Wackoland.

"Who else is on there? Let me see that." I snatched the paper from his hand.

Chief Page was there all right, as was just about every citizen of Sachem Creek, including some children.

"You've listed just about everyone except for yourselves. And me."

I watched as Neal's face turned red. Buster's went white, and Walter's went green; standing next to each other, they looked like the Italian flag. Then Walter went from green to blue.

"You okay?" Buster had a concerned look on his face.

"Asthma's acting up," Walter said.

He pulled an inhaler from his pocket and took a couple of puffs.

"Well, actually..." he said between wheezes.

I realized what Walter didn't want to tell me. WTF! "I'm on it! Where?"

Neal handed me another sheet of paper.

"You kind of made a list of your own. The Prime Suspect List," he said.

"You've got to be kidding!" I looked from the paper to Neal to Buster to Walter and then thrust the paper back to Neal.

"I don't mean ours. I mean, as far as the rest of the village is concerned, you're #1. That's why we came up with this other list. To help you out." Neal waved the paper as if that were proof of their sincerity.

"I don't need your help."

"Yes, you do. You had motive," Neal said.

"You had opportunity," Buster said.

"You were dumb enough to go out to that island and crash the wedding," Walter said.

"So were you!"

Walter seemed offended. "It was a social obligation for me. But let's talk about you. The fact that you told us—"

"And just about everyone else," Buster chimed in.

Walter gave him a dirty look for interrupting.

"The fact that you told us, and just about everyone else, that you were going out there, proves to us that you didn't do it."

"But, I said I wasn't going out there!"

"Work with us," Walter said. "We're trying to help you."

"Right," said Neal. "You would have kept your plans a secret. Developed an alibi, instead of setting yourself up."

"That's why we made up the list," said Buster.

"But everyone is on it. What good is that?"

"Because everyone had a motive." His voice dropped to a whisper. As if anyone could have overheard him. "Don't forget, Amanda was destroying the Creek. Nobody wanted to see that happen. At least none of the locals."

"But a list with everyone on it except the four of us isn't much help."

"Maybe they all did it. Like in that movie *Murder on the Fancy Train*," Neal said.

"If you did do it, no one could really blame you," Buster added, a smirk tugging at his lips.

I couldn't take it anymore. The audacity of these guys was too much. I had to leave before I said something I'd regret. Because the truth was, they had plenty of nerve—and plenty of motive. Buster and Walter's historic-home restoration business had taken a hit every time Amanda bulldozed another antique house, giving the couple a good reason to resent her. And Neal? His barbershop had fewer regulars with every step toward gentrification.

"Okay, I'm out of here," I said, rising abruptly and heading for the door before I said what I was really thinking.

Buster stood between me and the door. "Well, take the list and read it later." Buster handed me the list, and I stuffed it into my pocket.

"That's Doris' job, but I'll take a look at it." I gave in just to get out of there.

"You want this one too?" Walter said, waving the paper with my name on it.

"No!"

Neal, Buster, and Walter; the triangle of old codgers was enough to drive me crazy. I had to get out of there while I still had my sanity. Then it hit me. The thing that was evading me was right there in the personification of these wonderfully eccentric relics of Sachem Creek that I had known and loved since boyhood. I was so excited that I began shouting.

"That's it! How did I miss it?"

Walter squinted and wrinkled his brow. "Miss what?"

Neal put out his arms in front of his two cohorts and held them back. "Don't go too near him. I think he's gone mad."

I gave Neal a high-five. "Mad! I'm not mad." Neal looked stunned.

Then I gave Buster a high-five. "You guys are geniuses!" Buster looked bewildered.

I attempted to high-five Walter, but he closed his fist, put his thumb out, and jerked his hand back, giving me the beat-it sign. "Walter, I love you guys!"

Old Walter wasn't moved. "You need help, you know that? Real serious help!"

I think Neal was relieved to see that I was leaving the shop. "Where are you going?"

"Out to Doubloon Island. I want to talk to Ed Teach."

Buster shook his head. "That old pirate? You should be finding the killer instead of playing pirates."

The three of them watched from the doorway as I headed home to get the kayak. They shouted in unison.

"Bring your sunscreen!"

Chapter Thirty-Six

For once, my habit of gravitating toward that loony bin paid off. While I wondered how much they were exaggerating about what people were saying, I couldn't be happier. If I was right, I would have a big piece of the puzzle solved. I actually laughed out loud, thinking that they had put Doris, not to mention practically the whole village, on their suspect list.

There was a slight headwind as I paddled up the channel toward the islands. An invigorating paddle was just what I needed to clear my mind enough to think this out. The tour boat was about to leave the dock for the island tour, and passengers waved at me from the top deck. I lifted the paddle out of the water and gave them a hearty wave back. A bit up the channel, I moved out of the way as the water taxi came in from its hourly loop through the islands. It carried only two passengers, probably people who rented cottages on Money or Governor Islands, hitting the mainland for supplies. The boat used to be packed before Amanda bought up so many of the islands. I wondered how the economy of the Creek would be impacted now that Amanda was in a coma and near death.

I paddled hard, keeping the race in mind, but I kept going back to the fact that practically the whole village had reason to try to kill Amanda. Buster himself said if I *had* done it, no one could blame me. Not only had Amanda alienated the locals by making it possible for her rich friends to change the face of the village, but now she was going to stab the summer people in the back by sinking the value of their properties with a lithium mine. If word was out that put the newcomers and the natives in the same boat. So

211

basically, my friends in the barbershop were right. Everyone in town, from rich to poor, was a suspect. I had a hunch I'd find out more when I got to Doubloon Island.

Doubloon Island is another of the Nutmeg Islands, reputed to be the hideout of Captain Kidd. Today, it's the home of a private association of sun-worshipping pirate aficionados. If anyone could give me information on the subject of pirates, Ed Teach could.

As I approached the island, I could see small, crooked pine trees growing out of the thirty-foot granite palisades. I beached the kayak in a small cove by a boulder with the initials W.K. carved into it. Legend has it that they were carved by Captain William Kidd himself. I had my doubts. I always suspected that they were carved by one of the early tour boat operators.

A large sign with the picture of a camera in a circle with a bar through it stood by the wooden stairs that led from the rocky beach to the top of the cliff: *Private Association. Keep Out. Trespassers will be prosecuted.*

As I sprinted up the stairs from the beach, I could see a large Jolly Roger flying from a flagpole. A woman whom I knew to be Livy Teach, was planting flowers in front of a cottage that had been painted black, as were all of the cottages in the association. Her back was to me, so I called out her name so that she would know I was there.

"Livy! Is Ed around?"

Livy stood, a necklace of seashells the only thing breaking a deep, even tan from her head to her toes. She must be pushing seventy, but she looked half her age with hardly a wrinkle. So much for the sun being detrimental to your skin, I thought.

"Al! Well, what brings you here? I heard you were back in town."

I focused my gaze on her white teeth, which gleamed in the sunlight. She approached me and I gave my old friend a peck on the cheek, carefully arching my body away from hers.

"I have to talk to Ed."

"Quincy…"

"What?"

"You know the rules of the island."

I pretended I didn't understand what she was saying. "I don't have a camera."

"You know what I mean."

"But I'm only staying for a minute."

A couple, sporting the same all-over tan as Livy, strolled by with their Basset Hound. They eyed me suspiciously.

"Rules are rules, Quincy. So everyone will feel comfortable."

"But I wouldn't be comfortable."

"Then you'll have to talk to Ed when he goes into the village for supplies."

I stripped off my T-shirt.

Livy stood there patiently, shaking her head.

"Rules," she said.

I acquiesced. Holding my shirt in front of me, I dropped my cargo shorts and kicked them in the air, catching them with one hand and holding them in front of me.

"So, where's Ed?"

"He went to the village to get supplies."

"You're kidding. Right?"

A smile unfolded across her face.

"Yes, yes, I'm kidding you. You look so stressed. Don't worry. I wouldn't blame you if you did it. Nobody would."

So, they were speculating on my guilt even out here on the islands. I shouldn't have been surprised.

"That's reassuring," I said. "But I didn't do it."

"Of course, you didn't. Now you go talk to Ed. He's out by the shed working on an outboard."

I took off in the direction of the shed.

"You know the rules. Non-members can only stay for thirty minutes," she called after me. That was fine with me. I guess these nudist-pirates never heard of skin cancer.

It was easy enough to find Ed. All I had to do was follow the growl of an outboard motor, roaring like an angry wasp inside a rain barrel. When I spotted him, he looked like a walrus come to life, fat and bald with a sweeping mustache, but with none of his wife's sweet demeanor. Thankfully, he'd managed to cover himself with a pair of ragtag shorts.

Figuring it wasn't wise to startle a walrus, I stopped about twenty feet away and shouted over the racket. "Ed!"

No response. He was engrossed in his tinkering.

"Ed!" I shouted again, louder this time.

A wrench zipped past my head, close enough to ruffle my hair.

"What the hell! Are you crazy?" I bellowed.

He glanced up, cupping a hand to his ear. "Can't hear you!"

"Cut it off!" I gestured at the motor.

"What?"

"The motor!" Frustration flared, and I marched forward, flipping the switch to silence the infernal noise.

Ed stared at me, wide-eyed. "Why in the hell did you do that? Took me an hour to get it running!"

"Well, if you fixed it right, it'll start again. What's the matter with you, throwing a wrench at me?"

"What's the matter with *me*? You sneak up on a man like that. How'm I supposed to know you're not packing?"

"Packing? I'm naked, for Christ's sake! Where would I hide a gun?"

Ed let loose a laugh like rolling thunder. I seized the moment to pull on my shorts.

"Whatever," he muttered, waving a hand dismissively. "Still shouldn't have startled me."

"Look, Ed," I said, reining in my temper. "I need information. Someone in a Boston Whaler tried to kill me right before I found Amanda."

"Why're you telling me?"

His tone was pure orneriness, the kind he was known for. If I'd had one handy, I might've tossed the walrus a fish.

"Because the Whaler was flying a Jolly Roger."

"So, you automatically come here. That's profiling, isn't it?"

"If he had been flying a martini banner, I'd be at the yacht club. It's only common sense. I'm not accusing you or anyone else on the island. But

I've seen that boat a few times, first when I found the body, then over by Faulkner's island, and last night over by Kittle," I nodded toward Kittle Island in the distance. "And I thought you may have spotted it around too."

He seemed to be thinking. I was sure that I saw something dark pass over his face.

"Yeah, I know the one you mean."

Good walrus. "Doris was assuming that it was Abe's, but since I saw it last night too, I doubt it. Abe has been missing. Do you know who it belongs to?"

"Nope."

"Too bad. I was hoping you knew who was on the boat."

"I said I didn't know to whom the boat belonged. The guy who was driving it was named Rondell. He was with another guy named Warner."

"Rondell and Warner. That's unbelievable," I said.

"Well, believe it. They came here a while back. Warner said Amanda wanted to buy Doubloon Island. Said our lifestyle didn't fit into the image she had for Sachem Creek."

That sounded like a motive to try to kill Amanda to me, but I couldn't imagine Ed, even being as cantankerous as he was, killing someone. Although the wrench incident was still fresh in my mind.

"Warner's dead."

"I heard you killed him, too."

"I didn't kill anybody! Ed, I have to ask you something else."

"Well, go ahead, because when Livy comes, she's going to give you hell about breaking the rules."

"Well, you're not following the rules either."

"These motors get hot. You got to be practical sometimes. You know what I mean?"

"Yeah. Yeah, Ed, I know what you mean. Tell me something. Would Captain Kidd have known about triangulation?"

"You writing a book or something?"

"You might say that. I'm writing a book...or something. So, would he have known about triangulation or not."

215

"I suppose he would. The sextant was around back then."

"Well, I'm not talking about navigation, exactly. But from use of the sextant, he would know triangulation. Right?"

"Like I said. I suppose."

"Tell me something else. What unit of measure did they use back in the 17th century?"

"Measuring what?"

"Distance. I mean the colonists didn't use meters and kilometers, did they?"

"Of course not, they were English. They used Imperial measure. They had feet, yards, rods, and the like."

Rods. I hadn't thought of that. From my paddling magazines, I knew the term was used to measure how far a canoe was portaged; a rod being about the length of a canoe. "So, a rod is about what, sixteen feet?"

"Sixteen and a half to be exact."

"Thought so. So, Captain Kidd—"

"What about him?"

"He was English, and he used the Imperial Measure for distance. Right?"

"He was from Scotland, but yeah, he used the Imperial Measure."

"Scotland, huh? Isn't that where Freemasonry started?"

"Yeah, he belonged to the Masons. You said you're writing a book?"

Livy was racing over and yelling at me about the rules.

"Thanks, Ed. Have to go before I'm thrown off another island."

* * *

As I paddled back to the village, I mulled over what I had learned. I had gone out to Doubloon Island to find out about Captain Kidd and triangulation. I came back with the knowledge that not only would the good captain know about triangulation, but that he was a Scottish Freemason to boot. But what I found out about a couple of modern-day pirates was even more interesting.

Not only did Rondell and Warner know each other, but they were seen on a Boston Whaler similar to Abe's. Which also made it similar to the one that was in the vicinity when Ginny Lawson was keelhauled. And on top of that, they worked for Amanda. Rondell was president of Big Apple, but I was willing to bet that Amanda was behind the company. If he knew Ginny wanted to put the kibosh on the lithium mine, that was motive enough to kill her. Could Rondell have killed Warner to keep him quiet and attempted to kill Amanda as well? I had this feeling that I'd better be on my toes from now on when it came to Oscar Rondell.

I called Max as soon as I got home.

"I went out to Doubloon Island to dig up more about Captain Kidd, and I found out Rondell and Warner knew each other."

"You're losing me."

"Not only did they know each other—they were working for Amanda. I'm betting Rondell killed Warner at Bulls Bridge to keep him quiet."

"Okay, now I'm starting to understand. What does this have to do with Doubloon Island?"

"Rondell and Warner had been on the island on behalf of Amanda. She wanted to buy it. She claimed the present use doesn't fit her image to create an upscale resort. But what if she wanted the island for another reason?"

"Like using it as a processing site or shipping dock for her lithium mine?"

"Exactly!" I said.

"That tracks. But where does Captain Kidd fit in?"

"I think we might be dealing with two separate issues. Remember Ginny Lawson planned on meeting with her brother and Abe on Outer Island? I'm thinking while she was researching Abe's property at town hall, she stumbled onto something bigger."

"Don't tell me she's treasure hunting."

"I'm not saying anything until I figure this out."

"Hold on, I'm getting another call," Max said, cutting off the line.

* * *

I wanted this thing concluded. It was the day before the Fourth of July and the big race. I needed a clear head. I went to see Doris and spilled my guts.

I presented the evidence to Doris, who nodded but made no comment. I did my duty as far as I was concerned. For now, I had to focus on the race and then find Abe. Max was right, I had to speed things up and get back to Savannah before she hired Phil to work for the Blue Palmetto.

I surprised myself by getting a good night's sleep.

Chapter Thirty-Seven

Monday, July 4

The Fourth of July, the day I'd been waiting for. I felt good. I did my part in the investigation of Ginny Lawson's murder and the assault on Amanda. Now it was time to do something for Abe. I only hoped he was alive and would benefit from my efforts. Max was the only disappointment. I really thought she would be at the starting line to cheer me on.

More than fifty kayakers showed up off the village green, including Ernie Fitzgerald. I wondered who was minding the store at Tide and Griddle Tavern. The biggest surprise was Tom, who seemed to have put off the honeymoon so he could compete. Poor Kim.

The kayaks ranged from eight feet to twenty, and judging from appearances, the paddlers seemed to be of every skill level. Already, there were collisions and tipping, and the race hadn't even begun. There seemed to be a direct correlation between the skill and dress of the paddlers. The fancier the wetsuit, the lower the skill level. I dressed in shorts and old sneakers.

I'd worked my ass off training for this race, despite all the distractions. There was a lot riding on it, so one precaution I took was to ensure that my paddle and I didn't get separated. I decided to use a bungee cord paddle leash in case I dropped the paddle in rough water. I knew an untethered paddle could get away from you in no time, and the last place I wanted to be was in the middle of Long Island Sound without a paddle. Ernie saw me attach one end of the leash to the paddle and the other to the deck lines. Before I knew it, he'd paddled over to me.

"Hey, Tom! Get a look at this guy's paddle leash. I guess he's expecting rough going."

Tom was quick to pick up on the ribbing. "Aw. Ain't that sweet. Are you using a seatbelt too?" They both had a good laugh at my expense.

"Yeah, well, let's see who has the last laugh if a storm comes up." That's when I noticed his robin egg blue kayak. "Talk about sweet. Where'd you get the pretty kayak, Tom?"

Tom's face turned a deep red. His reply was almost inaudible, "It's Kim's. Why? You got a problem with that, DeLucia?"

"No. No problem."

"Good. Then enjoy the race because when they pull you in for what you did to Amanda, it'll be the last fresh air you get for a while.

* * *

I knew Tom was trying to rattle me, but I wasn't going to let him break my focus. The only thing that mattered was the course, which was fairly simple. The race would start at the Sachem Creek dock, head south for two miles through the Nutmegs channel to Outer Island. Then southeast eight miles to the Central Long Island Sound Buoy. After rounding the buoy, the course veered southwest twelve miles to the Friars Head Yacht Club on the north shore of Long Island. From there it turned around and bee-lined back due north eighteen miles to Sachem Creek, a total distance of forty miles.

Doris fired a replica 17th-century pirate cannon to start the race, and we were off at exactly 10:00 a.m. The water in the harbor was calm, but the stiff offshore breeze told me that we were in for some rough water once we got past the islands. My paddle leash just might pay off. With my chart under the deck cords in front of me, I glanced at the compass, but I didn't need it. On a clear day like this, the course was a piece of cake, unless a fog rolled in. Even then, I wasn't worried. The biggest challenge at this point was to keep away from those people who didn't know what they were doing.

The field was crowded until we passed the last of the sailboats moored to vertical poles on the west side of the channel. As soon as we passed the buoy marking the no-wake zone for powerboats, the group thinned out a bit.

The wind was at our back, that is, out of the north, which was favorable, but the 2-knot current was going to be pulling us westward. It would be a challenge, but I knew it would also weed out the weekend paddlers who still hadn't dropped out.

In less than ten minutes, we were between West Crib and Money Islands. Straight ahead, in the channel between the islands, several large motor yachts filled with spectators were moored just about where I had found Ginny Lawson.

I was happy with the progress on the murder case. Just a few more pieces had to fall into place. With Max's help, I was confident that would happen soon. But right then, I had to concentrate on the race. There were only about twenty of us left as we passed between Horse and Outer Islands, and I realized these were the true contenders. The rest apparently had been there only for kicks. As I had predicted, Tom and Ernie were among the group that remained.

Open water and Long Island lay straight ahead. I knew I had to be mindful of the shipping lane that ran the length of Long Island Sound. Huge ships can't see kayaks in the water, no matter how brightly colored the small boat may be. If you're lucky, the sunlight reflecting off the paddle might give a warning to the pilot of one of those seagoing monsters, but I wouldn't count on it.

It would be at least two hours before I spotted the bald-topped hill that marked Friar's Head. But first, there was that diversion to the southeast where I had to find the Central Long Island Buoy. There we had to pick up an official race tag proving we followed the course. Finding the buoy wouldn't be easy since its anemometer, the device that measures wind speed, sits only twelve feet above the surface of the water. In the distance, I could see the rotating white light of the ancient Faulkner's Island Lighthouse. For now, all I had to do was keep the Faulkner's light to port and the smokestacks of the power station on Long Island to starboard, and I would find myself in the vicinity of the buoy I was looking for.

Simple triangulation. Who would have thought it would play out to be the key to Ginny Lawson's murder and possibly Amanda's assault as well? Damn! I was thinking about those recent horrible events again. I had just promised myself that I wouldn't let them distract me right now. I had to keep alert and focused. That was the key to winning this race: alert and focused.

My strategy for winning was simple. I viewed the race as more of an endurance test than one of paddling skill. I felt I had a pretty good chance, as long as the weather cooperated. As far as I was concerned, the clock was my only competition, and the only way to beat it was to maintain a steady pace. I didn't want to expend all my energy in the first half of the race to Friar's Head and then have nothing to bring me home to Sachem Creek. Mentally, I would use that first half to prepare my mind for the second half when my muscles ached and I would want to quit. For every minute my opponents would gain on me in the first half, I would gain two or three on them in the second.

Once we reached the Friar's Head Yacht Club, each racer would be given exactly fifteen minutes to rest before setting off on the return trip to Sachem Creek. I preferred simplicity; that's when I found the most success. Running the race against no one but myself, I aimed to maintain a clear head, focusing solely on conserving energy for the later stages when my muscles would be pushed to their limits. Calculating that maintaining about a nautical mile in seventeen minutes, just under four knots, would keep me in good shape, I aimed to cover the course to Long Island in about four and a half hours, with the direct return course taking an additional four hours. That totaled thirty nautical miles in a little over eight hours. Adhering to my plan, I deliberately kept my pace down in the first half, avoiding the temptation to be a jackrabbit, as I believed a steady pace would lead to victory. Even while pacing myself, I found myself ahead of everyone except for Tom and Ernie.

At last, I spotted the buoy. It belonged to the University of Connecticut and looked like a huge yellow and blue hockey puck with a jungle gym sitting on top of it. Fitted with wave and water quality sensors, it bobbed only eight miles from the north shore of Long Island. Tom and Ernie got there first, but that went right along with my strategy. It seemed like it would be a three-man race. I grabbed a tag off the buoy as proof that I was there and then turned southwest toward Friars Head.

A chase boat ran back and forth along the course to observe the racers and assist in any emergency. Once or twice, I looked behind me when I heard it coming. But I decided that it was a foolish waste of energy and time, not to mention the loss of concentration.

As we approached the Friar's Head Yacht Club, several craft came out to greet us. We were about a mile offshore when a thirty-foot Sundancer racing east, and disregarding every rule of navigation, cut off a smaller Grady White that was coming out from the yacht club. The Grady cut hard to starboard to avoid a collision. The resulting wakes from the two boats swept up Tom and Ernie. Tom was able to ride it out, but Ernie was swamped. As I passed him, I could see that he was swimming around his kayak looking for his paddle. I didn't try to help him because I knew either the chase boat or one of the other boats would bring him to safety. It looked like it would be just me and Tom. He got to the yacht club first and began his fifteen minutes of rest. I was a couple of minutes behind and caught up with him at the refreshment table. He was stuffing his face with a hot dog. When he saw me coming, he grabbed another one.

"Damn. I just took the last one, old sport. Sorry, I bit into it already." With that, he took a giant bite out of the hot dog.

"No problem. A water and one of these energy bars are good enough for me. Wouldn't want the hot dog to sit on my stomach. I wonder how Ernie made out."

Tom started to laugh with his mouth full. I swear, if he choked, I wasn't about to waste time giving him the Heimlich.

"I just saw them bring him in. He's fine. He lost his paddle. It looks like it's just you and me now. And I predict that you're going to lose this race to me, just like you lost Kim."

I was about to make him take it back when one of the judges approached and told Tom his fifteen-minute rest was up. He made a great show of dancing his way down to the beach like he was the coolest dude in kayaking history. As he shoved off, people from the club cheered him on.

"I finished my power bar and threw away what remained of the water before walking down to the beach. Three racers came in, in quick succession. I guess I was wrong about everyone else dropping out. When I was told my break was over, I shoved off. Once more, well-wishers from the crowd let out mighty cheers.

I paddled as hard as I ever did in my life. This was when I had to make up time. I spotted a racer coming in, about a mile and a half out from Friar's Head. He seemed like he had given up all will to race. Behind him was a woman who paddled consistently but slowly. No problem from them. They still had to take their fifteen minutes. I didn't see anyone else until I passed Tom. He was dead in the water and vomiting up the hot dogs and other junk with which he had stuffed himself. Now, I was in the lead, but I didn't let up on my pace.

Two and a half hours out from Friar's Head, I could see the Nutmegs ahead of me, but I knew I still had at least an hour and a half more to go. I was well ahead of the other racers, and I didn't want to spend too much time looking over my shoulder, but as far as I knew, the race was mine. About five miles off the Connecticut shore, I saw a tug approach. Holding my hand up before my face, I checked the angle of the tug's bow to mine. If the angle didn't change, we were on a collision course. A tug pulling barges filled with crushed stone and weighing thousands of tons can't maneuver. So, it was up to me, non-power craft or not, to avoid being run over.

I adjusted my angle. As I did, I noticed that distinctive yellow and red hull of Harry Carter's river kayak barreling toward me. He wasn't in the race, so what the hell was he doing out here? I had a good lead in the race, and I didn't want to lose it. Harry obviously didn't realize how important this race was. What seemed at first to be only a well-intentioned spectator turned ominous when I realized the funny-shaped kayak was chasing me. Could my first impression that Carter was trouble be right after all?

Still determined to finish the race, I dug my paddle in with a quick side-to-side motion to maximize my speed. His kayak being much shorter and more suited for the rapids of the Colorado River than the currents of Long Island Sound, he had to compensate more than I did. Then, from the corner of my eye, I saw the river kayak beside me.

I stopped paddling and grabbed the bow of his kayak, ready for a mid-Sound chicken fight. The two kayaks rocked violently, with neither of us able to flip over the other. That's when I realized it wasn't Carter.

Chapter Thirty-Eight

"Damn it, cut it out!" Max's scream startled me enough to loosen my grip on the kayak.

"What the hell are you doing in Carter's kayak?" I growled.

"Never mind the kayak," she snapped. Her voice was sharp, but something in her expression stopped me from arguing. "I was waiting at the finish line with Carter when I got a call. Someone I used to work with. They had information I've been chasing. The state police picked up Rondell yesterday. He's the president of Big Apple."

"I know that," I shot back, shoving my paddle into the water to keep us moving. "What's your point?"

She looked me dead in the eye. "Do you know your friend Charlie is behind the mortgage company?"

My paddle froze mid-stroke. "What?"

"Rondell's talking," she continued, her voice steady now. "He claims he worked with Charlie. Says Charlie was the mastermind behind the scams, the laundering, all of it. Worse, Rondell says Charlie helped take out Lawson. And Charlie's the one who shot Warner."

"Hold it, hold it," I said, shaking my head. "You're saying Charlie is a killer? That's insane."

"Is it?" Her voice tone serious. "Rondell gave details—dates, places. Things only someone involved would know."

I glared at her, denial fighting off the uncertainty she was trying to plant in my head. "And where's this all coming from? Don't tell me—Phil?"

She sighed, clearly frustrated. "Yes, Phil. He followed a paper trail linking

Big Apple to Charlie, then had one of his FBI contacts confirm it."

"That's just perfect," I muttered. "Phil swoops in with some wild accusation against my best friend, and I'm supposed to buy it? He's just trying to make himself look good to you.

Her eyes narrowed. "This isn't about Phil," she said, her voice tight. "It's about the truth. You need to face the facts. Charlie might not be who you think he is."

I turned away, staring at the Connecticut shoreline in the distance as if it held some magical answer. My mind raced. Charlie? The guy who'd stood by me through every mess? Who'd never flinched when things got ugly? No. This was a mistake. Or worse, a setup.

"I need proof," I said finally, my voice lower, rougher. "Not just Phil's word. Not Kondell's either. Real proof."

Max's shoulders relaxed slightly. "Fair enough," she said. "But you need to keep your eyes open."

"Fine," I muttered, shoving my paddle back into the water, "I'm in the middle of a race here."

Her jaw tightened. "I just wanted you to know. Charlie hasn't been picked up yet. Watch yourself."

"Charlie's not going to bother me," I said with defiance. "We've been friends since we were kids. I don't believe any of this. Now let me finish this race."

"Fine," She said, "But don't say I didn't warn you."

She didn't get to tell me much more because a Boston Whaler was headed toward us in a hurry, and it was flying that Jolly Roger. This time, it was close enough for me to read the numbers 322 under the crossbones. Charlie was at the wheel.

The Whaler had created an enormous wake. I turned my bow into it and braced my paddle flat on the water. I was sure that Max would be swamped, and I prepared to go to her aid, but there was no need to. She rode to the crest of the wave and then, in an amazing maneuver, turned her kayak in midair with a twist. She crashed onto the surface, landing upright.

The quick maneuvering on both our parts was to no avail. The Whaler had forced us into a collision course with the tug, which was bearing down on us all too fast. Charlie buzzed us again, forcing us to stay in harm's way. I knew Charlie. I trusted him. Even after what Max told me and what seemed like a deliberate attempt to sabotage the race, I still held on to the hope that Charlie had a good explanation for what was going on.

A shrill blast of a horn from the tug split the air. The prow of the powerful boat looked to be the size of the QE II as it sped closer. Its horn blasted again.

With nothing else we could do, we both jumped in the drink. I dove deep and swam away from the tug. When I got to the surface, I was beside the second of the four gigantic barges loaded with gravel that the tug was towing. Max was nowhere in sight.

"Max!" I called several times but got no response. I dove and spotted her deep below the murky water. I could make out a rope wrapped around her hand. When I got down to her, I ripped the cord away. Whatever was on the other end sank to the bottom. I led her to the surface, but she fought me the whole way. We finally broke into the fresh air not far from her kayak. She thrashed at the water angrily as I led her to the overturned hull. In the movies, they slap hysterical people to calm them down. I was considering this when she clocked me.

I saw stars for a minute. When I realized what she did, I was as angry as she was.

"What the hell was that for? I saved your life!"

"My dry bag was on the other end of that rope! My gun was in it, you idiot!"

I didn't have enough time to explain that I thought she was tangled in the cord, and it looked like whatever was on the other end of the rope was pulling her down. The Whaler was barreling down on us. We both pushed off from the kayak just before the Whaler hit it. There was a loud thud, and I watched as the kayak spun around in the air several times, making a weird whooshing sound. When it landed, it struck Max in the head. She seemed to be knocked cold, so I started to swim toward her, but the Whaler got to her first.

Charlie hauled her on board and then made a wide turn. He buzzed me, and I was able to grab a bumper hanging over the side of the Whaler. I hung on to the rope that tied the bumper to a cleat on the boat. The water seemed as hard as pavement as my body slapped against it with each bounce of the hull. I tried to pull myself up onto the boat, but Charlie left the wheel and kicked at my hands. I was determined not to let go. The boat was running in circles now, and Charlie had to return to the wheel to keep it from hitting a barge. I took the opportunity to heave myself into the boat. Charlie reached for a wooden paddle. The last thing I remember was thinking, *Live by the paddle, die by the paddle.*

* * *

When I woke up, Charlie held a gun on me.

"Charlie, what the hell? We've been like brothers." His eyes held an emptiness that I'd never seen before.

"Things change," he said.

"I never thought you had it in you. Did you really kill Ginny Lawson?"

His voice was so calm that I don't think he really got it. "Did I have a choice? Do you really believe I had a choice? I knew from a chance conversation with Chelsea that this…this abstractor," he spat out the word, "was digging way more than one normally would in researching a title."

"She was only searching historical records. She was a treasure hunter," I said.

"Was I supposed to know that! Unfortunately, Ms. Lawson expired before she could tell me what she was up to."

"Expired? For Christ's sake, Charlie, we're not talking about a driver's license. You killed her. You killed her because you thought she was looking into Rondell's Mortgage Company, the company that you're behind." Charlie looked very surprised that I knew that.

"Well, there. Point proven. You see, I had no other choice but to kill her."

He had no other choice but to kill her. I could tell by his voice that it seemed perfectly logical to him. I wondered where along the line he had turned into a madman. Why had I never noticed?

"I have to know how this happened," I said.

"I messed up, okay? Things spiraled out of control. Rondell had this geologist buddy from his Yale days, part of the Skull and Bones crowd. I kind of remembered him. The geologist had this theory about spodumene deposits around here, similar to the ones in Portland, just twenty miles away."

That actually made some sense. I remembered from a history class that lithium from Connecticut spodumene was used for military lubricants during WWII.

"Now that everyone wants electric cars, it's turned into a goldmine," I said.

Charlie nodded. "Exactly. The geologist paid Abe to run a geophysical survey on his land. Abe was broke and thought it was just some academic study funded by Yale."

I thought back to the rocks lining the walkway at the Cromwell home.

"Let me guess—Abe's property was loaded with the stuff," I said.

"Right. Once they confirmed the deposits, Rondell's Apple Mortgage started scooping up properties. Rondell came to me for funding and asked me to bring Amanda on board. I was really hoping you wouldn't notice that sample on her desk."

"So, she *is* behind all of this," I said.

"No. She wanted nothing to do with it. She was smart, saw the risks. I never should've gotten involved in Rondell's scheme. Who could've predicted that supporting the company would lead to—"

"Murder?" I said, finishing the thought.

He tossed a life jacket at me. "Enough, put this on."

I knew Charlie wasn't concerned about my safety in the water. "I can swim, thanks."

I could hear Max in the cabin kicking and yelling.

"Put it on or I quiet her permanently. I need some help up here!"

Much to my surprise, Summer emerged from down below.

"You too? Can't I trust anyone?"

Summer didn't look directly at me as I put on the life vest. Charlie gave her a short piece of rope to tie my hands behind my back. Then he had her feed a longer rope in the right armhole of the jacket and out the left, with the rope passing over my back. I tried to resist, but once again he threatened to kill Max. Summer seemed to have no qualms about stringing me up.

"Did you help keel haul Ginny Lawson, too?"

She didn't answer, but just looked.

"You would have thought that I learned my lesson about trusting people. Next time I'll know better."

Charlie laughed. "I think you've used up your next times."

"Like Warner did? That was his Benz leaving your home that night, not your accountant's. You killed him at the falls because you thought he was going to talk."

"You are the one talking too much. Maybe if you shut up, you can put off drowning for a bit."

He tied one end of the rope to the side rail and then pushed me over. Walking to the bow of the boat, he brought the line around and pulled it and me under the boat. I struggled, but with my hands tied behind my back, I couldn't do much. I knew he was tying the other end of the rope to the side rail on the port side because I was pulled up against the bottom of the boat, where I bumped my head. Luckily, modern boats don't have many barnacles, or I would have been shredded. It really didn't make a difference because I wouldn't be able to hold my breath for long once the boat started, and he would keep me under until I drowned. My hands were between my lower back and the hull, and I had just enough wiggle room to fumble with the rope. Summer didn't seem to know much about knots because I was able to get my hands untied. I thought I was home free, but the boat started moving forward, and I was dragged toward the motor. I knew the propellers would do far more damage than the barnacles ever would have. They say you hear bells when you're drowning, all I could hear was the repetitive formation and collapse of the bubbles created as the propeller churned the water.

I was preparing to die when the rope on the port side let go. I popped up on the starboard side of the boat, and the rope ripped my back as it pulled out of the lifejacket. I found myself floating in the water with the boat speeding away. Then, to my amazement, I saw Charlie throw Max from the boat.

Thanks to its airbag, my kayak was floating nearby, and the paddle cord that Ernie Fitzgerald had made fun of kept the paddle from floating away. I climbed in and sped over to help Max.

But when I got to the person in the water, I saw it wasn't Max but Summer. My first thought was to leave her in the water. But I couldn't.

She sputtered water as she tried to talk. "He saw me cut the rope and threw me over. I'd tied your hands loose so you'd get them free."

I wasn't concerned about her explanation. "What about Max?"

"He's going to hold her hostage until he gets away."

"Where?"

Summer was treading water but didn't seem any the worse for wear. After all, she was a surfer and used to wiping out. "The old quarry is my guess. That's where he used to meet Rondell and Warner, so no one would see them together."

I saw Tom paddle past us in his kayak. I'd been so far ahead that it took him this long to catch up, even with the big delay. If it weren't for everything that just happened, I probably would've set some kind of record for crossing the Sound. But the race didn't matter anymore.

"Take this." I took off the life vest and threw it to her. I knew that in time, she could get to Carter's kayak.

I never paddled so hard in my life. Now it wasn't winning the race that made me work so hard. I had to help Max. Charlie went east in the direction of his house, where he had a dock. If he was bringing Max to the quarry, he had to get his car. There was no use in following him. Instead, I headed for the village where I had left the Mercedes on the wharf.

To Tom's surprise, I glided past him like I was the roadrunner and he was the coyote. Before I knew it, I had reached the harbor and aimed right for the beach.

The finish line was on the swimming beach from which Doris usually banned kayaks. I landed on the beach, hopped out, and ran up the sand. The whole town was cheering me, led by Neal, Buster, and Walter. Doris approached me with a ribbon and a cup. I ran right past her, up the beach, and to my Mercedes on the wharf.

I could hear Aunt Phoebe comment, as only Aunt Phoebe could. "He must have the runs or something!"

Normally, I would have been pretty embarrassed, but somewhere in this ordeal, I realized that this world isn't all about Al DeLucia.

Chapter Thirty-Nine

I parked on the dirt road that led to the abandoned quarry and hiked about a half mile through the woods. This time, I didn't take time to enjoy the cool shade of the trees. I hopped over downed trunks and ran splashing through small streams. Still exhausted after that grueling race across the sound, I thought my heart would burst. But I pushed on to Fat Man's Squeeze. Not far beyond, I came out of the woods at the quarry.

A quarry is a barren, scarred patch of land with no trees or vegetation, stripped bare by mining. Not exactly ideal for stalking someone. I moved in a crouch until I reached the edge and peered into the pit. The urgency of the moment made the familiar scene look even bleaker. The derrick loomed like a giant gallows, its reflection rippling in a pool of murky green water. The scattered granite blocks on the quarry floor looked like tombstones. I glanced across the pit to the far side, about three hundred feet away.

I spotted Charlie's BMW next to the engine room shack on the opposite rim of the pit and made my way around to it. Again, staying low and hiding behind blocks of stone when possible. At the back of the shed, I peeked through a window and saw Max bound in a chair with a gag in her mouth. I couldn't see Charlie, but I did see a gun on a table. Max blinked to let me know that she spotted me. Then she jerked her head to the side to tell me to get away from the window. She began to bounce in her chair as she directed loud mumbles at Charlie through her gag. He came into view, standing between her and the window, and snapped at her to quiet down. This wasn't the reserved Charlie I had known most of my life. Max only got louder, and he paced in front of her. He seemed about to lose it, and that was dangerous.

Charlie told her again to be quiet. He was pacing near the table with a gun now.

With no time to call for backup, I picked up a baseball-sized chunk of granite and flung it at his windshield. The car alarm went crazy. Then I ducked back behind the building.

Charlie rushed out of the shack. I was hoping that in the excitement, he'd left the gun behind. No such luck. I tackled him from behind, and the gun flew out of his hand, falling into the quarry. That worry gone, now it was down to a contest between an ex-cop and an ex-Yale athlete. This wasn't a wrestling match between two friends. Those days were gone forever. Charlie shook off his confusion and came at me, punching, catching me on the side of the face. I staggered but it wasn't the first sucker punch in my life. I took it as a betrayal and came back determined. I grabbed his arm and pulled him downward, then tripped him.

I knew he was tough, and he proved it by getting back to his feet in a second.

"Okay. Okay. Let's discuss this like gentlemen," he said.

I thought I saw something move, and I glanced at the shack. A stupid thing to do on my part. He drove his head into my stomach, wrapping his arms around my legs. I flew backward, my head hanging over the rim. With my neck craned back, I could see the rock bench halfway down below, where Max and Big Al had lain, taking in the sun.

Determined that one of those *tombstones* down there wouldn't have my name on it today, I kicked him off. He managed to get away from me and scrambled down the path that led to the bottom of the quarry.

I followed him into the pit but lost sight of him behind a pickup truck-sized block of granite. As I inched along the side of the block, he got me from behind. He locked his hands around my stomach and lifted me off the ground as he squeezed the breath out of me.

Pissed for letting my guard down, I locked my hands together. I brought them up and over the back of my head, catching Charlie in the forehead. The move from my police days stunned him enough for him to drop me. We both ended up on the ground facing each other. I scrambled to my feet first and spotted the gun next to a long-abandoned rusty sledgehammer. I lunged for it, picked it up, and pointed it at him.

"You know I can't just let you walk away from this, Charlie."

"But the thought is crossing your mind. I can hear it in your voice. We're 'brothers' and loyalty means everything to you."

I couldn't ignore two people dead and another in a coma because we were friends. I knew then not only how deranged he was but how little he knew me. Now I had to question if we ever were friends. The centuries-old love-hate situation between town and gown had come to a head. Amanda legitimized the struggle between the haves and the have-nots in Sachem Creek. But the truth was, it had been there long before she and her super-rich friends had arrived.

"It seems I have more 'brothers' than I can handle at the moment."

Charlie had a hurt look on his face. Did he think I was going to let him go based on our friendship?

"As you said, things change. People change, maps change. Have you changed like the Allotment Map? Maybe you're here not looking for justice but treasure."

Charlie was trying to mess with my head to escape. I actually felt a little sad because I knew gaslighting was a sign of a personality disorder.

"If you're saying I noticed the same thing Ginny did—that over the years, islands disappeared and merged with the mainland—you're right, Charlie. But if you think I'm after treasure, you're way off."

I'd figured out that a peninsula on Abe's property used to be an island, gradually joined to the mainland by storms depositing sand and people filling in the gaps.

I went on, "If you drew lines connecting Outer and Doubloon islands to that former island, you'd get a triangle with sides a little over a mile each. That's what Ginny intended to show her brother and Abe from Outer Island that afternoon, you killed her."

"Meaningless," Charlie dismissed me,

"It was. Until I converted the distance to rods—each side was 322 rods."

Charlie's face darkened. "What does that prove?"

"You've got a thing for the number 322."

"So do a lot of people."

True. The Skull and Bones society at Yale is big on the number 322. During my time with the New Haven Police and as a Yale Fellow, I learned a bit about them—it's connected to the year Greek orator Demosthenes died and means a lot to them.

"You belonged to Skull and Bones when you were at Yale, and you're a Mason."

Charlie pooh-poohed the idea. "Don't you think I can't see through you. You're thinking of what you could do with the treasure. You're thinking if you could kill me, you could have it all for yourself."

"Not at all," I admit that was a lie. But it was only a thought.

"Bull shit. You're no different than anyone. The problem, my friend—"

"We're not friends, Charlie. Not anymore."

"The problem, Al, is that you don't have the balls to kill me. That's where I have the advantage over you, being the villain, as they say."

"Are you sure, Charlie? I can shoot you right now. It would be easy to prove that it was self-defense."

"You could. But will you? Guys like you are always worried about their conscience."

"Money does a lot to soothe an aching conscience. I'm sure you know that it would be so easy to pull the trigger.

"Then go ahead and shoot me if you can. You're no different than me. Greed can make even Al DeLucia kill."

I aimed at his skull. The bullet would enter right between his eyes. It would be over before either of us knew what happened. He wasn't my friend. He was a killer who tried to kill me.

I tossed the gun into the pool of stagnant water. "You have it backward, Charlie. I have the balls *not* to blow your head off." I watched the rings from the gun's splash ripples in the pool. "It's up to Doris to deal with you. As for the treasure, I can walk away. Ginny Lawson wanted the treasure, and it cost her life. I don't need the bad karma. All I need is justice for her."

Charlie seemed pleased that he read me so well. "By the way, you were right about where Kidd hid the treasure. But you're almost two hundred years too late. Bonesmen found it in 1832 when they founded the society. Why do you think they call it Skull and Bones?"

"Score another one for Yale." I motioned toward Doris on the quarry rim. "You're still a murderer."

"Alright, I screwed up joining Rondell's scheme. I only realized how deep I was when I went along with disposing of the Lawson woman."

"And the antique dealer was collateral damage because he knew too much," I added.

"Yes, yes. You understand. Good. I knew I could count on you. And for the record, I had nothing to do with what happened to Amanda."

I couldn't understand why he would cop to two murders but deny an assault on Amanda.

"I'm not so sure about that."

"I didn't need to harm her. She didn't have any concrete proof against me."

"Well, they have proof against you now. Rondell talked."

Charlie's face expressed shock, but his words didn't betray him. "It's Rondell's word against mine."

I turned my back on him and walked away in disgust.

"Behind you, Al. Behind!" Abe's unmistakable gravel voice rang through the quarry. Had he been hiding in the pit all this time?

I spun around just in time to see Charlie wielding the long-forgotten sledgehammer, poised to strike me. As Charlie pivoted toward Abe's voice, the hammer collided with the gaff. The rotted wood couldn't withstand the impact, swaying as the hefty guide wires at the quarry's edge snapped and lashed around. The derrick started to fall. In a desperate move, I lunged forward, attempting to pull Charlie out of harm's way. But he resisted and darted into the path of the falling timber.

I vaguely remember being tackled. The world went black, but I still heard the creaks, groans, and cracks. And then a thud, and I felt the vibration. When I opened my eyes, my skull ached from hitting the quarry floor. Max was slapping my cheeks.

"You don't need a guardian angel, you need a bodyguard," she said.

"You?" I asked.

She nodded her head and kissed me.

When we came up for air, she gestured toward Abe, who was standing over Charlie, crushed against a granite block by the falling derrick.

"You had no rights, no rights at all to my land. Neither did Amanda," Abe was saying, his voice thick with rage.

That's when it clicked. The anger in his voice, the vehemence with which he spoke of Amanda—it wasn't new. I had heard it before, in the way he talked about anyone he thought was trying to take something from him. It wasn't proof, but it was enough to confirm my hunch.

Abe came over to me, extending a hand to help me up.

"Don't touch him, Abe," Doris warned, stepping between us. "An ambulance is on the way."

I looked up at the rim of the quarry. Doris, Big Al, Phoebe, and half of the village stood there, watching.

Chapter Forty

The EMTs recommended a hospital visit, but there was no chance I was setting foot in one for the second time in a week. They finally convinced me to at least see a doctor. I called Lenny Rodriguez, who arranged for the Force Police Surgeon on duty to check me over. We agreed I could recuperate at home, as long as I promised to take it easy for a few days. Max offered to let me stay at her place with a visiting nurse dropping by to keep tabs on me. With the case wrapped up, I was more than happy to lie low and enjoy the island views for a while.

Max and I had plenty of time to talk about everything under the sun. Eventually, the conversation turned to the idea of moving in together. We tossed around the options—Savannah or Sachem Creek—without making any firm decisions, but there was a glimmer of hope for the future. If we finally decided on Sachem Creek, I knew I'd have to sit down with Big Al and discuss closing the chapter on Savannah.

Then there was Phil—he'd done some impressive work uncovering information on Charlie, but I wasn't ready to bring him into the agency yet. We'd deal with that later.

On the second day, Doris came in, wearing a rare smile. I wish I'd had a camera. I decided not to tell her or anyone else that the treasure had been found long ago. Sachem Creek had already lost too much; the legend needed to stay alive.

I asked about Amanda. She said Amanda was making progress and would likely recover fully.

"As for Abe," Doris said, sighing, "he confessed."

240

I raised an eyebrow.

"He didn't mean to hurt her, at least not like that," she clarified. "He was furious when he thought she was trying to steal his land, same as Ginny Lawson, but he says he just wanted to scare her off. Things got out of hand."

"Do you believe him?"

"Enough to let the courts decide. I talked to the prosecutor, who's willing to cut him a deal. Instead of jail time, he'll do public service—fixing the department's cruisers until he's too old to turn a wrench. Saves us money and keeps him busy. Plus, there are things in the works for him to get his land back. It's a little complicated, but there's a good chance."

It wasn't perfect justice, but in a town like ours, sometimes you worked with what you had.

"For the record," Max said, "Doris deserves the credit for finding Rondell."

Doris shrugged. "I work in my own way." Then she turned serious. "You missed the town meeting. They voted to block any development out of character with the village."

"Whatever that means. But it's a start." I wondered how that would play out when Amanda was back in action.

Doris was about to leave when she paused and turned back.

"Hey, I almost forgot. The Pirate's Day committee asked me to give you this." She reached into her pocket and pulled out a check for twenty-five thousand dollars, handing it to me. "You earned it. Consider it their way of making up for you not getting a fee for solving the case."

I stared at the check, then glanced at Max, who gave me a small nod. We'd already decided what to do with the money.

"It's going to Abe," I said. "If he gets his land back, he'll need it for next year's taxes."

Doris left, and I was ready to take a nap. I don't think I'd been sleeping ten minutes when Max shook me awake.

"Phoebe and Big Al are here," she said.

When they came into the room, Big Al acted like it was a party rather than a visit to see his recuperating son.

"Hey, there he is," he said. I wasn't sure if he meant me as his son or as a colleague. Either way worked. "I told you I didn't like that guy."

"You mean Charlie?"

"Yeah, that guy who goes around praying." Big Al pressed his hands together in a mock Namaste gesture.

At least he seemed aware of what had happened. "Look, Dad, we need to talk."

"There he goes with that 'Dad' stuff," he said to Phoebe, laughing. "What's with you?" he asked when I didn't join in the joke.

"It's just a headache," I said, though I'd felt fine until my father showed up.

"Let me feel your head," Phoebe offered.

"I'm fine," I said. "Just disappointed. I thought Charlie was my best friend, but he tried to kill me. I never liked Abe, and he saved my life. But even after all that, I still can't see him as family. It's just a gut feeling." I tapped my chest.

Phoebe sat on the bed, her expression serious. "I need to tell you something." Her tone reminded me of Mom's when she had something important to say. "Your mom and I looked alike, but we were different people."

"You're you, and that's a good thing," I said.

She shook her head. "You're not getting it. Everyone adored Betty, and the more I saw that, the more I rebelled."

I still wasn't following. "What does this have to do with Abe?"

"I had a baby when I was young."

That caught me off guard. "I'm listening."

But as I thought about it, the pieces started to fit. I put an arm around her. "Abe?"

She nodded, mouthing the word *Yes*.

The room tilted as the implications sank in. "You're saying you're my mother?"

Phoebe straightened, mock horror in her eyes. "Hell no! I'd have killed you by now if you were." She grabbed my hand as a smile spread across her face.

"But you said you're Abe's mother."

"I am. But he's not your brother."

"The DNA says otherwise."

"Do you know what quaternary twins are?" she asked.

I raised an eyebrow, assuming it was some medical jargon. "Is that another term for quadruplets?"

She explained, "It's when two babies are born to two sets of identical siblings. Genetically, they're closer to siblings than cousins."

"Even I know that," Big Al chimed in; his voice confident, but his expression slightly foggy.

I knew he was bluffing, so I pulled out my phone and typed "quaternary twins." Sure enough, the definition matched what she'd said.

"You're right. I guess the DNA test was flawed," I admitted.

"More like the person interpreting it lacked the full picture. Are you satisfied now?"

"Not really. You need two sets of identical twins for that to work."

"Did you know your father had a twin brother?"

"Not until recently, when he mentioned it. I thought he was confused. No one ever told me about him."

"Andy was your father's identical twin."

I shuddered at the thought of two Big Als. "Too bad he never stepped up."

"He couldn't," Phoebe said. "Andy died in a car crash the night I told him I was pregnant. I was in the car. Two broken legs made it easy for me to disappear for 'rehab'—she used air quotes—"and have the baby in secret. The nuns took him before I even saw him. Years later, I learned he'd been adopted by the Cromwells, right here in the village. My son was living under my nose, and I never knew."

"So, you never told Abe?"

"What good would it do? He was fourteen when I found out. I gave him a job helping in the garage and got him out of trouble a few times. Eventually, we became friends. That was enough. He wasn't just like a son to me—he was my son. I'm going to rectify that. He has the right to know."

So, Abe was my cousin. Not ideal, but better than him being my brother. I was happy for Phoebe, and him too, that things seemed to be working out for him.

"I told you it was complicated," Big Al said with a faint, wandering grin.

I waved him off. "We need to talk."

"Right, right. But I have to tell you something first," he said.

Here we go, I thought, bracing for whatever curveball was coming.

"No, I need to tell you something," I insisted.

Big Al turned to Phoebe. "He never listens to me. You tell him."

Phoebe sighed. "What your father's trying to say is that we went to see a specialist at Yale. They got him into a memory program."

"Wait—what? He lives in Savannah. The Blue Palmetto..."

"The Blue Palmetto II," Big Al corrected, his voice tinged with pride, but his eyes unfocused for a second.

I looked to Phoebe, confused.

"It's going to be on the wharf in that empty storefront next to Neal's," she said. "It's yours if you and Max want it."

"So, we're closing Savannah?"

"What are you? Crazy?" Big Al said, his tone sharp despite the hint of uncertainty. "I built that place. We need to hire."

"Greenleaf can run the place blindfolded," Max said. "And I was thinking—"

I cut her off. "I have an idea," I said. "Phil Malkovich would be perfect."

I could see the *thank you* in Max's eyes.

"Now, what was it you wanted to tell us?" Phoebe asked.

I glanced from her to Big Al, then back again. "I forget," I said.

Big Al's expression didn't change. "Like father, like son."

When they left, I retreated to the back porch to process how everything had fallen into place. Except for one thing. As the sunset cast a warm glow over the islands, I sat on the swing, lost in thought. Max joined me, settling close. "You're a good man," she said.

Was she referring to my decision about Phil, or something deeper? I couldn't quite place it. Whatever it was, it made my heart race. I wanted to say something nice back, to explain my feelings, but words failed me. I'm not the type to come up with sweet nothings, but she seemed to understand.

She shifted, her hand tracing gentle circles on my thigh, sending shivers down my spine. "What are you thinking about?" she teased.

"Things." I tried to play it cool, though my voice betrayed my nerves. "A lot's been on my mind lately."

"Work or me?" she asked. Her gaze was intense, her eyes both confident and alluring.

"You," I admitted, my heart pounding. "Only you."

She leaned her head against my chest, her breath mingling with mine. "I've been thinking about us," she said softly. "And I think you should stay."

I chuckled.

"Find that funny, do you?" she asked.

"No, it's just...I'm surprised you thought you could get rid of me."

She playfully swatted me with a pillow. "Oh, you!"

She climbed onto the swing, her knees tucked beneath her. I took her hand, pulling her closer. Our lips met in a passionate kiss. The world outside faded. Her hands tangled in my hair, pulling me in deeper.

"We're doing this, aren't we?" she asked, her breath catching.

"Absolutely," I replied, my voice filled with certainty.

Finally, we were on the same page. And damn, it felt good.

Acknowledgments

As always, thanks to my writing group, Lucy Burdette (a.k.a. Roberta Isleib) and Christine Falcone, for over twenty years of support, sharp critique, and unwavering friendship.

Also, to my daily write-in group—Eileen Doyle, Lisa Harkrader, Chris Falcone, Louise Robinson Talotta and Mary Nunn Maki—thank you for helping me stay focused, showing up every day, and reminding me that writing is a habit as much as it is an art.

Special thanks to my good friends and fellow writers, Elise Hart Kipness and Tessa Wegert, for taking an interest in this project and always offering help and encouragement.

I'm especially grateful to my wonderful agent, Nadia Lynch at Talcott Notch Literary Agency, for her guidance, insight, and steady belief in my work.

And of course, to my wife, Annette Pompano—for your love, your patience, and your belief in me, even on the days when I didn't believe in myself. This book, like all the others, wouldn't be possible without you.

About the Author

Ang Pompano is an Agatha Award-nominated author, as well as an editor, publisher, and blogger. He writes the Blue Palmetto Detective Agency and Reluctant Food Columnist series for Level Best Books. His short stories have been featured in numerous anthologies, including one that won the Anthony Award. He blogs about food and mystery at *Mystery Lovers' Kitchen*. A recipient of the Mystery Writers of America's Helen McCloy Award, Ang co-founded Crime Spell Books and co-edits Best New England Crime Stories. He also serves on the New England Crime Bake committee and the Sisters in Crime Connecticut board. Ang lives in Connecticut with his artist wife, Annette, and their two rescue dogs.

AUTHOR WEBSITE:
www.angpompano.com

SOCIAL MEDIA HANDLES:
Facebook: https://www.facebook.com/AngPompanoMystery/
X: @AngPompano

Threads: angpompano
Instagram: angpompano

Also by Ang Pompano

Novels
When It's Time for Leaving
Diet of Death

Short Stories
Quincy Lazzaro Short Mysteries
"The Copycat Didn't Have Nine Lives" in *Still Waters*
"Promises to Keep" in *Deadfall*
"School's Out Forever" in *Best New England Crime Stories*
"Diet of Death" in *Malice Domestic Mystery Most Edible*

Mike St. Martin Short Mysteries
"Sand Bar" in *Stone Cold*
"The Noir Before Christmas" *Audio Recording*

Also by Ang Pompano
"The Bucket List" in *Red Dawn*
"Stringer" in *Seascape*
"Directions to Justice" in *Bloodroot*
"Minnie the Air Raid Warden" in *Snakeberry*

Anthologies (edited by)
Bloodroot
Devil's Snare
Snakeberry

www.ingramcontent.com/pod-product-compliance
Lightning Source LLC
Chambersburg PA
CBHW020617110726
47899CB00002B/543